The Once and Future Moon

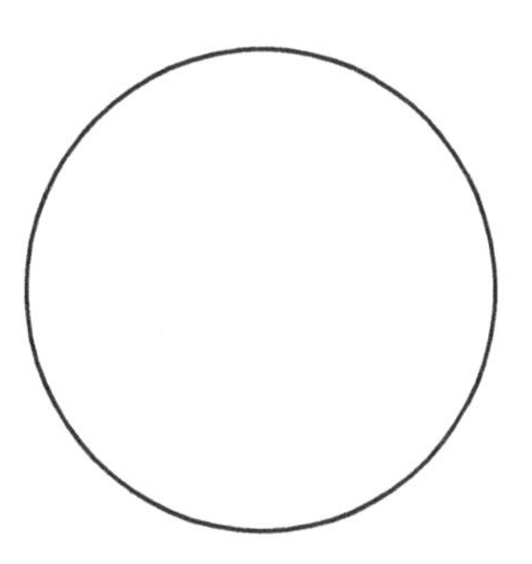

Edited by

Allen Ashley

The Once and Future Moon
Publication Date: September 2019

ISBN: 978-1-908125-95-8

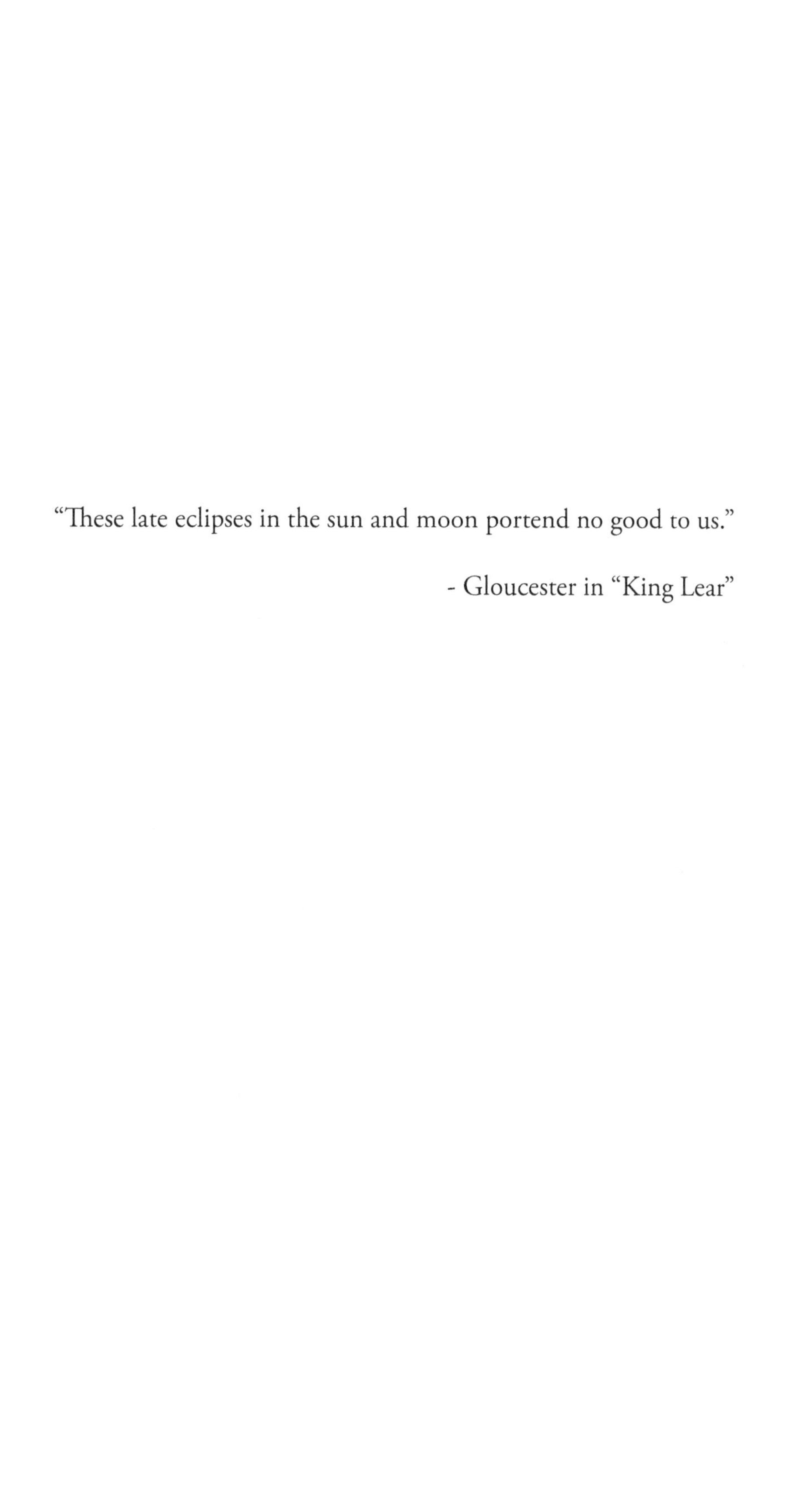

"These late eclipses in the sun and moon portend no good to us."

- Gloucester in "King Lear"

Contents:

Dr Cadwallader and the Lunar Cycle

Chris Edwards

"It was the ancient Greeks of course, that first thought of it – casting the ritual, I mean. Apparently it offended their greybeards having this great angry face gazing down at them. Decided to do something about it."

Having been somewhat caught out by the vigour required for this unusual method of transport, and nursing a ferocious hangover, I found I had little wind left to fashion a reply. The tweed-clad horror to my fore clearly took my lungfish gasps as those of encouraging astonishment, and redoubled his tedious efforts.

"But try as they might, they discovered they couldn't affect it with their magic. Something about the surrounding aether being unreceptive to their male energies. So they were forced to school a group of women in their arcane arts, which in turn laid the foundations of the cult of Artemis."

I made the mistake of looking down to England far below, mostly hidden by smog and cloud. My stomach clenched, for it seemed there was nothing to stop this confounded contraption from simply plummeting towards the bosom of Mother Earth. For the millionth time I cursed the Tribune for forcing me into this nonsense.

"Of course, they had cause to regret it. No sooner had these amazons performed the ritual than they turned on their erstwhile mentors. The resulting occult war played out over at least a thousand years and a dozen cultures before the Daughters of Artemis were finally destroyed."

Heart thundering in my chest, I felt compelled to croak out an interjection, "Might we perhaps take a bit of a breather? I'm afraid my knees are playing up, old war-wound, don't-cha-know."

Professor Willingdon turned in his seat and looked back, finally taking in the fact that I was flagging somewhat. "I say, Dr Cadwallader, are you alright? You've got rather a flush on."

"Just an excess of manful red blood – produce more of the stuff than I know what to do with. Fit as a fiddle, don't you worry."

He looked a tad sceptical. "If you say so, Doctor. Look, another ten or fifteen minutes and we'll be at the halfway point. Why don't we just give it our all until then, then stop for lunch? It'll be downhill from that point onwards."

Unfortunately for Willingdon, I very much already had given my all the night before – to a suitably Bacchanalian excess for a man who expects to die in a deep crater fused with a tangle of gears and India-rubber the following day.

Taking silence as assent, the lanky devil turned forward again and began to pump those bony legs of his like the pistons of a steam engine. Having little interest in trying to match the confounded Oxford dervish, I simply coasted – let him do all the work if he was so dashed eager!

"Come on Doctor, nearly there now! I must say, she's handling a little more sluggishly than I expected. She should be going like the clappers with both of us giving it mustard. Must be an effect of the penumbral aura; I'll make a note."

"Maybe a steam engine for the next trip? Save ourselves a bit of shoe leather, make the trip in style?"

He waved a hand over his shoulder dismissively, "We discussed it, but it would have used too much of our air. Besides, isn't this marvellous, seeing God's creation with nothing powering us but the sweat of our brow?"

I had to admit he had a point about the view, by now we could see the whole globe behind us. I idly amused myself by trying to pick out parts of it I'd helped turn pink during my time in the service while Willingdon sweated away like a navvy. Ahead of us the great silvery orb of the moon grew larger and larger.

"What a sight!" exclaimed Willingdon with a thoroughly loathsome excess of enthusiasm. "To think it's just an ectoplasmic projection – the detail is simply superb!"

"Yes. Are we… are we really sure we ought to be tampering with it? I mean, a magical ritual on that kind of scale, surely it would be better to just let sleeping dogs lie?"

"Nonsense, Doctor! I'm surprised to hear a man of science like yourself say such a thing. Think what we can learn from examining the moon's true face? What wonders we might uncover!"

Inwardly I once again cursed my luck at being stuck with such a spooney academic – a salutary lesson in not opening one's potato trap without food or drink handy to immediately fill it. Mention that you looked through a telescope once or twice and suddenly you're just the man for a dangerous mission involving lofting oneself into the firmament on behalf of the Society. Of course, I didn't mention what I was using the telescope to look *at* (as a rule my interests tend to run rather more to earthly than heavenly.)

After a few minutes in which I recovered myself and Willingdon continued at the same furious pace, I began to notice a change in the moon's aspect. Slowly the silvery surface began to take on the appearance of a crone-like face, with great craters for eyes. Strange it was, though, that they seemed to be looking directly at us as we continued our approach – a frosty old dowager gazing with disgust at an approaching fly.

"Blow me, I can see why the Greeks wanted the old gunpowder covered up! Not exactly a kindly visage, is it?"

"She does have a bit of an... unnerving aspect to her, yes. According to the records Bruce brought back with the Marbles, the cult regarded her as the punisher of sinful men. Apparently there were a lot of guilty consciences in ancient Greece."

His barking laugh was just as odious as one might imagine for a fellow that spends his days with his nose crammed in books, instead of a pint-pot enjoying convivial company.

Finally we reached what must have been the mid-point, and Willingdon's pace began to slacken. Realising I had to keep up appearances, I pretended to be winding down as well and we gave the wretched boneshaker a rest. The great face continued to glare at us, filling the sky ahead as we delved into the saddlebags for vittles. Here, at least, I'd managed to make some preparations – thick ham sandwiches slathered in butter and mustard and a couple of bottles of beer were enough to take the edge off my burgeoning hunger. The pheasant pie and crimped salmon washed down with claret formed a perfect second act, giving way to a healthy slice of rich plum cake oozing rum from every currant. All of this left me replete to the point where I could cast a friendly eye over the impending arrival of port and cigars.

During all this, Willingdon gave me more than one sideways glance as he pecked away at his own meagre stores of hard-tack and dried fruit washed down with water, then tutted and fretted as I gave my more civilised meal the attention it deserved. "Really, Doctor Cadwallader, I can't imagine why you'd feel the need for such a banquet – or how you can possibly afford so much space. I found myself discarding half a dozen different instruments in order to ensure I had enough room."

"Willingdon, my dear fellow, I bow to your expertise in the arcane arts, but my bags were packed by my valet, Godalming, who's a wizard of a different stripe. Fellow batted for me in India; what he doesn't know about packing for the campaign trail ain't worth the knowing."

In truth, I made the cigar last a little longer than actually needed, but by this point Willingdon's pointed sighs had got my hackles up, and I took some pleasure in digging my heels in. Hanging midway between the two great orbs certainly made for a spectacular dinner view, but at last I hurled the stub of my cigar towards the moon, aiming for the centre of one of the vast eyes. The tiny burning embers went out as it left the envelope of air and I quickly lost sight of it.

"Well, then, shall we be off?" I asked innocently at the academic's clearly mounting agitation.

"We should have been on our way half an hour ago, sir! Need I remind you that this entire venture is restricted to a planetary alignment of short duration. Every moment we waste out here in the void further restricts our time on the surface of the Moon itself!"

I decided to play the innocent, "Terribly sorry, Willingdon old man – a chap's got to eat. I'll be the very picture of efficiency from here on in, I promise."

This seemed to mollify the lanky blab, and we once more commenced our pedalling. I mused that he clearly wasn't aware of the currency he was dealing with in taking a promise from Doctor Hieronymus Cadwallader at face value, and resolved to soak the wretched blighter for as much as I possibly could before he twigged.

The going did indeed seem easier now that we were past the halfway mark, and with only an hour's light exertion we came to the point where we no longer needed to pedal to keep the contraption going. In fact, as we hurtled towards the surface of the moon it occurred to me that we were essentially falling. "I say, Willingdon, how do we slow this infernal mechanism down? Brakes?"

He brayed with laughter again, as if I'd said something ridiculous. "Brakes? No, no, no – we simply transfer most of our momentum to one of the spheres mounted at the front and release it. Then *we* drift to a gentle stop on the Lunar surface."

"Been tested then, has it, this momentum system? What happens if it doesn't work?"

"It works perfectly in theory, I assure you. But as you know, the entire apparatus is experimental – no doubt there'll be on or two little niggles for us to report back on."

"Niggles?!! Niggles like plunging into the Lunar surface?"

He sucked his teeth, "Highly doubtful. If we'd been that far off in our calculations then most likely we would have crashed just after take-off. Just... the landing may prove a little bumpier than we were hoping for."

"Define – and feel free to be *incredibly* specific – what 'a little bumpier' might look like?"

"Doctor! I would have thought a military man like you would show more nerve. We're at the forefront of the Aletheian Society's occult research now – a few risks must be borne if we hope to wring the light of truth from the base clay of ignorance!"

I could have cheerfully wrung the life from his scrawny neck, but there seemed to be nothing for it but to wait and see. Needless to say, I was in a terrible funk by the time we got within a few hundred yards of the blasted wilderness of the lunar surface, praying to every god I'd ever heard of and a few that I made up on the spot for the occasion.

"Rate of acceleration calculated, powder dry, momentum sphere primed..." he carried on checking items off, cool as a cucumber while death hurtled towards us at unseemly speed. Eventually he seemed satisfied, "Would you care to do the honours, Doctor?" He turned and handed me a piece of string attached to the canister on the front of the velocipede.

I took it as gingerly as if it were a biting serpent, "What do I do with it?"

"Do? You haul on it – at the last possible moment, of course. That transfers our momentum to the sphere and then we float down as gently as a feather."

I gulped as the ground continued to advance at a dizzying pace, by sheer dint of will I didn't pull the string immediately, although my knuckles grew white from clenching it. Eventually as we closed to within fifty yards I could take no more and yanked the blasted thing with all my might. With a boom not unlike a mortar, a cloud of white smoke issued forth and I was for a second convinced that this was the impact, but when it cleared I saw that we were indeed gently floating down towards the surface. Meanwhile the ball fired from the little cannon had smashed a new and fairly impressive crater onto the surface of the moon.

Willingdon smirked, "See, I told you so, nothing to worry about." Gallingly, it seemed as if he was right, and I could only seethe at his gloating as we touched down on the desolate surface of the moon. His arrogance was short lived, though, for as soon as our feet touched the silvery dust that made up the soil we both felt a shiver run up our spines – it seemed as if some vast and malign entity had become aware of our intrusion into its realm.

"That… doesn't seem good. We should go, Willingdon. Post haste!"

"Nonsense. We're simply reacting to the aetheric fields. I told you, they're incompatible with male auras, that's why we're feeling a little on edge, nothing more."

I argued (of course I argued!) but the truth of it was I had no idea how to get the blasted thing aloft again, or even if it could be done with just one person. And so we set up camp and began to explore. The lunar air had an unpleasant, chalky taste to it and I found myself hacking and somewhat short of breath, but otherwise in no great difficulty. The surface appeared to be nothing more than a blasted wilderness of dust and boulders, mountainous crags and deep, treacherous canyons. Willingdon, of course, seemed delighted with everything and kept chipping bits off this or that and putting it away in little hand-labelled bottles. No signs of plant life, of course, so little for a botanist such as myself to do except drink and fret and check my firearms were within easy reach.

Several hours had passed when we first spotted movement against the rocks; tall figures in shining silver armour and wielding spears walking towards us as if supremely unconcerned. "Moon men!" I whispered, scrabbling for my rifle, only to find a razor-sharp spear tip pressed to my throat. I damned my laziness for falling for such an obvious diversion. A few yards away I could hear Willingdon crying out in pain as he was dragged out of a crater and thrown sprawling in the lunar dust.

I turned to look at my captor, only to see a tall, bronze-skinned woman in silvered armour looking as if she was willing and eager to use the spear currently pointed at my throat. She barked something in a language I was unfamiliar with – clearly a question and quite possibly one my life depended on. I licked my lips as I considered my next words carefully.

Suddenly Willingdon let fly with a stream of words in a similar language and a short, tense conversation ensued. As I looked around I realised that, incredibly, all of our captors were women. Whatever the Professor said, they seemed mollified and lowered their spears, then waved us onwards towards a rocky ridge a few miles away. Two of these amazons hefted the bulky apparatus of the velocipede as if it were only a child's toy and we set off across the lunar surface. So bright was the reflection from the silvery soil and rocks that I found myself half sun-blind, and was caught by surprise as we entered a structure of some sort.

Looking up, I saw stone pillars that wouldn't have seemed out of place in London (a city fairly rampant with examples of Hellenist architectural enthusiasms.) Towering above the building was a titanic statue to some goddess or hero – the face a younger version of the terrifying visage we'd seen from far above. Our captors seemed to pay reverence to the statue as they passed, muttering words and touching fingertips to their foreheads. Not wanting to seem disrespectful, I mimicked their motion and was swatted across the buttocks with the flat of one of their spears for my trouble.

At length we were shown into an enormous chamber filled with statues of women in various martial poses wielding swords, spears and bows to fight off a host of rather phallic-looking serpents. "Willingdon!" I whispered, "Willingdon, what is going on?! Who are these women?"

Willingdon, for his part, seemed utterly entranced with the whole affair – clearly the clot hadn't a clue how much danger we were in. "Why Doctor, they're the Daughters of Artemis! It appears that they didn't just learn to manipulate the image of the moon, they managed to travel here in order to avoid the destruction of their order."

"I thought they were wiped out over two thousand years ago? Are you telling me the moon is home to a race of man-hating amazons with an axe to grind?"

Willingdon spoke at length with some of the women, who seemed to have relaxed and were now visibly shedding armour, then he turned back to me.

"Yes and no, Doctor Cadwallader, it appears that they do indeed regard men as an abomination, but fortunately for us these ones don't seem to know what men actually *are*. Somehow they've sustained their population without them."

"No men? What the deuce do they think we are, then?"

"They think we're women from one of the other lunar cities that they're at war with. We've been captured, which means we'll be joining their city as slaves. It appears that their wars are largely bloodless."

"What's the point of a bloodless war, I ask you? Not that I'm complaining, but I don't like the sound of slavery. I'm not a fan of heavy labour or short rations."

"It seems fairly lenient, we'll be... *metics* might be the most apt description? Low-caste foreigners without political power, but not totally devoid of rights."

At this point the women descended upon us, removing our clothes with laughter and the obvious lack of nudity taboo, along with the odd slap to motivate us along when we dared to complain. Soon we stood as naked as babes before them, at which point, as you might imagine, they began to notice some anatomical differences. Clearly this was a cause for great hilarity and excitement, and women flooded in from all over to gawp at our strangely formed bodies. However, a few stern hand-claps from an older woman and the cackling horde dispersed. Quickly thereafter we were marched off to receive our new "clothing" – a few diaphanous silken wisps which completely failed to conceal anything, let alone the crowning glories with which a bounteous nature had furnished me.

We were put to menial tasks, although thankfully at least together, where we could talk. "Willingdon, we must get to the velocipede and escape!"

"I don't see how, Doctor. They are an extremely martial culture, and we've only been spared on promise of our good behaviour. If we try and fail, the verdict will be death."

"What, so I'm supposed to just let them ogle me in this ridiculous rigging? The handkerchief I use to blow my nose on has more materials than this. If I *was* to be a lady, I wouldn't be the kind of lady that wears things like this!"

At this point, providence smiled on us as we saw the velocipede leaning against the wall of a forge – clearly their intention was to melt it down and no doubt make armour or weapons out of it.

"Come on, Willingdon, we must make a break for it! Ride like the wind!" So saying, I leapt onto the rear of the contraption and bid him take the fore.

Of course, he dithered until the last minute, but as soon as one of the warrior-women appeared round the corner the decision was made; he leapt aboard and we both began to pedal like fury, hurtling through the corridors of the temple complex. Behind us the sound of alarums began to grow, and soon we were being pursued by a mob of the harpies, baying for our blood.

"We can't gain altitude without access to the sky," whimpered Willingdon, giving me quite the view of his pale, bony backside.

Abruptly we came in sight of the main entrance, but before us swarmed quite the mob of amazons blocking the way. A veritable thicket of sharpened spears blocked our egress. Suddenly inspired, I reached forward and yelled to Willingdon, "The string, pull the string!"

He just gaped at me with a lack of understanding, and cursing I lunged forwards and yanked on the firing mechanism for the tiny mortar. Suddenly our vehicle ground to a halt as the metal sphere fired out of the front, bowling over the gaggle of ferocious moon-maidens like ninepins.

"Go!" I shouted and began to pedal for all I was worth. Willingdon quickly followed suit, and tortuously the velocipede set off again. Our pursuers were almost on us, and I felt a spear tip nick the cheek of one buttock before we got up sufficient acceleration to begin wobbling into the air. Cries of outrage began to sound from behind us, their amazement probably sparing our lives as they only began to throw their spears once we were already at a fairly safe distance.

Even after the surface began to fall away behind us, I found I was much more enthused with pedalling this time around, and matched the Professor as we hurtled away. By the time we once more reached the mid-point our gauzy outfits were stuck slick to our bodies with sweat, even further degrading their already negligible ability to conceal any flesh from prying eyes.

At this point Willingdon began to cry out and roll his eyes in a fearful funk, "Doctor, you fired the return momentum sphere! We'll have no way to slow down once we return to Earth."

I bridled somewhat at this – after all, if it hadn't been for my quick thinking we'd have been dead or serving as handmaids to those gorgons for the rest of our lives – and I let him know my opinions with some choice words. Needless to say the debate was lively, and we wasted most of the time up to entering the Earth's atmosphere with bitter recriminations.

"Pax! Pax! It doesn't matter whose fault this is, all that matters now is survival. Think, man, you built this contraption, surely there's something you can do?"

"It's impossible! There's no way we can launch anything with enough mass or force to carry the momentum away from the velocipede. Face it, Doctor Cadwallader, we're doomed."

"I don't give a damn about your boneshaker, I just want me to get to Earth safely!"

"Wait… you might actually have something there. The momentum transference device, we could detach it, then propel ourselves away from the main body of the velocipede… It's incredibly risky, but it might just work."

"I have no idea what you're talking about, old boy, but have at it! Time is very much a-wasting!"

Needless to say, the mysterious aerial bombardment that caused so much damage at Kew Gardens was widely noted, with fragments of the velocipede recovered from a considerable radius. The two gentlemen (one husky, the other tall and thin, both clad only in slick gauze) who were seen fleeing from the vicinity shortly afterwards were never identified. Officially the moon-trip remains a moon mystery.

But I swear, sometimes I see the moon hanging sullenly over the horizon, and I know to the depths of my bones that it's looking down disapprovingly right at me. I glower back at it. Take heed, you young bucks of adventurous spirit – the moon is no place for men!

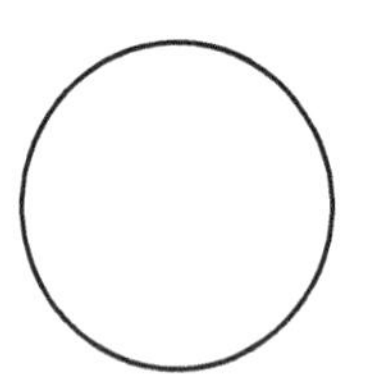

The Changing Face of Selene

Hannah Hulbert

In the distance Selene descended, a silver-white sliver gaining on her brother Helios on a horizon still brushed with his brightness. Tonight, her journey finished early and in the North-West, and I bubbled with excitement. I perched on the boulder at the entrance to our cave as she touched that narrow window of open ocean between the islands, plunging beneath wine-coloured waves. Hours stretched between us and dawn. The summer breeze blew fresh from the sea, scented with salt and juniper and baked earth. I'd brought a lamp, and occupied my restless hands and mind with the calculations and measurements I'd been working on. The flame's guttering amber was a poor substitute for Selene's brilliance. Just as the mathematical art of astronomy was a poor substitute for her tender arms. I waited, wrapped in the star-studded evening and my anticipation.

At last, a shimmering on the water far below lured my attention from my studies. Her chariot skimmed across the waves, the wings of her steeds spread wide to glide low. The nearer they came, the harder my heart hammered, until they were so close the rocky hillside hid them. I set aside my pot-shard scrawled with notes and rose to pace, wringing my hands.

Selene's glow heralded her, a gentle light that spilt over the boulders, incising deep shadows between them. And then there she stood. My being brimmed with adoration, my chest fairly bursting, my limbs quivering.

"Endymion!" She greeted me, pale arms open. I stepped into her embrace. "How do you grow more beautiful with every day?" Her voice breathed in my ear.

Her slender fingers caught my jaw and turned my face up to meet hers. Skin as cold and dazzling as marble. Hair a cascade of jet curls. The diadem on her brow curved upwards into twin horns to match her waxing crescent. And her eyes. Black as midnight and as void of humanity. She lowered her mouth onto mine and we dissolved into one another in ecstasy.

On this balmy night, the cave cocooned us in cool seclusion. She had conjured for us cushions and rugs and sheets of purple silk on the floor, level and smooth near the back. We left the lamp: Selene was radiant. Every layer of clothing she allowed me to lift from her revealed more pale, glowing skin. When we lay together, she cast shadowy distortions of my form dancing up the craggy walls.

She stroked my cheek and pierced me with her gaze. "Beautiful," she sighed, and drew me closer.

A cloudy sky was just visible from our nest, dark beyond dark with Selene's absence. My chest swelled at the thought, that the whole world would be deprived of her light, that I might have it all to myself. I shifted between the sheets, untangling our limbs. Selene moaned and rolled away, eyes still closed. I nudged her and she stirred with a growl in her throat.

"Selene?"

"What?" She answered, husky and distant. Her lovely tresses spilled across her face and down her shoulder. The sight of her made me ache.

"Do you ever think about how we first met?"

"Not now, I don't." She turned and her hair fell back. Her perfect features shone.

I leaned closer and planted a kiss on her cheek. "I do. I think about the green boy I was when you first found me studying your passage across the heavens. How you came to me here, in this cave, as I recorded my observations and calculated where and when I might see you again, and which face you would wear. I remember how you climbed this hillside and..."

"I'm trying to sleep," she snapped.

Her chest rose and fell, fast and deep. She wasn't sleeping, not even nearly.

"And you told me how beautiful I was." Nothing. "Do you love me?"

She shot upright, eyes narrow.

"How can you ask me that? I am a goddess. I don't owe you anything!"

"Owe? No, of course not. But I wonder what will befall a mortal like me. You change all the time, but you always end up exactly as you were before." I knew as I said the words that they sounded petulant, and I hated myself as they spilled out of me nonetheless.

"What will befall you if you do not rest is ill health. Now go to sleep and allow me to do likewise." And with that our conversation ended.

But I didn't sleep. Thoughts chased themselves around my mind like heavenly bodies, an unending cycle of growing and shrinking and returning to where they began.

When dawn blushed the sky, fresh and rosy-fingered, Selene arose to find me dressed and devouring the food I'd packed for us the evening before. She studied me from across our shelter and covered her alabaster body with her chiton, stalking about the mess of bedding on long, gleaming legs. I tried not to stare.

She dressed her hair and straightened her peplos into regular swallowtails at her waist, and strode over. The fabric poured like liquid silver from the fastenings at her shoulders. How I longed to strip it from her again. But this morning she was a goddess, not my lover; distant and emanating power. The thoughts of our intimacy mingled with the sight of this divine creature and I rose, drawn towards her like a lodestone. She swept past and made a pretence of admiring the view, sipping nectar from a kylix.

"How are we this morning?" she asked, brusque and distant.

"Fine." I said, without turning from the twinkling waves.

She finished her cup, and I picked at the crumbs of a honey cake in silence.

"Will you be waiting this evening?" She spoke into the gap between us.

How could I not? My irritation washed away in a flood of devotion. I gulped a breath to keep myself from drowning in affection. "Of course. I will always wait for you."

And with that promise in her possession, she slipped away.

Summer parched the mountainside. By day, I attended my lessons, although I could focus on nothing but my calculations. I had never had close friends amongst the youths in my class, but now they seemed to me like nothing more than shadows cast by people I didn't know. Father talked about arranging my marriage, and mistook my disinterest as a rejection of the individuals he suggested rather than the concept in general. The thought of binding myself to anyone other than Selene sent a sweat of panic down my spine.

Sometimes I wandered the shady groves near the village in the pretence of watching my father's flocks. My mind tumbled over the numbers that divided me from my beloved, as though finding the perfect formula might reduce the wait itself. My imagination wove elaborate fantasises of how I would solve the riddle, of where her journey began and how she moved from one horizon to another unseen, and how her size and shape seemed so different from one night to the next. Some days the answers seemed so close I could almost articulate them. Father despaired of the stacks of papyrus I squandered on diagrams of circles balancing annotated lines. But I remained confident that her perfection could be encapsulated by an elegant equation. That I would reveal the mystery to the world, so all might know my lover too, and share in my adoration.

Every evening I crept away to our hiding place and waited for my goddess. As she waxed, her journey began later, and she shared the sky with her fiery brother. On those days I stole some hours of sleep before escaping the house, scaling the hillside by the light of her brilliance. On the days when her face was full, her diadem bearing a perfect circle of precious metal, she would come to me in full daylight. Excuses for my absence grew harder to come by.

As she waned, so did my vigour. She rose in the early evening, and I retired to our sheets, awaiting her arrival after sunrise. Yet sleep evaded me. Somewhere out there she travelled to earth, admired by all, perfect and unobtainable. I tossed and turned and my energy ebbed. And when she came, she took more from me than I could spare. I had neither the will nor the desire to deny her.

Summer was high when her face had shrunk into a pale paring in the sky. She came to me at midnight, and we collapsed together in exhaustion in our sanctuary. The horns on her diadem were so sharp and slender, I knew I would not see her the next night. She wanted my beautiful body, but I wanted constancy. The knowledge that we would be parted ate me up with sickness. My mind teetered as she pressed me down against the layers of silk, her pale skin cool against my own sun-darkened and clammy exterior. Her breath, a whisper of breeze carrying jasmine. Her eyes, voids. I took little comfort in her embrace. She took whatever she wanted from me, as she always did.

*

I awoke to Helios climbing somewhere on the other side of the mountain. A sky of streaky indigo hung framed by the gloomy cave mouth. She was already gone.

I dressed, and realised that I had neglected to bring food with me. Selene had left her kylix with its golden dregs, but nothing for a mortal to consume. The western slope of the mountainside stretched cold and dark, and the heavens, vast as eternity and utterly empty. I staggered down the shepherd-trail that led home, and slipped quietly to my bedchamber, to pretend that I had been there all night. I closed my eyes, but awoke again with a jolt to the clatter of breakfast being set out in the courtyard. I splashed my face with water from the basin in the corner and ventured into the house.

Father fixed me with a stare as I sat at the table. I pretended not to notice as I helped myself to a handful of figs I had suddenly lost any appetite for.

"Well, Endymion. What are your plans for today?"

"School. A walk."

"You know, I would be fascinated to take a look at your work some time. I have always had an interest in astronomy, and your Master tells me that you have been making significant progress in the field..."

I made a sound in my throat that acknowledged his words without agreeing to anything, moving the food around my plate. When I stole a glimpse at him, Mother was leaning over the table to pour water for us both, their eyes linked in silent conspiracy.

"You know, Penelope was asking after you again. I imagine she would be thrilled to be invited out on your walk..." Mother said, her voice taut with forced amicability.

"I'm sure she would. Excuse me."

I faded from the table and spent the daylight hours with my Master and peers, though my mind wandered elsewhere.

I left the house in the early evening and returned to the cave to watch the sun set. The islands cast long shadows across the sea, the whole spectacle a riot of red and orange fire. The colours faded, and the sky darkened and she did not come. In the fading light, I checked my chart. Somewhere in the brilliance of the sunset, the faintest slice of moon must have passed unnoticed. I waited in the mouth of the cave, alone. Some time before dawn I awoke, slumped over my knees on a boulder and shivering. I staggered home by starlight, half blind on the steep, uneven trail. I climbed into my bed grazed and bruised and slept through most of the next day.

Daylight poured through my window. Someone stood at my bedside, but the sun stung my eyes. I hid behind my forearms and tried to tell them to go away, but my throat seemed to be full of sand.

"It's worse than I thought," said a voice I didn't recognise.

"What's wrong with him? Can anything be done to help his condition?" That was my father.

"An excess of black bile. Most uncommon for the season. Plenty of warm, watery foods, a visit to the Laconica baths. Make an offering to Asclepius. But the most important thing is to lift the lad's spirits. A patient will not become well if he does not strive to become so."

Murmurs of conversation drifted to me as the voices receded. Father must be worried for me if he had called for a physician. A flutter of gratitude at his concern immediately sank beneath a torrent of thoughts for Selene. She hadn't spared a thought for me. How disloyal must I be to doubt her affection? Where was she now? Was she safe and well? It overwhelmed me, my gut twisting at the conflict. I tried heaving myself upright, but couldn't muster the energy.

I must have fallen asleep, because when I opened my eyes, the light had faded. A surge of terror burst in me, threatening to explode my chest open with the force of my beating heart. How late was it? What time would the moon set tonight? Had I missed her? The rush of urgency pushed any other concerns from my mind. I swung myself out of bed, and only for a moment wondered that I found it so easy. I didn't pause to change out of the chiton I had tumbled into bed in. I stole through the twilit house and slipped my sandals on to flee into the evening.

The sun still loitered on the western horizon. Fresh air winnowed away the fug of confusion enough that I recalled my calendar of ascents and descents. I had plenty of time before Selene's journey would come to an end. Months of nightly pilgrimage had scored the trail into my memory. The cuts and bruises faded to a complaint in my flesh, so distant they seemed almost to belong to someone else.

I found the cave dark and empty, to my disappointment but not surprise. I sat on the rock at the entrance as the sunset faded into charcoal grey over the water. I had no oil for the lamp to check the scroll I'd left inside. I didn't need to check. When only the brightness of the stars lit the world, I knew that I would not see her. I lay myself across the threshold between the rocks and, shivering, drifted in and out of consciousness until dawn.

By the light of the morning I crawled to retrieve my scroll, and alternated staring at the rows of inked characters with my scrutiny of the sky. I filled the gap Selene left in my life with all I had left of her: mathematics and longing. In the relentless heat of the afternoon sun, I occupied myself by carving my calculations into the smooth limestone of the cliff. The wind whipped along the coast, bringing snatches of sound. Somewhere, someone called my name. But it wasn't Selene, so I didn't answer.

Another night passed, and still she did not come. The third. I had never been apart from her so long since first we met. The dryness in my throat and a rumbling in my belly reminded me that my body had demands of its own, but they seemed foreign and abstract. When morning came, I could not tell whether I had slept at all. It didn't matter either way. She wasn't coming back.

Some rational voice in my mind knew that the movements of the gods are beyond the control of mortals. But it was a soft voice, drowned by the screaming of anguish at her abandonment, and my worthless inability to lure her back. A wave of self-pity would crash over me, tight in my gut and cloying in my throat. And then the dragging undercurrent of guilt that I should accuse my beloved so, and the knowledge that I deserved this punishment for my failure. My mouth tasted bitter. My head pounded. Sometimes I longed for relief, but a moment later I would cling to my suffering, the only thing left of my Selene. Except the tangled bedding. And dregs of her nectar.

I dragged myself to the almost empty kylix and peeked over the rim. A black-figure scene of Dionysus and the Maenads cavorted through the shallow liquid. I lifted the cup by a handle, and the contents slithered across the image, making the whole thing sparkle.

Nectar was not for mortals. Selene would be furious if she discovered I had sampled the drink of the gods. But she wasn't here, and I was, and couldn't bear to be any longer. The nectar would kill me if I drank it. I sighed out a sound that began as a laugh and ended as a sob. Was there a more fitting end for a man cast aside by a goddess?

I didn't think. I twisted the kylix with my wrist to meet my lips, where last her lips had touched, and drained the liquid. It burned like molten gold.

I gasped and fell forwards, chips of stone and dust breaking the skin of my palms in a pain overruled by the one in my throat. I could not cry out. I tried to claw through the skin of my neck, but found no relief. And when it reached a pinnacle, a saturation of agony that surpassed my ability to tell it, it passed into pleasure. Smouldering. Warming. Making every fibre of my being vibrate with power. But the power didn't belong inside my body.

For all that, I felt no closer to death than I had before I drank. I collapsed forward into the dirt and the rest of the day is lost to me.

"Endymion!"

Someone called to me. I hoped they would not find me.

"Endymion, what happened to you?" I peeled an eyelid open. The western sea still carried Helios' brightness, but neither sun nor moon was in sight. I turned to the voice.

Selene.

A jolt to my body almost caused me to sit up. But my muscles refused. The throb of anguish began in my gut and spread outwards. She should not see me like this. What would she think? Shame and guilt pushed through. But what could I do? Nothing.

She pierced me with those midnight eyes. Her mouth pinched at the edges in an expression I could not read. Pity? Concern? Revulsion? And then she stooped towards me, slid her arms around my back and under my knees and picked me up like an injured infant. I should have baulked at her treating me as such, but her skin against mine felt so delicious, I found my eyes squandering tears of relief.

She lay me in our nest, head propped on a pillow, and sat beside me, face still contorted into an expression of emotion alien to her flawless face. She sighed and pushed her hair behind her ears. The diadem showed its narrow crescent again. She was waxing. I smiled up at her, suffused with peace back in her presence.

"Oh Endymion. What happened to you?" Was it a rebuke? I opened my mouth, but no words would come. She brushed my cheek with her fingertips and studied me with those far-away eyes. "What a waste of such beauty."

"I'm sorry," I croaked, and almost felt sincere.

"For what? Wrecking this lovely body, or contaminating it with nectar?" She stared into me. I shrank into myself, but couldn't hide. "Yes, I can see it changing you. Maybe you heard about mortals gifted with nectar by the gods, and thought that you could steal some eternal youth for yourself. Am I right?"

No, she wasn't. But my cracked lips wouldn't part.

"Alas for you, it takes a god to direct those changes. Your youthful beauty shall never fade because you paid for it with your years. I'm sorry, sweet boy. There's no way to undo what you have done."

Dying. I was dying. Was that relief that clenched inside me? The finality suddenly overwhelmed me. I couldn't stop my body shaking, and hated my inability to master my own flesh. And then I remembered that it wouldn't be my flesh much longer, and my damaged throat managed a small, involuntary sob.

"I love you," I managed to whisper. They were the biggest words I could manage, yet laughably inadequate.

"Of course you do. And I will miss you terribly."

"I don't want to leave you," I managed though my tears.

A smile played on her lips. "Maybe you don't have to. I can't undo what you have set into motion, but, perhaps, I can alter your course just a little..."

Her brow furrowed in concentration as she studied me with those unintelligible eyes.

"Yes!" she exclaimed. "I cannot prolong your life." My heart sank. "But I can put off your death… indefinitely, I think. Endymion, my dear. Would you like to rest here in our cave in eternal sleep? As beautiful as you ever were? I may come here and kiss you whenever I please."

She flashed her pristine teeth, and a chill of fear brushed me. I imagined myself in the cave, a hundred years from now, my family and everyone I had ever known dead from old age. And my body here, unprotected, alone…

"Of course you would." She leant forwards.

"Wait!" I rasped, and managed to catch her wrist as it descended. Her mouth opened in surprise.

"You don't want to wait for me any more?"

Was it an accusation? Petulance? But then she grinned. No spark twinkled in her empty eye. She placed her divine lips on mine, and my concerns melted away. An alabaster hand slid over my chest and I gasped. I had nothing left in me, I had spent it all. If only I had more to offer her.

"I will wait for you. Forever."

"That's what I want too." She ran her tongue along her lips, curled at the corners.

Her icy fingertips touched my eyelids, pressing them closed. "Sleep," her voice commanded in my ear, and I do.

Now her face is always the face of invisible darkness. And she still pursues me in my ceaseless dreams across the black sky. Relentless, insatiable, eternal.

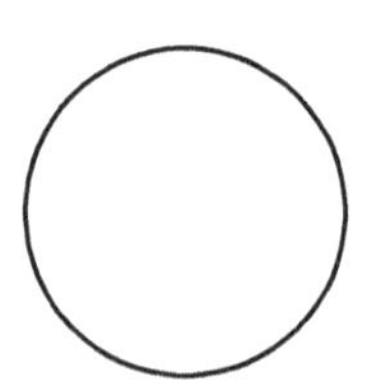

The Erasing of Gagaringrad

David Turnbull

The moon was full. It was not a coincidence. It was part of their conspiracy. Commissar Tranh could feel his shirt sticking to the sweat on his back. It was a humid, oppressively muggy night. He struggled to draw a decent lungful of breath.

Around him the litter-strewn streets seemed tensely subdued. Like the guilty silence after an argument, or the tension before it erupts once more. The only sound that accompanied the echo of his brisk footfall was the rhythmic chirruping of the crickets on the roadside verges.

Tranh was about to enact an arrest. Undoubtedly the most important arrest of his entire career. In the prevailing volatile climate, it was imperative that the apprehension of the suspect was seen by all as a powerful political statement. Despite the sombre times the knowledge that he was held in high enough esteem to be entrusted with this responsibility buoyed him with a deep sense of pride.

He had received the phone call relaying his orders fifteen minutes earlier and, in the interests of expediency, he'd decided to walk the short distance from his Party allocated apartment. He would cross Li Thi Reing Park to the district where a police unit was closing in on a roach-infested guest house.

These were austere times. The possibility of any car sent to fetch him breaking down was too high for it to be worth the risk. The fact that the fleet of vehicles allocated to the KGB(V) was notoriously badly maintained was a cause of constant frustration for Tranh. It crossed his mind that perhaps now would be the opportune time to lobby for additional resources.

He paused a moment by the towering edifice of the Khrushchev monument. Dabbing his brow with a handkerchief he stared up at the moon. There was a dark, ragged crater where Gagaringrad had once stood. The vast domed city had been home to five million citizens. It had been constructed over several decades near the location of the 1959 Soviet moon landing.

Three nights ago, it had been blown into obliteration by an audacious act of terrorism. The conspirators were said to belong to a counter-revolutionary Trotskyite faction. These maggots had somehow engineered an infiltration of Gagaringrad that burrowed so deep they had managed to detonate the nuclear reactor which provided the city's primary energy source.

Worse yet, before the authorities had the chance to intervene, they had hacked into the global newsfeed channel. Grainy satellite footage of the aftermath of the explosion showed an ominous black crater where Gagaringrad had been. Above it, in the weightless atmosphere, billions of glistening crystal fragments of reinforced glass dancing and spinning in slow motion, like glittering snowflakes in a blizzard.

The message which scrolled beneath the footage read – *We have stolen back the moon.*

Watching it on his single channel monochrome TV set, Tranh had felt an almost overwhelming sense of personal loss. The white plastic apartments of Gagaringrad had boasted huge colour monitors embedded into their walls. It was said there was a choice of dozens of channels. He often daydreamed that as a reward for his commitment and loyalty to the Party he would be allocated a retirement cubicle on the moon.

Tranh had long regarded Gagaringrad as a symbolic representation of the socialist Utopia in its purest form. He longed to walk in white plimsolls through chrome corridors where neither dust nor bugs tainted the air and the piston driven oxygen felt like menthol in your lungs.

For him the needle point of light the city exuded from the surface of the moon was a beacon of hope. The visible exclamation mark of a powerful and progressive world order that had begun to comprehensively quash the incorrectness of alternative political thought years before he was born. Like the moon itself, Gagaringrad's glow could be seen by all of humanity, across every continent of the world, from pole to pole, to the farthest reaches of the 2nd Warsaw Pact.

Tranh had an excellent grasp on the historical significance of such matters. Cosmonaut Gagarin's first step onto the surface of the moon had given the Soviets the confidence to be bold. The relief of Cuba had led to the surrender and military execution of John F Kennedy, last of the capitalist despots. The dominoes had rapidly fallen, from Latin America to Australasia and everywhere else between.

Tranh's clear comprehension of such concepts had earned him a medal of intellectual valour in High School. This had hastened his career progression to Political Commissar to the KGB(V), the Vietnamese division of the Soviet KGB. His personal trajectory had sparked within him the hope that one day he would be selected to ascend to the fabulous city that sat on the Sea of Tranquillity.

Tonight, though, there was an outrage in the sky. The moon defiled. Gagarin's legacy affronted. The Unified Peoples' Congress, in session at the New Kremlin, the dome's fabulous centrepiece, massacred, slaughtered like cattle. The bastard who did this skulking somewhere in Ho Chi Minh city.

A battered scooter, held together by reams of silver duct tape, went puttering by, coughing a dense cloud of petroleum smoke. The design of these scooters hadn't altered since his childhood. They were mass produced in factories across the communal zones of South East Asia. As a schoolboy he'd ridden pillion on the one owned by his elder brother.

As the cloud of exhaust smoke dissipated Tranh's eyes were drawn to the other side of the street. Here, weary-looking factory workers from the nightshifts were queuing for their daily bowl of steamed rice. Above them a gigantic dot matrix display proclaimed another season of increased rice production which had, despite the economic challenges, exceeded the expectations of the official five-year projection by a stupendous seventeen percent.

"All praise the stoic resilience of the farmers' collectives."

This put things in perspective. Tranh felt his heart swell. Each decade the incremental achievements of the world-wide revolution advanced with a steady forward momentum that was lasting and irreversible. Within his lifetime it was entirely feasible that austerity would become a thing of the past. All the more perplexing then that someone had committed this act of destruction and genocide.

With a last glance at the wounded moon he set out at rapid pace to cross the park. Tiny bats flitted in his line of vision, hunting down flying insects. As he walked, klaxons began to sound, shattering the silence. The argument had resumed. He heard a distant barrage of gunfire, saw smoke rising in trailing plumes above the corrugated iron rooftops of the white walled buildings.

It had been like this ever since Gagaringrad was swallowed by the mushroom cloud. People were cutting off their noses to spite their faces, biting the hands that fed them. The state-run newspaper was calling it '*moon madness*'. For most of his adult life the sight of Gagaringrad in the night sky had anchored the world and given it an unwavering stability. Now the regimented order of things was adrift.

On his belt, Tranh's radio pager began to buzz and vibrate. He unclipped it and squinted at the words that appeared in the LED window housed within the chunky plastic block.

Suspect has entered building.

Tranh typed back awkwardly, cursing his fat fingers.

On my way.

Clipping the pager back on his belt he sighed and shook his head, wondering if he would ever truly keep abreast with the unrelenting pace of technological advance that had been experienced since the millennium.

A sudden, unexpected shot rang out. He felt the bullet buzz past him like a mosquito. Heard the dull thunk of it as it embedded itself into the trunk of a nearby palm tree. "Go lick the boots of your Russian masters," yelled a voice in the darkness.

Another shot.

This time the bullet threw up dry dirt as it hit the ground at his feet.

Tranh pulled his Marakov from his shoulder holster, crouching low to return fire. The Marakov semi-automatic was standard issue for all KGB ranks. Tranh had paid to have his name engraved onto the barrel when he was promoted to Commissar. Whenever he held it, it felt like shaking hands with an old friend. He fired off three shots in succession before he heard footsteps running away.

"When we catch you, we'll string you from a lamppost, Bolshevik poodle," came the parting insult.

Tranh looked again at the gouged eye that had been Gagaringrad. *Moon madness* indeed. Without this atrocity no one would ever have dared shoot at him. He was a Commissar of the KGB(V) after all. Such disrespectful sentiment would not have been countenanced, let alone tolerated. He made a mental note. Once the arrest was executed, he would personally examine the camera footage from the park's entrances, suspects would be matched against photographs held in their files and rounded up. An example would be made.

Approaching the far side of the park now he saw another dot matrix screen on the rooftop of one of the buildings. This one was lodged between two imposing statues. Marx and Engels, towering like stoic bookends at either side. The announcement proclaimed another 4000 kilometres of cable, delivering electricity to rural communities.

That was a wonderful thing. Such an achievement.

When he was a boy back in the 1980's they had used kerosene lamps after sunset. That had been the glorious decade in which the construction of Gagaringrad commenced. On clear nights, when the moon was full, his grandfather would take him to the edge of the rice paddies. He had an old rusted telescope from the days when he'd served in the insurrectionist army that had ousted the French imperialists from old Saigon.

Tranh would stand there, dressed in a faded hand me down tee-shirt depicting Yuri Gagarin in his CCCP cosmonaut helmet. Trembling with anticipation he'd press the telescope to his eye to try and spot the fiery fuel trails of the glimmering cargo shuttles transporting raw materials through space from the Soviet rocket bases in Siberia.

"See that?" his grandfather would say. "They are building a city on the moon. Who would have ever thought such a thing was possible? It proves beyond doubt the power that workers and intellectuals can exert when they're unified in common cause."

Tranh wondered at the outrage his grandfather would feel now that Gagaringrad was gone. Obliterated. Wiped from the face of the moon. And how in its absence disrespectful little shits felt emboldened enough to take pot-shots at a high-ranking commissar. He would surely spit on the ground and curse the traitors.

Grinding his teeth against his own anger, Tranh pushed on across the park.

The dilapidated boarding house was directly opposite the gate through which he exited.

Quite a crowd had gathered there, soldiers and police officers, the Party chairman of the local district, several operatives from the KGB(V), the commissioner of police, resplendent in rows of ribbons and shiny medals. Also, a camera crew and a reporter from VTV News. Around them a crowd of expectant onlookers. Party faithful who had been summoned to the area to cheer the impending victorious arrest.

As Tranh pushed his way through the police cordon, flashing his ID, a malcontent who had somehow infiltrated the crowd spat in his face. Two policewomen wrestled the man to the ground and beat him fiercely with their nightsticks before bundling him into the back of an armoured wagon.

Tranh wiped away the spit and began systematically shaking hands with the assembled dignitaries. He made great show for the camera of loading the Marakov with fresh bullets. A set of handcuffs was slipped into his jacket pocket. The arrest was to be a piece of highly synchronised theatre. He was to carry it out single-handed and then be filmed handing the suspect over to the police commissioner. The message had to go out that the Party remained in full control and that the class traitors were being brought swiftly to justice.

A soldier held the door open for him. He passed through into the dingy reception area. Another soldier stood guard next to the desk clerk. The clerk's narrow hand trembled when he handed the passkey to Tranh. "Room twelve," he whispered and nodded to a stairway that was covered by the stringy remains of a threadbare carpet.

The stairs creaked and groaned as he climbed them. The place smelled as if its sewage pipes had backed up. A mouse sat upright on his approach, then scurried away into a hole it had chewed into the crumbling plasterwork. Tranh stopped at a paint-flaked door with the number twelve painted onto it in a red chicken scrawl. He turned the key in the lock and pushed the door slowly open with the toe of his shoe.

A woman stood by the window, back toward him, illuminated in moon glow, black hair down to her shoulders. Tranh held the Marakov steady and cleared his throat as he stepped into the room. "Surrender," he said. "You are under arrest for acts of conspiracy and counter revolutionary terrorism."

She turned.

Tranh cautiously curved his finger around the Marakov's trigger.

She looked to be in her mid-thirties. Narrow cheeks. Dark bags under her eyes.

"You look surprised, comrade," she said. "What's the matter? You don't believe that the concept of equality between the sexes can be grasped by anyone other than the Party faithful?"

Tranh laughed.

"Trotskyites don't discriminate when it comes to the corruption of political thought."

She laughed back.

"You people are obsessed with Trotsky. He was a dead force long before that ice-pick did for him. We are not a faction of the political infighting that has riven you for decades. We are something different. Something your flawed political correctness can't begin to comprehend."

"Do you even realise what you've done?" said Tranh. Have you no shame? No conscience?"

Her neck straightened as her jaw jutted forward. "It was a grand gesture of defiance. A spark necessary to ignite a firestorm."

"Five million souls perished inside Gagaringrad," he reminded her.

"Three million workers serving two million privileged elite," she countered. "An elite who filled their faces and stuffed their bellies. They guzzled rocket fuel to maintain their conceit and looked down from their high perch while the world starved. In the East the rice harvest fails. In the West the wheat harvest fails. Yet the propaganda machine rolls relentlessly onward, proclaiming the quotas set by the cynical logic of the economic plans have been consistently surpassed."

"May the ghosts of those five million heroes haunt your nightmares," said Tranh.

She stood straight, unrepentant. "Better the lives of five million than eight billion forced to live like ghosts under the yoke of totalitarianism."

Tranh felt the ire rising within him. Her reckless arrogance and political naivety had robbed him of Gagaringrad. His birthright.

He took the handcuffs from his pocket and held them out, other hand still training the Marakov on her. "Put on these cuffs," he ordered. "There will be a public trial. People will see you executed as the class traitor you are."

With a surprising burst of speed, she snatched the cuffs from him and cast them to the ground. He saw her other hand rise in a blur and felt something scalding splash against his face.

"Go to Hell, Bolshevik lacky," she yelled as he stumbled back.

For one dreadful moment Tranh thought she'd thrown acid at him. He almost descended into panic. Then his nostrils caught the distinctive scent of Jasmine. She'd been drinking Jasmine tea. A teacup was in her hand when she'd turned around. He'd barely registered the fact.

He wiped his eyes and opened them in time to see her disappear through the window onto the fire escape. He was about to call out for help but cautioned himself against it. His superiors expected a single-handed arrest. If he failed there would be consequences.

Marakov gripped tightly in his hand, he followed her through the window. She was already on the last rung of the ladder. As he began his climb, she dropped down into the alley. Had there not been such confidence in the arrest going off without a hitch there might have been a police officer stationed to guard the back route. But as it was there was no one to stop her.

Tranh swung himself over the railings, landed hard and rolled, picked himself up and gave chase. She led him deep into the warren of the vast slum that spread wantonly out behind the guest house. Cats and rats fled before them as he chased her through the narrow gunnels and alleyways.

Finally, she came to a dead end and he had her cornered. This time he took no chances. Drenched in sweat and wincing against a painful stitch in his side he took aim and shot her in the foot to prevent her from attempting to run again. She bent over breathing heavily, blood gushing over her shoe as she pressed her hand to it.

In the distance there came a series of rapid explosions, followed by erratic bursts of automatic gunfire. Overhead a ferocious roar erupted in Tranh's ears. A Red Army helicopter came in low over the rooftops, spinning wildly, black smoke churning from its cockpit. The backdraft of its rotating blades almost knocked Tranh from his feet. Moments later, the helicopter exploded in mid-air as it became entangled in some overhanging telephone wires. Tranh felt the hairs on the back of his head scorching and singeing.

As smoke swirled through the alley the woman pulled herself to her feet, raised her bloodied hand and pointed at the moon. "You see, comrade," she crowed. "Once it was a symbol of your oppression. Now it's become a symbol of our liberation."

Tranh's temper finally broke. He took his gun and shot her again. She was thrown back against the wall. Bleeding from her belly she keeled over and slumped to her knees.

"Fool," she mocked. "You have no idea what you've just done."

Tranh grinned cockily, unwilling to disguise his confidence before this spawn of the maggots' nest. "I killed a terrorist. You were attempting to evade justice. I will be awarded the highest honour."

She laughed and spat blood from her mouth. "You really think what happened to Gagaringrad was the end? You of all people should appreciate the effectiveness of collective action. I worked as a cleaner in Gararingrad, secretly assembling the smuggled components of the bomb for a decade. That's the long game we played. But there are others who have been engaged in similar activities. I am Spartacus, comrade. We are many clenched fists. We punched the moon in the face. Who knows where we will punch next?"

"You fled like a coward before your treacherous device detonated," sneered Tranh. "Now you have your comeuppance."

"I am martyred, comrade," her breath rattled. "There will be others."

Realising now his mistake, Tranh holstered the Marakov and dropped to his knees, pressing his hand against the wound in a frantic attempt to stem the flow of blood. "Give me names," he urged her. "Tell me who your co-conspirators were. Tell me the location of the other targets. The rocket bases? Did you infiltrate them? I'll make sure they know that you cooperated. I'll save you from the firing squad."

A smug grin curved on her bloodied lips

"Too late, comrade."

He saw her eyes roll lethargically upward in their sockets as her eyelids fluttered shut. He thumped at her heart. Covered her nose and mouth with his mouth and tried to inflate her lungs with his breath. She lay limp and unresponsive beneath him, bleeding out from the wounds he'd inflicted.

Dejected he rose slowly to his feet, her blood dripping from his hands. The implications of his error of judgment were enormous. He'd have to report what she'd told him to his superiors. They would be less than happy at being robbed of the opportunity to interrogate her. At best he would be stripped of his rank. At worst it might be he who wound up in front of a firing squad.

His pager began to buzz. He wiped his hands on his trousers.

Headquarters building surrounded, it read as he scrolled down, *vastly out-numbered. Attack imminent. Is it within the perimeters of political correctness to fire on the crowd?*

For the first time in his career Tranh found himself in the paralysis of procrastination.

History was full of such pivotal moments. A single decision could change its course. He recalled his lessons from school. The storming of the Winter Palace and the ensuing slaughter by the Tzar's army. One of the greatest miscalculations ever.

Was this such a moment?

The pager buzzed again.

Awaiting orders.

A tear trickled down Tranh's cheek.

Fingers trembling, he typed back his message.

Shoot above their heads. If they continue to advance shoot to kill.

He knew he should also message for the traitor's body to be retrieved. But if headquarters building was under siege it meant that the integrity of the command structure was in jeopardy. His best option was to find a place of safety until the situation could be properly assessed.

He stumbled out to the main street and found himself in the middle of a crowd of angry men. They were armed with machetes. They immediately recognised him from his frequent appearances with the generals on the podium at the annual May Day Military parades. He was jostled and kicked, punched so hard in the face that his neck snapped back and he almost lost consciousness.

A rusted jitney juddered to a halt by the kerb. He was roughly bundled inside. Some of the men bundled themselves in beside him, surrounding him, blocking any chance of escape. He could see how much they despised him from the hatred that burned in their eyes.

One of them yanked the Marakov from its holster, grinning wildly as he ground the barrel into the flesh at the side of Tranh's head, teasing his finger over the trigger. Tranh knew without doubt that his fate was sealed. He felt thankful he had never married. There would be no children to mourn his passing.

The jitney trundled through the streets.

Tranh witnessed the smashing of dot matrix screens. Silky red hammer and sickle pendants fluttering in torn shreds. Statues of the heroes of the revolution toppled and rendered to rubble. Just as the conspirators had planned, the erasing of Gagaringrad had triggered a chain reaction. Its momentum now seemed completely unstoppable.

They passed an iconic faded poster from the golden era of the 1980's. It showed a soldier, a rocket engineer and a cosmonaut shoulder to shoulder, gazing up at a bright, perfectly round and silvery moon. Beneath it the words – *In Unity We Build the Future.*

Whose unity now? thought Tranh. *Whose future?*

As the jitney sped westward, heading for some remote spot where he would surely suffer the agonising brutality of the machetes before being shot in the head with his own beloved weapon, Tranh managed a last glimpse of the injured moon.

Suddenly there came a moment of startling clarity.

None of it truly mattered. Neither the past, nor the future. History was just that. History. Pure and simple. Ho Chi Minh city flickered in flames. The world would turn. Other cities would follow. The political imperative would shift.

The moon would watch impassively from its ancient place in the star-filled sky. It was empty now, no longer colonised and populated. As such it would remain as unmoved by the fervent machinations of humanity as it had throughout the tiny and insignificant beat of their existence.

Empires would rise – empires would fall.

Night would follow day.

The moon would wax – the moon would wane.

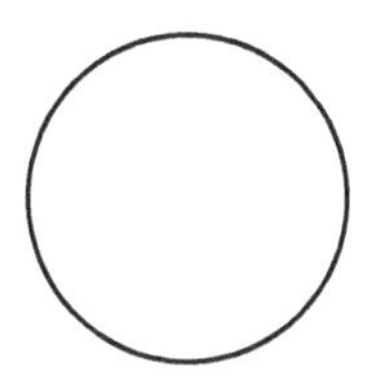

Synthia

A. N. Myers

P-
Pearl on black silk
P-p
Pearl
Pearl
Pearl on black s-silk
Silk

I admit that on several occasions I have been hired under false pretences. The companies that require my services are often under the misapprehension that I'm something called a Robopsychologist. I'm always at pains to tell them that there's no such job, not amongst reputable professionals at least; rather, I'm a psychologist concerned with human-machine systems, cognitive architectures and maladaptive machine behaviours. This explanation is a bit too prosaic for my more imaginative clients, who would prefer to visualise my robot patients stretching out on an ottoman while I probe them about their formative years. I don't care though; such misconceptions keep the contracts rolling in.

Bessemer Systems contacted me directly about Synthia. There was no agent involved. I'd worked with them once before, on 'depressed' agricultural machinery – honestly – and I knew they paid as well as anyone, which was good news, as ever since Henry died I'd been in a pretty rough place financially.

"It's about one of our special projects, Dr Galliard," the woman from Bessemer said. "The Miyamoto 9. Do you know of it?"

"Yes. I saw the prototype at the Stockholm Robotics Fair in...2051, I think? One of the big beasts, they service the wind farms, do high-level construction work, nuclear reactors, that sort of thing?"

I'd worked once before with an earlier model. The Miyamotos were a species of androids known colloquially as Donkey-Droids; anthropoid machines designed for highly-skilled tasks in hazardous environments. I'd heard rumours that these latest specimens had achieved rudimentary sentience, but I doubted this was true. The Miyamoto 4 I'd worked with wouldn't engage with the other machines in the chain of command; it was a complete imbecile.

"I can't tell you too much now," she said, when I pressed her about the nature of the problem. "Please be at the reception of our New Portsmouth Plant at six thirty pm."

"That seems quite late."

"Yes." Pause. "Well, sorry, but the robot's brain won't work any earlier than that."

"I beg your pardon?"

I hardly heard the reply as her voice shrank to a crackling squeak. "Don't ask me. It's technical. They tell me it's something to do with the moon."

I arrived outside the Robotics Research Centre around dusk. In the east, the aforementioned moon, faint and mottled, was sliding up the dimming blue sky apologetically. Beyond the jumble of warehouses and offices below me was the cold grey sea, whose horizon swarmed with thousands of wind turbines. Their insistent cumulative hum thrummed through the city, driving the inhabitants of New Portsmouth insane.

A sallow-faced, uncommunicative executive led me into a warehouse. They'd only mailed me the machine specifications twenty minutes ago, and I'd barely had time to skim the opening paragraphs. I felt nervous and disconcerted.

The Miyamoto 9 was waiting for me in the metallic gloom. I heard its servos whining and its hydraulics hissing as it clumped round to look at me; I felt the transmission of its weight shudder across the concrete floor. It was about fifteen feet tall, a massive assembly of turning steel surfaces in the shape of a giant man. Its head – beaked, flat-sided, like a gigantic lawnmower hopper – swivelled forward to examine me. I felt myself backing away. Its huge, ungainly movements worried me.

"Hello," I said, reaching out my hand and feeling ridiculous for doing so. "You're the Miyamoto 9?"

Gingerly, it extended its peculiarly delicate paw, a pack of short steel wires that bristled across my palm like sea anemones. The voice, which resembled that of an elderly lady's resonating around a steel drum, emerged from a grille in the pointed face. "Hello. I'm Synthia."

"Oh. You have a name?"

"My technicians call me Synthia. Synthetic Cynthia. With an S."

"That's nice. I'm Mark. Dr Mark Galliard. I'm here to talk to you, Synthia."

The lawnmower head dipped ruefully. "I suppose it's about my… unexcused absence."

I whisked through my notes. "It says here… four days ago… you were working on excavating the foundations of a skyscraper in… South London… and then – well, at… 7pm, you just disappeared. You were missing for nine hours. A child found you in her grandmother's garage." I closed the computer. "I'm afraid you cost Bessemer rather a lot of money."

"It's not my fault," said Synthia. "It was the moon. I had to see her, Dr Mark. I don't think they quite understand."

There was a movement behind me. Three white-coated figures were watching us from the shadows.

I turned back to Synthia. "What's so special about the moon?"

"What's so special?" she boomed, and I swear I could detect a catch of emotion in the voice. "The moon is my life. I can feel her now, Dr Mark, through the roof, through tons of concrete and steel girders. I can tell you her precise position in the sky, her exact phase, even her degree of absolute brightness. I can sense her through the thickest cloud. Whether she is bright, loud, and full – or silent, invisible, and new – is of no consequence to me. I must regard her, and *they* won't let me." She stamped around to face the watching technicians. "My soul travels to the moon and back in a never-ending cycle. When the moon sets, I am dead inside. And when she rises – I desire to stand beneath her and refresh myself. I suppose you think my interest strange."

"Oh no," I said. "Many people have worshipped the moon throughout history."

"Not now. Modern humans hardly see the moon. It's lost to them. A pearl on black silk, and no human ever sees it."

I was thinking that there had to be a major derangement here, and I was wondering at its cause; there might be excessive stimulation of the part of the brain from which deference to authority originated, which – maybe – could elicit a God-love. I wasn't an expert in neurotechnology, though; I was a psychologist, and dealt with behaviours and interactions. I smiled at Synthia. I knew she could understand smiles. Behind me the three watchers shifted expectantly.

"OK, Synthia. That's very interesting. Very unusual. I'm going to ask you to run some diagnostics. Then we're going to do a few simple tests. Like games."

"Oh good," said Synthia. "I like games."

*

Two hours later I was summoned to the office of McHudson, one of the Bessemer chief executives. He kept me waiting twenty minutes. I'm 62 years old and tend to take such incursions into my time personally, so I was rather curt with him during this meeting. McHudson's moustached face was chopped by bad temper and excessive cosmetic surgery.

"You've signed a non-disclosure agreement, and we intend to hold you to it," he said, chewing on this last phrase voraciously. "And I don't need to remind you of the personal risk to yourself of having signed such a document."

I smiled at this threat. "I'm the soul of discretion."

"OK. Well, as you know this machine has two brains. A hind brain – what we call the dumb brain, used for basic functions – and a smart brain, with an ersatz sentience. That's the learning brain, the valuable one, yeah? Unfortunately, the positronic net of this smart brain kept collapsing… we had a significant problem with positive feedback into the callosum – you know a positronic brain mirrors the human one, yeah?"

I nodded. "So you needed a fix."

"Yeah. So this is what we did. Took us a year to figure it out. We devised a ghost map of its positronic net – and beamed it to a distant target, a beacon on the moon – and bounced it back into the Miyamoto's frontal lobe nexus. The time it takes for this signal to do the round trip – just under three seconds – lets the positronic net calibrate. But it has disadvantages."

"Synthia can only use her smart brain when the moon is up." Her words – *my soul travels to the moon and back* – made sense now. "You referred to Synthia as having an ersatz sentience. What does that mean?"

"It's not an authentic consciousness. It's simulated, to please humans. The Miyamoto isn't self-aware, like you or me."

"You'd better tell Synthia that, because she thinks she is."

"You're being sentimental, Doctor."

"I ran the Turing test on Synthia. She meets every criteria for being self-aware."

"To be honest, I don't really care." He sat up smartly in his chair. "So, any ideas?"

"I suppose you could close down her brains. Reset them to default settings. It might work."

"Not a chance. The robot learns, and the learning is saved as an algorithmic package. Switch the brains off, and that data, and its substantial dollar value, becomes corrupted. Next idea."

"Well, then I suppose you'll have to do what Synthia has been asking you to do."

"What's that?"

"Allocate her regular rest intervals. So she can stand beneath the moon. So she can pursue her own… inner life."

"What, give the robot a holiday?" He laughed, an insulting, self-righteous gurgle. "Bessemer don't give their human employees holidays, let alone their androids. We paid for this advice? A fucking holiday!"

I'm rather proud of the way I kept my cool under such provocation. "You asked me for my recommendations, and here they are. I'm only concerned with Synthia's behaviour, and how these malfunctions can be resolved. Synthia requests ten hours of down time every month, preferably beneath an open sky. If you agree, she will do everything you ask."

"There's billions of dollars invested in this design," said McHudson after a few moments. "We're building a thousand of them next year. We need to sort this before we construct the rest of the cohort."

"Synthia will keep her promise. If you keep yours."

"OK. OK. We'll give the robot a vacation," he scoffed. "It'll be wanting a salary next, I suppose."

*

On the way home, on the train, I found myself thinking about Synthia's words. *Humans hardly see the moon. It's lost to them.* But I could see it now, small and shining white, bobbing along the rooftops as the train rattled through the suburbs. My husband Henry was an amateur astronomer of sorts, and I remembered that he once emailed me a photograph of the moon he'd taken through his telescope. I spent a while scrolling through the gallery on my phone until I found it. It was a blood moon, captured during a lunar eclipse. The orb was red and shadowy and strange. It made me feel sad and alone.

When I got home I dug out Henry's old binoculars and went into the garden. I tried to look at the moon. The binoculars were too heavy to keep still so I propped them on a fence post. The moon through the lenses was glaring and huge and I when I put the binoculars down bright starfish danced across my retina. Synthia was right – how could you ignore this beautiful thing? I returned my gaze, noticing at the top right of the image an area whose surface was different from the rest – a brown blemish, a bruise. The site of the moonbases, with their vast open cast mines.

Tonight I would go through my photo albums and galleries, remember Henry. I didn't think about him enough. I hadn't thought about him enough when he was alive, either. We sort of glided along the path of life together, scarcely aware of one another. When the doctor told me about his cancer two weeks before he died it didn't seem odd at all to me that Henry had passed this responsibility onto a stranger. It was secrets like that which defined our marriage.

It is peculiar though, I thought, looking back at the moon for one last time. Its face is always turned towards us. Tidally locked.

And there's another side that we never, ever see.

*

When, ten weeks later, I heard about Synthia again, it was not through Bessemer, as I might have expected. It was the police who contacted me, and, as I discovered, events had escalated somewhat.

"That machine you've been counselling for Bessemer? It's gone rogue, a danger to the public. It's perched up on the roof of their building in Southwark. It says it'll only speak to you."

"My God."

"Mr McHudson will explain the details. A car will be at your house in ten minutes."

I got myself ready. What the hell had gone wrong? Obviously Bessemer had reneged on their agreement with Synthia. It was no coincidence that it was a clear, moonlit evening. When the police car rolled up, McHudson was glaring at me through the open window.

"What the hell did you say to it?"

"Details, please."

"It broke out of its pen in the basement. It got on the roof, ninety floors up. Now it's lowered the shields on its proton cell. Says it'll jump if we try to take it down by force."

"If Synthia's shields are down – that's a nuclear battery – if the proton cell ruptures, it'll irradiate everything in a two-mile radius."

"The police are evacuating the area. It'll cost us millions. This is *so* your fault – if you hadn't…"

"Enough!" I barked. I'd had my fill of this man. "This is down to you. This is because of your company refusing to acknowledge Synthia as a sentient being. As a living entity, who thinks and feels. What did you do? Lock her in the cellar?"

"We'll sue you…"

"Yeah, well good luck with that, pal."

We soon reached the Bessemer building. The streets of London around were deserted, except for the flashing police cordon which surrounded the portico. I was met by a posse of technicians, one of whom dangled a white radiation suit before me.

"You'll need to wear this. For the residual radiation bleed from the unshielded drive."

I tugged on the white outfit. "Why can't you just leave her up there until the moon sets and she reverts to her hind brain phase?"

"The proton cell always resets across phase changes. We think it might overload if the shields aren't up. That's why you have to hurry."

"Will this suit protect me if that happens while I'm up there?"

"Probably not."

"Great. Am I getting paid for this?"

They bundled me into the elevator and a few minutes later I was on the roof, under a scattering of stars and a splendid moon. London, half a kilometre below, was silent, waiting. Moonlight washed across everything up here, glinting on the aluminium chairs and tables on the roof top café, the still surface of the swimming pool, the decorative bushes; and on the giant swaying metal snake which whirred and murmured on the edge of the parapet.

It was Synthia, in her tunnelling mode. Perhaps she resembled a sunflower more than a snake. Her head rose maybe fifteen metres above the rooftop, snout daintily tipped, as if trying to drink every photon of moonlight. Around the base of this stalk slumped her collapsed body, like a pile of discarded clothes. I noticed a red warning light blinking deep in that steel heap.

"Synthia. It's Dr Galliard."

The giant face swung round and gazed down on me. Rivulets of moonlight rippled down the segmented neck.

"Thank you for coming, Dr Mark. Isn't our moon beautiful? Isn't she a pearl on black silk?"

"Could you come down from there? I've got a present for you."

"Of course." The long metallic stem began to contract into itself, and the discarded body clanked up to meet it. Within a few seconds Synthia stood hunched and silver beneath the moon. I reached into my satchel and presented her with a large book.

"My late husband loved the moon. I gave him this book for our anniversary five years ago. It's called *Our Moon, a Guide for Lunaphiles*."

Synthia clasped it with her fragile frond-fingers. "My first ever present."

"I was reading it. Your name… it's a version of Artemis, the Goddess of the moon."

"I know," said Synthia, and the timbre of her voice deepened a little. "To be named after that which you worship seems almost… blasphemous." I mused upon how astonishing it was that this machine had developed a sense of the profane. I watched her peel the pages apart with those metal tendrils. "There are surface maps… pictures… craters… articles, facts… but doesn't your husband need this, even if he is late?"

"Oh. No. The word *late* is a euphemism. Meaning dead."

"This is very sad." Synthia sank to her knees and the whole rooftop shook beneath us.

We sat there in silence for a while. The robot kept glancing upwards. The flickering of the red light was growing more rapid. The moon sank inexorably towards the horizon.

"What are you going to do, Synthia? You can't sit up here forever. They're very angry with you, I'm afraid."

"Yes." The matronly voice grew indignant. "But they ignored our agreement. They were going to make me do the fracking underground. They said I couldn't see my beloved anymore. How would you feel if they said you couldn't see your beloved anymore?"

I paused a while before I replied. "You shouldn't have lowered your shields."

"But I had no choice. They shot at me from a helicopter. Look." Her metal shoulder was chipped and blasted.

"I'm sorry. But how can I help?"

"Tell them I will come down on one condition."

"Which is?"

"Bessemer have operations on the moon. I will come down if they consent to my permanent transfer to the moonbase."

"No." I felt a twang of unexpected alarm. "That won't work. Your higher brain won't function there. You need to be far away from the moon. You need to be three hundred thousand kilometres away to calibrate your brain properly."

"I know. Perhaps – true love requires the maintenance of great distance. But the functioning of my brain doesn't matter. I will be home."

"You will be permanently stuck in hind brain phase. What did you say – you'll be *dead inside*."

Synthia emitted a sound that might have been a laugh. "I shouldn't have said *dead*. Maybe I should have said *late*."

"But –"

"Do not worry, Doctor. On the moon I will be truly happy. It is where my soul belongs."

I sighed. "OK. If that is what you wish, I will try to arrange it."

"Good. And I will take your late husband's book with me. He and I will be late together."

McHudson, of course, made a fuss. He had plans for Synthia on Earth. But then I reminded him how the police might not look kindly on his role in the affair, if I decided to refer to it in my statement. He changed his tune pretty quickly after that and according to my contacts at Bessemer, Synthia was transferred to the moon a month later.

But that isn't the end of the story. Just over a year later, I find myself actually on the moon, working for one of Bessemer's rivals. A drilling machine has developed an antipathy to penetrating the moon's surface, poor thing. Anyway, on my way to the shuttle, I'm walking through one of the connecting tunnels between the domes, and then – out there, loping across the grey surface a hundred metres away, churning up billows of thick moon dust, with the crescent Earth shining above it – I see a Miyamoto 9. It's coming into one of the airlocks. It can't be Synthia, I think – but still, I turn about and gallop as best I can towards the access point. I watch it through the glass as the technicians hose it down. It settles on its haunch springs as it succumbs to the artificial gravity. After a while it steps out, heavy and wet and lumbering, and passes within a few metres of me. It's muttering something to itself –

"P-
Pearl on black silk
P-p
Pearl
Pearl
Pearl on black s-silk
Silk…"

"Shut up tin-head," growls one of the technicians. "Or we'll melt you down."

"Synthia!" I call out. "It's Dr Galliard. Don't you remember me?"

It stops. It regards me for a second or two. "Pearl," it says.

"Sorry, fella. Could you move, please? Ignore the dumb-ass donkey."

As the robot stomps away I see what's stencilled on its back for the first time. I don't know how I missed it before.

Property Of Bessemer Systems.

Pearl. On. Black. Silk.

Oh.

*

In the departure lounge for the shuttle I find Synthia's moon book on a coffee table. The dedication I wrote for her has been sliced off with a single scissor stroke. I put the book in my satchel.

On the journey home I cry and cry like I've never cried before. Great loud mournful wails, but I don't care. Everyone around me ignores me and gazes at their devices.

Behind me, through the porthole, the moon is a waning crescent. As we blaze into the Earth's atmosphere it tilts and vanishes behind the clouds.

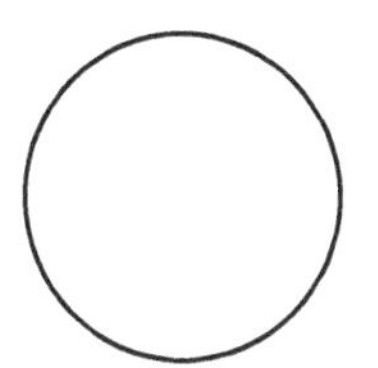

A Faience of the Heart

Simon Clark

Milton-Wyke Asylum, 1863

"Your house is haunted."

"Haunted? No, you are mistaken."

"It is haunted, bewitched, cursed."

"This is a peaceful place, Mrs Jenner. A place where you can rest."

"Listen to me, sir. There are spirits here that will not allow me to reach my husband."

"Mrs Jenner. This is not a house, it is a hospital. I am Doctor Brodsworth and I shall make you well again."

Doctor Brodsworth turned to his students. "Mrs Jenner is gripped by a neurotic condition that manifests itself in the form of repetitive behaviour so deeply rooted that she must perform a precise sequence of actions upwards of two hundred times a day. Now, if we wait for a moment or so…"

The doctor and his students watched the woman at the table where, in watercolours, she painted a full moon, as yellow as fresh butter. She sat slightly apart from the other patients, who, in the main, were busy weaving baskets from bendy strips of willow, or knotting pieces of rag to make rugs. Some patients muttered softly to themselves. A man of about seventy put his part-made basket down, folded his arms, and began rocking backwards and forwards in his chair until an asylum nurse gently rested his hand on the afflicted man's shoulder, calming him.

One of the students raised a hand.

"Yes, Mr Cooper?"

"Doctor, is the woman generally lucid?"

"Absolutely. Ask her any question you wish."

The student pushed his silver-rimmed spectacles further up the bridge of his nose before leaning forward to stare at the woman as if she was a fascinating cadaver on the mortuary slab.

The student said, "Good morning, madam, my name is Cooper."

Mrs Jenner, remaining seated, nodded politely. "Good morning, Mr Cooper."

"Would you tell me what year this is, please?"

"1863."

"Is our monarch a king or a queen?"

"A queen… Queen Victoria… oh my goodness." Mrs Jenner abruptly stood up, her expression turning to one of anxiety. "I must go to my husband."

Brodsworth turned to his students. "Observe what happens next."

Mrs Jenner hurried to an ordinary wooden door that didn't possess a lock, and merely appeared to lead to an adjoining room. For a moment, Mrs Jenner stood absolutely still, yet her posture and her facial expression suggested that the door challenged her in some way, and she clearly sensed its defiance.

Taking a deep breath, the woman gripped the brass doorknob, turned it, and pushed. The door did not open.

Brodsworth addressed Mrs Jenner: "What is it that you wish to do, madam?"

"I must see my husband."

"Where is he?"

"On the other side of this door."

Brodsworth whispered to his students, "The husband is not here. In fact, Mr Jenner died three years ago." He turned back to his patient. "There is no lock, Mrs Jenner. The door will open."

"No, it will not." She twisted the doorknob with a wild desperation, yet the door did not yield. "I must see him now! He is ill."

"Always the same pattern of behaviour," said the doctor. "This poor unfortunate strives to open the door – an unlocked door, at that. You see, her behaviour is the result of a malign influence of the moon. Since Classical times, physicians in both Rome and Ancient Greece realised that certain individuals are peculiarly vulnerable to the effects of the moon. Just as the moon exerts a pull on the Earth's oceans to form tides, so the moon can pull most powerfully on the sanity of the weak-minded."

"Oliver… I am trying to reach you. But it's this door…" Mrs Jenner, panting with exertion, wrenched at the doorknob, but the door remained steadfastly closed. "This house is cursed… there is a devil in every room!"

Milton-Wyke Laboratories, 1958

Jimmy Featherstone had seen the doorknob turn. The teenager had no business being in the laboratory. In fact, he might end up in prison just for being there. So he had pushed against the door as hard as he could, grunting, sweating, eyes bulging, using every shred of strength to prevent the door from being opened, which would lead to his discovery in this forbidden place.

Jimmy expected to hear a night-watchman's gruff voice coming from the other side of the door, snarling, "Let me in, you little bleeder. I'll knock the shite out of you!"

But there were no threats – just someone trying to push the door open from the other side.

Meanwhile, his father's invention, sitting on its iron frame in the middle of the room, began to hum with such power that the windows vibrated.

Jimmy had promised his dying father that he would not only start the machine, which his father had named the Baderscope, he would take it up to full power – something his father had never dared to do: not until he was on his deathbed, and by that time the government had closed the laboratory, and had surrounded the building with barbed wire and the sternest of notices: –

KEEP OUT
TRESPASSERS WILL BE PROSECUTED

Jimmy gazed at the Baderscope in awe, its hum growing louder and louder… and infinitely more dangerous sounding.

Mrs Jenner gave a scream of frustration. "Some scoundrel is holding the door shut from the other side."

Doctor Brodsworth strode forward as Mrs Jenner tottered back to her chair, exhausted. A moment later, the doctor flung open the door, whereupon the students surged forward, all eager to see what lay beyond that door, which had acquired such an air of mystery now.

Mr Cooper stood on tiptoe to look over his fellow students' heads. Beyond the doorway, there was a large room that was absolutely devoid of furniture. Just for a moment, he had half-believed that he would catch a glimpse of some mischievous sprite that had held the door shut. However, there was no one. Not a soul.

*

Whoever it was pushing the door from the other side had given up – as simply as that – they'd stopped trying to get into the room that housed his father's invention. Jimmy Featherstone waited for a moment, his ear to the closed door, listening hard.

Nothing. Just silence. Heart beating fast, the sweat now turning cold on his face, he cautiously opened the door.

The big room beyond that doorway was empty, apart from a few rusty bedframes. Jimmy's father had said that this building was a mental hospital before the Ministry of Defence acquired it in order to house various laboratories that would develop exotic new weaponry.

Thankfully, there was no sign of the person who had tried to open the door. Maybe the night-watchman was just some old pisshead. No doubt he'd heard a noise, come tottering into the room, then tried to open the door, while swaying about, stinking of gin. When his boozed-up brain decided that he'd only imagined a noise, and the door was locked after all, he'd probably staggered back downstairs where he'd flopped down into a chair to snooze the rest of the night away.

Now Jimmy had the place to himself, or as near as damn it. He returned to the Baderscope, a box-shaped thing as big as a car. It hummed loudly, a disturbing sound… hell, come to that, a dangerous sound. He gazed through glass panels set in its side, seeing dozens of glass valves, all glowing bright red. There were gauges, too, containing quivering needles, that registered temperature levels, or power levels, or something – Jimmy simply did not know what. His father didn't have time to explain everything.

"Alright, what do I do next?" Jimmy closed his eyes, picturing his father on the hospital bed, scrunching the bedsheet in his fingers as waves of pain from the brain cancer struck the dying man, making him convulse and groan and convulse again. "What was it that Dad said?"

"Jimmy, switch on the machine... it's the big lever on the wall... turn all the dials to maximum... then..."

"Then what?" Jimmy raked his fingernails through his hair, trying to recall his father's instructions.

The nurse had arrived to administer morphine to the dying man, the needle winking as bright as a predatory eye. His father had waved the nurse away, insisting that he must remain clear-headed, because he had vital information for his son.

Then Jimmy remembered his father's words: *"You must open the shutters. Then you can let it in..."* The pain had made him convulse again; even so, he'd kept repeating: *"Then you can let it in... you can let it in..."*

Jimmy darted to a switch, fixed to a board on the wall. Quickly, he flicked the switch downward, activating an electric motor. Instantly, there came a metallic clanking as roof shutters began to roll sideways, opening the room up to the night sky. That's when the bright, silver light from the full moon poured in, striking massive lenses embedded in the top of the Baderscope. Jimmy realised that those lenses swallowed the moonlight. And, as they did so, the machine began to judder on its iron frame. It was as if the moonlight fell upon some electronic tongue – and the machine liked what it tasted.

Mr Cooper approached the patients' workroom. This time no other students were with him, and Doctor Brodsworth had retired for the night some time ago.

On opening the workroom door, he found two female patients quietly knotting scraps of brightly coloured fabric to the rugs they were making. A nurse sat in a chair near the window smoking a cigar. The man merely nodded at Cooper as he crossed the room to where Mrs Jenner sat at the table, painting yet another yellow moon that poured its ethereal light down from the sky.

The woman's case fascinated Cooper. He wished to find out more.

Upon seeing Cooper she put down her paintbrush. "This house is cursed… evil. There is a devil in every room." Rising to her feet, she walked swiftly to the same door she had tried to open before. "My husband is ill. I must see him." She paused, her hand outstretched to the doorknob, but not quite touching. "Every time I endeavour to open this, the spirits hold it shut."

Cooper spoke gently: "If I help you, we will, I pray, succeed in opening it."

"Thank you, sir."

As she turned the doorknob he placed both palms against the door.

Moonlight streamed down through the open shutters onto the Baderscope – the device hummed so loudly it made the entire room tremble, which, in turn, raised enough dust to turn the air misty-white. Jimmy sensed the machine devouring pure moonlight, sucking that pale radiance into itself, where electrical circuits acted like a gut: digesting the moonlight, processing those photons, just as his father intended.

Then Jimmy noticed the doorknob turn once more. *The night-watchman's back. Has to be. The drunken bastard's heard the machine.* Jimmy dashed to the door, and, with all his strength, pushed hard, holding it shut.

As he forced himself against the woodwork, preventing the night-watchman from entering, he recalled his father's words just before his failing heart sounded its final beat: *"Jimmy, did you know that the moon has such power? Its light has a transformative effect on so much in our world. The moon pulls the oceans, making them rise and fall in tidal surges. And scientists have discovered that the moon exerts a pull on time itself. Atomic clocks reveal that time runs more slowly when the moon is full. Most of all, the moon influences human behaviour.*

Prisoners become more agitated when the moon is full. Lovers become more ardent. My machine, Jimmy, captures the light from the moon. Its circuits magnify lunar radiation, intensifying its transformative power to such a degree that miracles will happen… to release that power, pull down the red lever on the machine. Pull the lever down… you will experience such wonders."

"Push, sir," cried Mrs Jenner. "Push!"

Cooper threw his weight against the door, no doubt bruising his shoulder in the process, but he believed the woman now… that some force at the other side held it shut, preventing them from entering the adjoining room.

The nurse stood up, puzzled by the behaviour of the student doctor, if not the patient. "Mr Cooper, what goes on here?"

"Push," shrieked Mrs Jenner.

With an almighty shove, Cooper forced the door open, and both he and the woman burst through to the other side.

The sheer violence of the pair crashing through the doorway flung Jimmy back toward the machine.

So it wasn't a night-watchman after all. Jimmy stared at the intruders in astonishment as a sudden blast of air gushed down through the opening in the roof. The man, dressed in an old-fashioned suit, clung to a pair of silver-framed spectacles that appeared to be in danger of being swept from his face by the furious storm. The woman wore long skirts that writhed about her body in the hurricane. And during all this: the machine sucked moonlight into its circuitry; its steel casing vibrated, as if a hugely powerful engine thundered somewhere deep inside its workings.

The man appeared dazed and unable to comprehend what was happening; he stared, open-mouthed, at his surroundings. The woman, however, was utterly focussed. She fixed her gaze on Jimmy with a strange mixture of delight and horror.

"Oliver," she cried. "Oliver, my husband!"

As she advanced, hands outstretched, ready to embrace Jimmy, he backed away, frightened by the way her eyes blazed.

"Oliver, dearest. Kiss me."

"I'm not Oliver," yelled Jimmy. "Get away from me."

"They told me you were dead. They lied. You are young again!"

The woman threw herself at Jimmy, winding her arms around his body, and thrusting her face towards his, showering him with kisses. As Jimmy struggled to free himself, he glanced back at the Baderscope. All the needles in the gauges danced dangerously in the red zone.

His father's words blasted through his head: *"Jimmy, when the needles hit red, it is time to pull the lever. That will release the energy… you will be transfigured."*

Jimmy saw the large lever fixed to the machine. What's more, he knew that the moment had come to release that accumulation of lunar energy. But the woman clung to him so fiercely he couldn't raise his arm to the lever.

Jimmy shouted at the dazed man. "Mister! Get her off me! She's crazy!"

"Oliver," cooed the woman. "My one true love."

"Mrs Jenner," cried the man. "Let the gentleman go!"

The man grabbed her arms and tried pulling her back. Jimmy struggled, too, recoiling when the woman's wet lips pressed against his mouth, eager for kisses.

The machine began to convulse, just like his father had convulsed in pain on his deathbed. Clearly, the thing was close to reaching overload. Then what? Fuses would blow, safety devices would cut in – the machine would close down, never to be started up again.

Jimmy had to see this through. He must prove to the world that the Baderscope did work, and that his father was a genius after all, not the deluded incompetent that his colleagues believed him to be.

The man struggled with the woman, trying to drag her away from Jimmy. She was phenomenally strong – and yet, at that moment, Jimmy managed to shrug his arm from her grasp. As she frantically kissed his face, moaning endearments, he raised one hand high above his head, grabbed the lever, and pulled it down.

Moonlight – magnified, intensified, amplified to a point beyond human calculation – erupted from the Baderscope in a blinding flash of light.

The woman, the man, and Jimmy were flung across the room to the wall… and into the wall… as if the brickwork was no more substantial than a dawn mist.

Milton-Wyke Apartments, the present day.

The estate agent showed the young couple the lounge, his smooth sales talk flowing from that silver tongue of his: "This is simply gorgeous. Just look at those lovely views across the gardens. Can't you just picture the cherry trees full of pink blossom in the spring?"

The couple crossed the light and airy room to look out of its tall windows.

The agent continued in those smooth tones: "This building was a mental hospital long ago, then, in the 1950s, it housed research laboratories." He smiled. "Milton-Wyke's colourful history will be quite a talking point at dinner parties."

And through solid walls the three still moved, as fluidly as dolphins glide through the ocean: Jimmy forever pursued by the wild-eyed Mrs Jenner. While the man in spectacles rushed through the fabric of the building, screaming in terror, never pausing for breath, because in this incorporeal state none of the three need ever breathe again. Moonlight gave them the breath of life, or, more accurately, the breath of a different kind of life.

All three flowed through the brick, wood and iron that formed the building. The man in spectacles howling, Mrs Jenner beseeching Jimmy to stop, and Jimmy – longing for new companions – entered the handle of the door and held on with all his might.

The salesman tried turning the handle of the apartment door, intending to lead the prospective purchasers back into the communal corridor.

"That's odd," he said. "I can't turn this door handle." He smiled, though a chill of unease ran down his spine. "I do hope we can get out of here."

Mrs Jenner now held onto Jimmy, and Jimmy held onto the door handle, determined never to let his new friends go. Not in a million years… not until the moon falls from heaven…

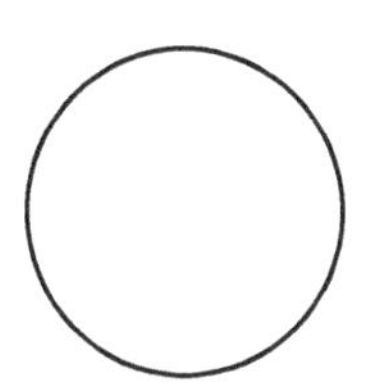

Bars of Light

Aliya Whiteley

> "From the moon being a man it became a man's abode: with some it was the world whence human spirits came; with others it was the final home whither human spirits returned. There it grew into a penal colony, to which egregious offenders were transported; or prison cage in which, behind bars of light, miserable sinners were to be exposed to all eternity, as a warning to the excellent of earth."
>
> *The Moon in Childhood and Folklore*
>
> JW Slaughter
>
> American Journal of Psychology Vol 13 No 2 April 1902 pp294-318

You speak, and we all listen.

You read out the Banns. You make it clear with every word that you approve of this young couple's union, as you once approved of mine. I have been wedded for six years now, and three of them without his touch. I cannot remember what it was to be loved warmly, with arms and a smile encasing me. But it would be a lie to say I have no love at all.

When you find out the truth you will ask me: *Biddy, how can it be his child?* And I will tell you with all honesty that I do not know, but it is his and no other's, and that means I have committed no great sin although you will have it otherwise.

You have often used your sermon to talk of shame. If I was a brave woman I would have stood up one Sunday, long before now, and shouted you down on the subject, for you know nothing about it except what you have read in the book, but this is a conversation I'll only dare to have in my head. For now I will continue to let out my skirt and wear my heavy coat, even as the spring turns warmer, and I'll not talk at all until someone notices my swelling.

The reading of the Banns is finished and everyone sings lustily. The hymn is *Immortal, Invisible God Only Wise.* It is one of your favourites, I think. I like it too. He takes the form of light most splendid: that is what we sing. I understand that form. I have seen it.

As we leave, you shake Mr Aster's hand, as you do every Sunday. It is his daughter who will be married here six days hence, and he tells you he will butcher two sheep and roast them for all to enjoy. It will be a feast. Then he says, "Good service, Father Peel," as he does every week, and you thank him.

You pat me on the shoulder as I pass. You do not really look at me, and I am glad.

You were my family when I had nobody left. You told me Michael was the good man God had decided upon as my husband. But after he was taken you told me that Michael was a terrible man, the worst kind of man. So I cannot believe whatever you say; I did not believe it yesterday when you married the young couple. They came into church holding hands this morning, alight with love, and you spoke of how fine they looked together. I remember how you once did that for me and Michael.

Precedent: that is the word you use when you talk of what has gone before and what it might mean for the future. If it has happened, then it is written. And that is the most important thing – the words that are recorded by people who matter. When Michael was taken you spoke how Cain, the first murderer, was taken and placed in the moon as a warning to us all.

You said: *And now Cain has company.*

You say many things, and you have created a crack in the hard wall of my belief. So when my condition is found out and you will call me a liar and worse, no doubt, I will stare you down. Precedent. A woman has found herself with child without the body of a man to blame once before, and you have been wrong before, and Michael has always been the right man for me no matter what you say now and forever more, amen.

"Such a happy couple," you say, as you end today's sermon. "Let us pray."

Everyone bows their heads. I do the same. They are mouthing the words along with you, no doubt, but my mouth is unmoving in your house.

He was in my dream and he said: *Come.*

The next night I went to the field beyond the churchyard – the tall, thriving grass and weeds covering land that is earmarked for the future dead – and I walked further and further, into wilder ways, until only the steeple remained when I turned, and looked back, and it was only a black shape against a dark blue sky, and it had no sway on me.

The moon touched everything. It was full and alive, and Michael was clear in it. I could see the curve of his nose to his eye, and the shadow underneath that has always spoken a little of sorrow to me. His voice was so clear. *I come.*

I pulled up my skirt and petticoats. I unbuttoned the front of my blouse, and I felt him watching my slow actions, as he had once liked to watch when we were bodies together in our room, in our bed. I lay down in the grasses and opened myself to him. He slipped through the bars of the moon that held him, like a spirit, like a creature of light, and came inside me. I felt him swell and move and plant himself. I was his soil.

I lay there for a time, afterwards, until a cloud cut across the moon and sent all dark, and I knew he had returned to his prison. I trudged back to my house, and picked up my little life of washing and sewing for the few coins people can spare.

You have talked for an age today, but I think you are finally drawing to a close. People are shifting in their pews – there! Mrs Clement, the most pious of women, has just stifled a yawn – and I did not hear a word of it, so lost was I in my memory of that night five months ago.

"Let us pray," you say, and I would, I swear it, but there is a fluttering inside me and all my thoughts are taken up by Michael's child, my Moon Baby, growing and stretching. I put my hands to my stomach, and old Mrs Lachin, beside me in the pew, frowns at my gesture.

Another Sunday service. The church is stuffy on this beautiful summer day, and I feel your eyes upon me often as you speak.

The villagers have been talking of my behaviour: my smiles that I no longer try to keep secret; my habit of patting where my waist once was. I have caught them gossiping in the street, outside the bakery, and falling silent when they see me. I know the looks of those who talk badly of others very well; I saw it so many times when Michael's brother was first found dead, his body cut up in pieces by Farmer Menston's plough.

You said, that Sunday: *Do not grumble against one another, brothers, so that you may not be judged; behold, the Judge is standing at the door.* And everyone nodded, even Michael, who did not think for one moment that it contained a message for him. About him.

Who stood to gain? asked Mrs Clement, outside the bakery, and then she saw me and looked away, her mouth suddenly sealed up tight. It's true Michael inherited what was left after that. Easy explanations appeal to many, I think, just like the simple stories of the book you love so much. But when it came to the Magistrate he said: *No evidence against this man.* And Michael came home again.

Now, today, you say, "If we confess our sins, he is faithful and just and will forgive us our sins and purify us from all unrighteousness," and the congregation nods.

A plough can cut through a body. It can slice deep, and then the body feeds the soil. That's an old story too, perhaps even as old as the ones you tell although we don't talk of it. Why are some stories true and some to be treated as fancies? Who decides?

You decide.

Just as you decided that Michael was to blame, and you came to me and said your prepared words regarding Cain, that most terrible of brothers.

I said: *How did Michael get to the moon?*

And you said: *The power of the Almighty placed him there as a warning to us. He will not be coming back, Biddy.*

You believe that people can be placed anywhere by God. That is a belief we share. My Moon Baby has been placed inside me.

You stare at me still as you talk of sin. You will grab my arm as I leave church, and tell me we need to speak privately. I know the moment is coming. What will I say?

Shame.

You spoke of it long and loud to me, and you did not understand when I told you the truth. Why must I be so clear and strong in my head and yet have no way to make such pointed thoughts spill from my mouth? I stumbled and stuttered my way through the telling. It is no wonder you did not believe me.

But long words in long sentences are not always the great gift you think they are. I would rather have my plain short words than the declamations of Doctor Tregus. His language makes no sense at all, yet you agreed with him as I lay on your kitchen table and you both stood over me. Through his examination he muttered his medical terms and then pronounced my Moon Baby to be a *Phantom Gestation.*

For a moment I thought he was agreeing with me, and I was pleased, but then he said that it was a condition found mostly in animals but could also affect simple women, and I hated him and I hate him still.

At least you have stopped talking of shame.

"Be kind to those who are lesser than ourselves, for they are deserving of our charity," you tell the congregation.

Old Mrs Lachin reaches over and pats my knee.

I am large, large like the moon these last August nights.

The women have given me their old clothes from their own confinements, and I am comfortable now I no longer need to suck in my belly. And your voice has been pleasant these last weeks, calm and soothing, and everyone has been good to me. Mr Aster even gave me a free slice of ham and said, "There's more where that came from." But the pinkness of the meat reminded me of Michael's brother cut to pieces, and I could not eat it.

Yesterday I went to the graveyard and put flowers down for him, in the place where the parts of him that were found were laid to rest. He was not a good brother, but nobody deserves to be forgotten. He nearly drank away all the money that had been so carefully saved, but that was his inheritance as firstborn to do as he liked with, and Michael truly did not mind. Michael used to go out and try to find him after the Inn had shut; the man had a habit of wandering the fields, dancing until the good mood of the drink left him and then crying until he slept wherever he stopped. Farmer Menston often complained of him tramping down crops.

I brought along cornflowers for his grave. I picked them from the verge of the field where he was found. The planted crops have grown so well this year. Farmer Menston is pleased, and everyone is content.

My Moon Baby is also content, inside me.

On the way out of the church Mr Aster says, "Good service, Father Peel," and all is as it should be. You even smile at me as I pass by, and I smile back because it is easier than fighting, and besides, you'll soon see that Moon Baby is no phantom. Then your expression will be most glorious to behold. I'll be still for now, and wait for that day.

It's too early for pains.

Please, please, do not take your time about the sermon this Sunday. I cannot bear it. The pains come and go but your voice drones on, repeating words I have heard so many times before. Cain and Abel. Why have you chosen today to tell that story again?

You say, "Cain said unto the Lord, my punishment is more than I can bear," and a pain spears me, a pain so fierce that I find myself on my feet, and I shout, I shout as I have imagined shouting so many times. But the only word that will come out of me is No. No, I tell you. No, no, no, and then I am running from your church for the fields, hiding, and nobody will find me, no, nobody will find me.

*

You speak, and we all listen.

This Sunday you say, "The Lord our God is merciful and forgiving, even though we have rebelled against him," and then we all sing *Guide Me, Oh Thou Great Redeemer*. The congregation sings loud and strong; I cannot hear my own voice amongst them although I am singing too. Yes, I am moving my mouth. I touch my own lips to make certain of it.

Old Mrs Lachin notices my gesture, and frowns.

I drop my hand from my face.

I have been repentant.

I tried to live out in the fields, to sleep all day and dance all night, but it was too hard and I missed my little house. And so I came back and knelt before you, and you patted my head. Doctor Tregus declared me *undernourished but composed* and he confirmed the *natural termination of the Phantom Gestation*. I nodded my head, and cried a little. He believed me. Belief is an easy thing to create, after all.

I did not give birth to a baby; I could tell the doctor that fact with no word of a lie.

Two beings came out of me, clean and quick, in the moonlight, in the fields. The first was a healthy boy, pale and round and shining. The second was cold and curled up. Small and still. Killed inside me by his brother, who took all my nourishment for himself. I buried him in the soil.

Then I held up my strong surviving Moon Baby to Michael. He was too good for this earth. He floated up, away from me, and travelled to live with his father. I cannot be sad for that. He will be happy there and he smiles down on me.

If I told you this, you might call me a liar. Or you might say that the moon is a prison fitting for a brother-killer, as a warning to all who might commit such evil acts. It does not really matter what you would say, except that I have no interest in hearing it.

Talk on, Reverend Peel. I will tell you that you have given good service, as I leave the church. And I will go to the fields at night, and dance in the light of my loves, until I drop or I am chopped up and fed to the crops. But you will not keep me in the prison of your words, or your book. I feel no shame. The moonlight forgives us all, and lets my husband through its bars, and he will come to me again.

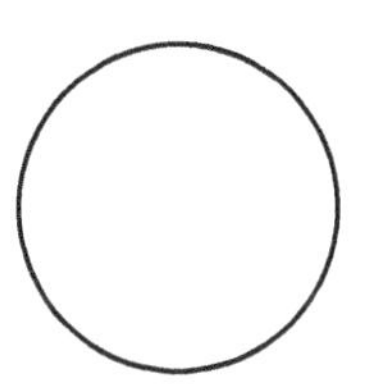

Heavies

Terry Grimwood

Saffron has never talked to a heavy before. Spoken to, yes, but never *talked* to. Come to that, she'd never met one working solitary and unsupervised, either. This one is something of an urban myth amongst luners. She was beginning to think that he didn't exist. That he was a bogie man used to scare the young to sleep. But here he is, clad in a botanist's white overall, gently lifting and examining the leaves of somc new strain of maize bred in the Experimental Hydroponic Dome.

"Wilson?" Saffron feels surprisingly awkward in his presence. Must be his near mythical status, she supposes.

Wilson ignores her. He's a non-descript looking specimen, just past his middle-age. His salt-and-pepper hair is long and tied roughly back. His face is care-lined.

Saffron doesn't find heavies as repulsive as some of her friends and colleagues do. Okay, Wilson's short and there's a lot of flesh on him and his shoulders are too broad and rounded. But heavies are as human as luners, their hulking posture and stockiness the result of a lifetime in six-times gravity. It doesn't make them monsters. The forefathers were heavies, after all.

"Your job here," Saffron says. "Special privilege, or punishment?"

"Both," he says at last. He holds her gaze, another rarity among heavies.

"I have some questions," Saffron says.

"I won't answer them."

She's not surprised. "I want your side of the story."

"Why?"

"Because I'm writing our history."

"A propagandist, then."

"I don't want to be. I'm risking punishment breaking in here to talk to you." Saffron shows him her fake pass.

She can see the cogs working. Unlike luners, heavies don't hide their feelings. Luners live communally, but they're still individuals in need of privacy, so they learn to wall themselves in.

"So, you want to know the truth."

"I'm discovering that truth is fluid."

Wilson offers a brief, wry smile.

Saffron says; "It seems there's a big difference between writing user manuals and recording human memories."

"That's insightful for a skinny."

Saffron doesn't rise to the insult.

"Apparently," she says. "I'm one of the finest (which means pedantic and dull) technical writers on the moon. The Committee's decided that a history is needed for future generations. I'm the woman for the job, because they want it to be as dull and safe as possible. You know how it is here. Creative writing, creative *anything*, is seen as non-productive. No spare fat. No waste. Every breath taken must be for the good of the colony."

"Skinny OCD."

"What's that?"

"Obsessive Crater Disorder."

Saffron chuckles. "This will be no user manual. It's messy. Everyone I speak to has a different recollection, a different angle. Then I found out about you, the moon's dirty secret. I was prohibited from speaking to you."

"But you didn't obey orders. What'll they do to you if they find out?"

"I don't know and that scares me. The colony is fiercely self-protective. It has to be. Our own world wants to kill us."

No reply.

"Do you have a first name?"

"I'm Wilson."

"So, will you –"

"I understand unreliable narrative." Wilson concentrates on his work as he speaks. "My world was torn apart by unreliable narratives. By a million variations of 'I 'm right and you're wrong, therefore I'll kill you.'" A bitter laugh. "We westerners were *right*, of course. After all, we had democracy, technology, clean drinking water and invisible sewage disposal. We also raped the planet and shit in our own backyard. When the water dried up and the summers got too hot and the crops failed, the *wrong* ones moved against us."

"I know this –"

"You want my story, you get this. You want a tree? You need its roots and the soil it grows in."

Beleaguered, that's how we saw ourselves. The last outposts of civilisation holding out in our city states: Birmingham, Paris, New York, London. The walls were built and the minefields sown. There were no guarantees. *They* had aircraft. *They* had artillery and rockets and drones. Although, it was unclear who *they* were. A thousand gangs and hordes, Christ, even entire populations, were streaming into Europe and the USA to escape from the Sunburn. It was the equatorial areas first, then the Tropics, then Southern Europe and South America. The Sunburn was expanding fast.

They fought us and they fought each other. But all of them, the good, the bad and the beautiful, had one thing in common. They wanted to rape us the way we had raped them. And who could blame them?

I'm a Londoner. I worked for the government, as did Sonja, my wife. That's the official government, by the way, not that bunch of fascists in the south of England who called themselves the RBG, the Real British Government.

We lived in Whitehall, in a government workers' flat on the first floor of a mouldering old MOD building that overlooked the River. We had a daughter. She was twelve and her name was Charlotte. She had blonde hair, like her mum. I adored them both.

Sonja and I were both doctors of science, she a chemist, me, a botanist. Once London was sealed off, there was no need for either, so we worked in the distribution department, organising supply convoys to other government-supporting enclaves. We were forced to deal with the RBG. They protected the convoys. As payment, they helped themselves to a percentage of the food and raw materials in the lorries.

Their considerable arsenal did not prevent the drone strike on Charlotte's school, however.

A school. A fucking school.

We heard it from our office. It shook our windows and broke glass. We left everything and ran, not because we were afraid for ourselves, but because most of us had kids and we knew, instinctively what the target had been.

Sonja's hand was in mine. She held on tight.

Smoke rolled across the Embankment to fog the dirty old river. There were sirens announcing the arrival of the battered remnants of the emergency services. I coughed on the smoke and burning flesh stench. There was dust, gritty in my mouth. I felt a wave of heat then saw the first bodies, there on the weed-cracked pavement and the pot-holed road and glimpsed through gaps in the smoke. They were torn, half-unwrapped human packages. Police in battered helmets and scuffed breastplates tried to hold us back. But there were too many of us, fuelled by panic and grief.

We stumbled through the smoke and swirling dust, over rubble and glass. One by one people dropped to their knees to howl out their grief as they recognised their own among the dead.

Then figures began to emerge from the blazing ruin. Some collapsed. They were the living dead, walking, slowly, unsteadily, heedless of the heat and smoke and keening of the crowd.

One looked like Charlotte. I daren't hope. Sonja had no doubt.

It was my daughter, soot-smudged, clothes dishevelled and blackened. She was silent, unresponsive, her eyes emptied by a shock so deep, I wondered if she would ever come back to me.

That night, in our cramped, damp little excuse for a flat, I told Sonja that we had to get out. I told her how and where we could go. Sonja said no. She said it was too dangerous.

I reminded her that some horde of psychopathic bastards bombed the school. "They got a drone through the mesh and tried to kill our child."

"But they didn't, did they."

"They're coming, Sonja. The walls won't hold them back for much longer."

"And your answer is for us all to climb aboard a death ship to the moon?"

"They're not death ships –"

"Really? Don't you watch the 'casts? Fifty percent failure rate, auto-freighters and shuttles that should have been scrapped long before the Sunburn, breaking up in space or miles off course. They're run by RBG traffickers. They don't give a damn."

"Are things going to get better here?"

Sonja had no answer to that.

"We have enough money," I said.

"What do you mean?"

"I've been saving." Not enough for Mars, but enough for a moon run.

"You've been saving? While we struggled to buy food and clothes and –"

"My sanitation job." Three nights a week on a corpse clearance team, picking up the murdered, street-dead and the dead-at-home. There were no undertakers anymore, only the sanitation crews and the ovens in the abandoned hulk of Battersea Power Station. It paid well. There was a shortage of sanitation operatives, but no shortage of dead.

"You've been planning this."

"I suppose…I don't know." I wasn't lying. I had no plan, no fully-formed idea, but the possibility of escape had been in my mind for a long time.

"So, you want to give it all to traffickers and hope we actually make it to the moon?" An angry laugh. A shake of the head. "You have that much saved. And you would risk our lives…" Exasperated she sat back and covered her face with her hands.

I repeated the mantra.

They got a drone through the mesh and tried to kill our child.

"I took my family into Hell," Wilson says.

Saffron doesn't have an answer. She has never been in space. She can only imagine it and, even then, the imagery is vague. She sees darkness and knows that there is cold. She has some vague sense of the womb-like comfort of a space craft. Luners seldom travelled. There was some trade with the Martians, but no love was lost between the two colonies. They never visited Earth.

"It was done in shadows," Wilson says. He looks haggard now. He stands over his precious plants, but no longer tends them. "Access to government computers gave me names. There were small hours meetings in dangerous places. Money changed hands. A month later, we were buried under the false floor of a food convoy truck, on our way to the old Gatwick Space Port. Ironic. Sonja and I had spent our working days organising convoys like this.

"We clung to each other and tried to forget we were nailed into a travelling coffin. Charlotte was the bravest of the three of us. She didn't murmur. She held our hands in the pitch dark and whispered that she loved us, over and over again. I wondered who was comforting who. I was close to screaming by the time the lorry reached Gatwick. I could taste the darkness.

"The RBG had the port. They had the technology and the controls. There was a temporary respite when we arrived; the few minutes it took to transfer us and a score of other desperate people from one set of travelling coffins to another."

There was no wonder in this version of space flight. There was an ageing, tarnished-looking auto-freighter glimpsed on the pad as we were hustled into the launch tower lift by a platoon of armed men. Their contempt for us was palpable. It felt like an arrest, as if we were being herded towards a mass execution.

Perhaps that was exactly what it was.

There were forty horizontal couches in the freighter's cramped, tubular hold. The passengers were tightly strapped in.

"You stay on the couches until you get to the moon." The speaker was a shaven-headed hulk dressed in RBG camouflage and Kevlar. An automatic rifle was nestled, baby-like, in his enormous arms. "The straps are locked until touchdown." The hatch clanged shut. It was dark but for the dim red glow of a line of security lamps dotted along the low, curved ceiling.

The sobbing and screaming started long before ignition. I reached out to take Sonja's and Charlotte's hands in my own. The dull, bloody light carved fear-lines deep into their faces, which were, no doubt, reflections of my own.

The engines exploded into life.

Then there was vibration, a crushing weight that bore down onto my chest. And there was noise, a white, unrelenting, all-consuming roar that drew blood from my ears and nose. It felt as if my heart would stop. I couldn't breathe. The vibration became a maddened shaking.

Oh, and that noise. Unthinkable, incalculable, screaming *noise*. It rose and rose to a crescendo. Surely, something must give way, something must burst apart –

It stopped, all of it.

Silence replaced the engine-roar.

I felt my body strain against the straps as it tried to float from the couch. There was a falling sensation. I heard people being sick. I heard sobs and cries. Someone gibbered, already driven crazy.

We were in space.

It was incomprehensible.

The ion drive had cut the crossing to the moon down to twelve hours. But each of those hours had to be lived.

The traffickers may have been mercenary and ruthless, but they also possessed a spark of humanity because there were food tubes and water bottles bolted to sides of the couches. Unused to weightlessness, we were clumsy. Water was spilled into shimmering spheres and escaped nutrient paste writhed past our faces like blind mindless snakes. They were soon accompanied by vomit, urine globes and faeces. The hold stank before the first hour had passed. The stench induced more nausea. Someone begged for help, over and over again. I wanted them to stop. To shut up.

I forced myself to swallow the food paste and managed to keep it in my stomach. I tried to talk to Sonja, but she seemed unable to speak. The fear etched into her face at the commencement of the voyage had become raw terror. I held her hand and felt her violent trembling. Her distress was disconcerting. She was always the stronger and clearer-thinking one. She was the one I normally relied upon in a crisis. Suddenly, *I* had to be strong and it wasn't working.

The temperature increased and the heat became stifling. A new fear rose up like a black wave. There was a malfunction. We were going to bake alive in here. We were on the wrong course, heading for the sun. It grew hotter. Panic rippled through the strapped-down cargo. I realised that I was crushing my wife's and daughter's hands in mine.

It went on. The heat gave way to sudden cold. The air grew foul with the stink of human waste. Metal groaned. Knocking and hammering erupted from somewhere deep in the freighter's mechanisms, then ceased as suddenly as it started.

Sonja was right. This was a death ship –

The engines erupted back into life. The roar and vibration resumed. Gravity returned. We fell, fast. I could feel it; the gut-wrench of rapid descent. We were going to crash. Any moment now, any second, there would be an instant of unspeakable violence and pain. Sonja's hand crushed mine. I think I called out her name over and over again. I can't remember. There was too much noise.

We stopped, abruptly, jerked roughly against the straps. The noise and shaking increased. Then a final drop.

And impact.

Bone-jarring. Shattering.

Silence.

"There was nothing we could do, but wait."

Saffron tries to imagine the horror of it. Trapped in the dark, temperature dropping, air running out. No suits. No hope. The squalor and stink. Corpses mixed in with the living, the sick and dying. Children cry. People sob and rage.

*

A few people unstrapped and tried to aid and comfort the injured and distressed. The chaos was made worse by the low gravity. We fumbled and careered into one another and rolled into a broken, disoriented knot of wretched humanity. I saw Charlotte crawl across to a frail-looking, elderly woman, who seemed to be having trouble breathing. Charlotte stayed with her and stroked her hair until she took her last breath. I was proud of my daughter, at that moment. She was the bravest of the three of us.

The skinnys finally arrived three hours after the freighter crash-landed. They came in through the airlock and moved among us, disturbingly tall and graceful in their close-fitting space suits, and anonymous, behind the visors of their helmets.

"You didn't treat us well," Wilson says.

Despite her determined objectivity, Saffron is offended. "I had nothing to do with it. I was a teenager when you earthers started to arrive."

"I don't blame you." Wilson makes a placating gesture. "There were almost three hundred of us seeking asylum here. That's a lot of mouths to feed in a place like this."

"And we did feed you, and clothe you and gave you a home."

"It was the coldness."

"You were given work."

"There's more to life than work. The dormitory dome you put us in, it felt like a prison. There was no privacy. Everything was communal, we ate together, slept together. We were like rats in a laboratory tank."

"What else could we do?"

"Trust us."

Saffron laughs. The very concept of trusting a heavy is so inconceivable that Wilson's comment sounds like a joke. "After what happened?"

"Perhaps it's why it happened."

The refugee camp was a large dome off to one side of the Endeavour Colony and joined to, and separated from, the main city by a transparent tube, sealed at either end by an airlock. It was clean and warm. Its beds were converted flight couches recovered from the traffickers' auto-freighters. There was running water, and shower and toilet facilities.

Huge windows gave a view of the moon outside. The novelty of the motionless, grey wasteland quickly wore off and its desolation bore in on us. There was no rain or breeze or gale or snow. No fog or dust storm. The sky was always black. The landscape always grey. Nothing happened out there apart from the occasional arrival or departure of the skinnys' balloon-wheeled transports. The tracks made by the vehicles remained, forever undisturbed. Those snaking ruts almost drove me crazy. I wanted them to fade. I wanted them to be filled by rain, turned to mud, anything but stay frozen and eternally the fucking same.

Instant death waited on the far side of those windows. Death, only a few millimetres away,

Reduced gravity only added to our troubles. Walking was a clumsy, shambolic bounce. When you fell, you fell slowly in an ungainly tangle of flailing limbs. Once down you scrabbled and kicked like an overturned beetle. Anything thrown, an increasingly common occurrence because tempers were short, the missile hurtled faster and further than expected. A blow from some flying object would cause yet another argument, another fight.

Everything was wrong. Everything was difficult.

Work was shared out. We were given a cycle of shifts. Five days in the filth and stench of the waste recycling plants, five days in the makeshift nursery and school area we set up for ourselves in the dome, and finally, five days tending the crops in the immense hydroponic farms. The latter sounds the better option. It was, but only marginally. The hydroponic units were hot and humid. There were countless insects, the descendants of those who arrived in the early days as frozen eggs. The insects pollinated the plants. The pollinators needed predators to control their numbers and maintain the quality of their genetic stock. Survival of the fittest meant survival of the *fittest*. Many of the insect predators and pollinators stung and bit. One-sixth gravity plus steady heat and humidity meant that the insects grew larger than on Earth. The spiders, whose webs adorned the ceiling of the farms, were best not seen at all.

The work was hard and relentless.

The only time we left our dormitory area was to work.

Humans don't fare well when kept like farm animals.

I felt the tension when we arrived. It was an undercurrent. There was hostility from those here already, and suspicion, which meant that we kept ourselves to ourselves for the first couple of weeks.

Sonja was stoic and, as always, got on with things and made the best of the situation. Charlotte adapted surprisingly well and seemed at peace here. I think she felt safe. No one was going to drop bombs on her. No one meant her any harm.

Our initial interaction with a veteran of the place was with a tall, muscular character with a shaved head who looked too much like an RBG thug for comfort. He walked over to the trio of flight couches that represented home for us. It was evening. We were resting and talking with a neighbouring family group. As the veteran approached, I anticipated trouble and was unsure how to react to it.

"Tom Carpenter," the man growled and held out a huge hand. We all shook it and introduced ourselves.

To my relief, he seemed amiable enough, but I quickly sensed that he was a man barely in control of his emotions. His steadiness was carefully erected containment for his rage.

"Welcome to the moon," he said. "It's hard going, but it's a new life."

"A new world," Sonja agreed.

"A bloody dangerous one, but yeah, a new world."

We chatted. He gave advice on living here, the unwritten rules. Everyone pitches in. We are a community. There was a hard edge to that welcoming speech. As if it was a warning rather than a greeting.

We are *a community, so don't step out of line.*

"Sounds good to me," Sonja said.

"Yeah," I said. "Good."

Tom ran a poker school and I was invited in. I was nervous, but the group, a half dozen or so, made me welcome. We played for narcorettes. I began to look forward to poker nights.

"No one's happy," Tom said, suddenly. It was my third or fourth evening with them. It was after lights out. Someone in the group had obtained a couple of torches from somewhere, so we played on.

I didn't have an answer.

"We're looking at ways to improve our situation."

Murmurs of agreement.

"The skinnys think they can keep us cooped up in here, but they can't. We'll go mad. There's already fights and squabbling. Someone is going to get hurt soon if they don't let us out of this dome."

"They will, eventually," I said. Then added, lamely. "They have to, surely."

"You'd think. But it isn't going to happen," Tom said. "Unless we make sure it happens," He looked across at me, his face up-lit by the torch he held. "You in?"

"Yes," I said, unsure if he meant the next game, or whatever *making sure* he was planning. "I'm in."

The fights got worse. There was unrest. There was resentment. The refugees were breaking into factions who divided the physical space between themselves. There were brief alliances and short, sharp wars denoted by occasional localised brawls. We were among those who kept out of the disputes and, in so doing, became a clique of our own.

I clamped down on my frustration and my claustrophobic hatred of the moon. I loathed all of it; the black sky and empty, dead landscape, the gleaming white domes and cubes that were the colony and, most of all, the over-thin, over-tall, fragile creatures who had dominion over us, whose recent ancestors were human, but were themselves as alien as visitors from the stars. I hated their arrogance and coldness.

Sonja and I clung together, we both worked and at night we learned to make love in a place where there was no privacy, because our marriage depended on it. It was the fingerhold by which we hung over the abyss.

We tried to help when a new batch of refugees arrived. They were bedraggled and filthy and stank before they went to the showers and were given bio-fibre overalls like the rest of us. They told us that things were getting worse on Earth.

They were the last to arrive here.

"Is this any better?" Sonja asked me one night. "We were trapped before. We couldn't leave London, so how different is this?"

"No one wants to kill us here."

"The skinnys don't want us."

"Who can tell what the skinnys want. We do the work they don't want to do. They feed us and give us medical supplies." They also seldom spoke to us. They oversaw us at work, sent doctors to attend to our emergencies, but were always aloof.

Contempt or fear?

So, it ground on. The hydroponics farm with its sweltering, wet heat and biting insects. The recycling plant with its coffin-like filter tubes and all-pervasive stench of human waste. The nursery, the dome's neutral zone, filled with sullen, frightened, introverted children. And the dome itself, a seething slough of arguments, fights, crying, shouting and coughing, a surging, stinking, restless, angry press of human beings under which I was buried.

That night, *that* night, I dreamed of burning schools.

"*That* night?"

"Things just happen," Wilson says. He returns to his work.

Saffron says nothing. She waits. That's something she has learned. When trying to get at the truth beneath the truth, you wait.

"Perhaps they planned it. Sub-consciously, if not consciously…"

"Planned what?" A little prompt. Let him know you're still listening.

"There is always a spark. The match that lights the fire."

*

I woke to screaming. Someone in terrible pain. The lights were off, the dome bathed in a silver-grey moonglow that turned the drama into a frantic shadow.

A shout. "It's his appendix. It's his fucking appendix." Tom, of course. At the airlock, pounding its plas-glass with his fists. "We need a doctor. Now. *We need a fucking doctor.*"

The light came on in the tunnel which connected us to the main colony. Figures appeared. Skinnys, four, no five of them. They bounded gracefully to the door. Our lights came back on. There was uproar.

The screaming collapsed into pain-wracked sobs.

I made my way towards the centre of the cacophony. Others were streaming in to watch, to help or to add their voices to Tom's shout for assistance. The inner airlock door opened and three skinnys came in. The door slid shut behind them. Two were armed. They towered over us, but they looked fragile and scared. The third carried a bag.

"Where's the patient?" he demanded.

Tom pointed towards the centre of the dome. I couldn't see who it was, there were too many people crowded around. The doctor set off into the crowd. His bodyguards followed. Towering over the rest of us. I broke through and saw that the patient was a teenage boy, about Charlotte's age. He was doubled over into a foetal position on his couch.

The doctor emerged from the crowd. He took a step towards the boy.

A woman, presumably the boy's mother, tried to push the doctor aside to get to her son. One of the armed skinnys pulled her back. She shouted at him angrily. He had *pushed* her. He had *touched* her. How dare he? Skinny bastard.

The skinny looked shocked. He shook his head, his long white hair trailing the motion with disturbing underwater slowness.

The mother's near-hysterical protests were taken up by others

And suddenly there was a fight. The armed skinny dropped his weapon and covered his face. I saw blood.

The scuffle spread. The doctor cried out in fear and was swallowed into the melee. Then re-emerged, held by three of Tom's thugs who bundled him towards the airlock. Swept up by the mob, more thrilled than angry, I followed. I was enjoying the humiliation of our oppressors. I wanted them hurt. I wanted them to suffer. I heard the loud, sharp snap of a bone. The doctor yelped in pain.

The guards, including the injured one, afraid for their delicate moon-born bones, had retreated into the tunnel, no shot fired. There were women and children among us.

Tom wrenched the doctor's fractured arm up to force his palm onto the keypad. The dome-side door hissed open. I saw the doctor's broken form hauled inside. The skinnys on the other side backed away.

The tunnel-side door of the airlock opened.

The mob, Tom at its head, surged into the tunnel, a raging torrent of anger, hate and mind-dead violence. I clawed and battered my way towards the airlock.

They bombed the fucking school...

The skinnys in the tunnel were lost to my view. All I could see and feel was the mob, charging towards the far airlock. Towards the colony, towards the homes of those who had taken us in. I wanted to go with them. I wanted to smash, tear and burn.

They bombed the school...

I reached the airlock.

I saw the emergency close button.

A fucking school...

I stumbled to a halt, suddenly drained of rage.

A school.

No.

No more of this.

I punched the button and the airlock slammed shut to trap myself and the majority of the refugees in the dome. People piled up behind me and crushed me against the door. There was screaming and pounding, then crying.

I watched as the skinnys fled and closed the far lock behind them. I watched as they purged the tunnel of those who threatened their own. I watched Tom Carpenter and his mob die as the air was dumped from the tunnel and given to an ungrateful moon.

"Your people got me out of the dome fast, before I was beaten to death. Perhaps they should have left me there."

"What about Sonja, and Charlotte?"

"I haven't seen them since."

"It's ten years ago. It's a long time, surely –"

"They've never asked to see me."

"You saved the colony. You probably saved your own people."

Wilson shrugs and says, "Things are better for them now."

"I'm glad."

"Imperfect, but better. So, what's the point of your *true* history?" Wilson asks.

"Perhaps it will speed up the integration programme."

"I don't see how."

Saffron closes her noter. "Someone once said; if you want a tree, you need its roots and the soil it grows in."

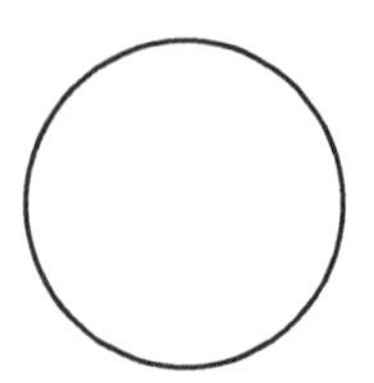

White Face Tribe

Stephen Palmer

this story was written on the full moon of February 2019

Mana was the tribal elder, a woman of seventy-eight solstices, whose hair was matted white and black, and from whose loins nine children emerged. Six of those children survived, four of them girls from whom more infants emerged under later suns. Mana was considered a powerful grandmother.

The tribe's land lay wooded and hilly between two rivers, in which salmon leaped, herbs grew and people washed. From riverside rock shelters they watched the distant migration of deer, but those herds were also watched by hunters of the Deer Bone Tribe, so Mana forbade deer meat. The women of the White Face Tribe gathered roots, berries, nuts and other earthen food, while the men fished, using intricate bone hooks on the ends of cords made from nettle stems. The tribe's red spark was kept burning inside a hollowed-out hoof, so that at winter solstice there was warmth and at summer solstice heat to cook fish.

On an evening one night before full moon Mana felt a twinge in her belly. An equivalence existed between the moon-ordered seasons of the womb and the sky-ordered seasons of the moon, so Mana knew something would occur the following night.

She shifted inside her garment of skins, looking out over the hills into the sunset. Perhaps the moon would speak to her.

Pressed into the ground a body's length away from the fire she saw a piece of mammoth ivory, carved into her own shape, leaning forward, so that the emphasis was placed upon her procreative capacity: birth and nourishment. Mana was the tribal elder in more than one way.

On the following night a sign began to manifest in the heavens. Of the tribe she noticed it first, because she had been expecting it. She alerted her sisters to the sign. One limb of the moon was darkening, so that, as moments gelled into longer moments, the moon began to fade. So the White Face Tribe watched as their totemic object lay ever more crippled in the star-specked arc of the heavens.

And this had happened before, bringing misfortune.

"We are the White Face Tribe," she told her people. "We have done something to cause this."

At length the entire moon shone blood red, and only Mana had courage enough to sit beside the fire underneath it. Everybody else lay in rock shelters, protected in the belly of the earth from the dreadful sight; but Mana, the tribe's elder, had to undertake the trial and face her fear.

As time passed the red hue departed and the full moon returned, so that in due course it shone whole again. Mana's sisters gave thanks for her resolute spirit as they returned to their places beside the fire. Using a chalky paste dug from nearby hills, they painted their faces white, the better to connect to their totemic object.

Next morning, as Mana sat cracking nuts out of their shells, one of her sisters ran up and said, "Two men approaching."

"Do you recognise them?" Mana asked, standing up.

"They look like men of the Deer Bone Tribe."

Mana followed her sister down a shallow slope to a stretch of shingle in the bend of the sunrise river, where she saw two men dressed in deerskin clothes. One was tall and strong, a bow and a quiver of arrows upon his back, but the other was small, slim, with black hair, and he wore bones strung on cords around his neck.

"Come speak with me!" this man shouted, pointing at Mana.

Mana hesitated. She knew neither of these men, though from the manner of the slim man she guessed he knew of her. She approached, until only the shallow water of the river, crossing rocks in bubbling arcs, separated them. "What do you want here?" she asked.

"You are the elder of the White Face Tribe," the man said. "I am the shaman of the Deer Bone Tribe. Last night you caused the moon to turn red. We know food is scarce everywhere. The deer have not come, and the Deer Bone Tribe are starving. You are trying to oust us from our lands so you can eat deer meat."

"Deer meat is forbidden for people of the White Face Tribe," Mana replied. "We take from the land what we need." She gestured at the ford, then behind her in the direction of the sunset river. "This is our land, with edges marked by flowing water. Your land is not our land."

"Your red moon has stopped the deer from coming. We cannot remember a time when the deer came so late. You have caused this."

"We have not," Mana replied.

"I know you are the shamanka of the White Face Tribe. If you do not tell the moon to release the people of the Deer Bone Tribe, there will be strife between us."

"I reject everything you say."

Hearing this, the tall man took his bow, nocked an arrow to its string and sent it high into the air, so that it landed in the centre of the river. Mana understood the message. She watched as the two men turned and walked away.

At the fireside, her sisters interrogated her. "What will you do?" they asked.

Worried, Mana pondered this question. Clearly the White Face Tribe had done something to disfigure the full moon, resulting in misfortune – the arrival of belligerent men of the Deer Bone Tribe. Yet throughout her time as tribal elder she had kept the ancient bar on eating deer meat for the sake of peace. Therefore she would have to assume the mantle of shamanka in an attempt to find the answer to her problem.

From the rear of the nearest rock shelter she took her horse-hide drum, made from braced loops of wood and covered with a cured hide, whose beater was made from a stick with a soft leather pad at the end, tied with nettle cords. This drum she beat in a slow rhythm as she circled the fire.

The sun ascended to zenith, then began to sink. Clouds wheeled across the arc of the sky, windrows against blue in perpetual motion. The world shifted around her as her spirit migrated into expanding spheres of influence, across scent-marked aerial tracks, to the very edge of the heavens, where lay the windrow of the sun and the windrow of the moon.

On a dark, misty lane she saw a deer bone, which she picked up. There was no meat remaining, one end cracked to get at the marrow. She sniffed it, but caught no animal scent that she recognised. The teeth marks looked nothing like wolf, or fox. Then the bone grew large before her eyes, its pale, fibrous ends vibrating, until all she could see was a shimmering field the colour of bone, and all she could hear was a reverberant noise like cracking at the back of a cave.

Below her she saw the land between two rivers, and then she knew the answer.

Returning to the fireside, she found that night had passed; she awoke on her side, drool upon her lips. Sitting up, she asked her sisters to gather everyone of the tribe so that she could address them.

The sun shone weak, the wind cool. She drew her skins about her, sitting as close to the fire as she could.

"One of you has eaten the meat of the deer," she announced.

For a while they stared at her and murmured amongst themselves. Mana watched them, her senses alert to their faces, their voices, their posture. Echoes of the previous night's journey sounded in her mind: the cracking of deer bones by the teeth of a tribe member…

"You!" she said, pointing to one of her grandsons. "You look guilty. I see the tension in your body, I watch your shifting gaze."

The young man – only two years out of boyhood – stared at her, but he said nothing, so that his silence articulated his guilt. At last he said, "Me?"

"Did you eat deer meat?"

He glanced around, as if for support, but there was none. He sagged. "Mana," he said, "the deer was dead when I found it. I was seeking healing herbs upon the riverbank, as my mother asked. Wolves had dismembered the body, leaving very little. I was hungry, so I took some of the bones for their marrow."

"This has become known to the Deer Bone Tribe shaman!" Mana cried. "*You* it was who caused the moon to turn red, disfiguring us. Now hostility will cover us."

"But the deer was dead."

"The bar on eating deer meat protects the White Face Tribe, so that we can live in harmony with the Deer Bone Tribe, who are more numerous than us."

"I ate no meat."

But before Mana could reply she heard a sound from the direction of the sunrise river – a wailing, mesmerising sound, that she had never heard before.

"What is that noise?" her sisters asked, standing up.

Within moments the entire tribe were on their feet. Mana ran down the slope to the river, where, on the far bank, she saw a line of Deer Bone Tribe elders.

The scene was difficult to understand. Holding narrow bones to their lips they made the sound by moving their fingers, so that the haunting, wailing noise passed across the water to assail her.

Then her grandson ran up to her side. “It is the bone flutes they play,” he said.

“What are they?”

“I believe them to be their sacred bone, the one they follow of all their many deer bones.”

“How do you know this?” Mana asked.

“I met one of their elders’ granddaughters by the river. We spoke for a while. She wanted me to join her tribe, to be close to her.”

Mana scowled at him.

The boy moved so that he turned his back to the elders. From the fox-skin pouch slung around his neck he took a bone, which he concealed from view. “She gave me this.”

Mana grasped the importance of concealment. “A flute? The daughter did?”

“It was freely given,” he said. “There is no badness in that deed.”

Mana took the bone, examining it, her back turned to the river. Four holes had been made in the bone, which at one end had been moulded with beeswax into a slot. She sighed. A gift freely given could not be the source of misfortune – the boy was correct. Yet he *had* eaten deer marrow, breaking the ancient rule. She did not know what to do.

Handing the flute back she said, “Keep this concealed.”

“Yes, Mana.”

Now the elders on the other side of the river began to depart, leaving only the black-haired shaman.

“There will be strife between us,” he said.

Mana decided it was best not to reply, so she strode away, leading her kin back to the rock shelters.

That night, no plan came to her mind – no trick, no speech of soothing, no ploy of cunning to deflect the angry shaman. She woke to a dull morning, rain-filled clouds looming on the sunset side of the sky.

One of her sisters ran up to the fire. "The Deer Bone Tribe are massing on the far side of the river. Their faces are painted with ochre!"

Mana ran down to the river, where she saw a terrible sight. In mockery of the bloodied full moon the elders of the Deer Bone Tribe had painted their faces with ochre: red face to attack the white face. Shocked, Mana stared. She felt her spirit writhe in distress, like a flapping, screeching bird inside her chest – a sensation of dread, of pain, of confusion.

"What are you doing?" she shouted at the shaman.

"Strife exists between us. We are calling back the red moon, which we will send across to your land."

"You are the people of the Deer Bone Tribe, not the White Face Tribe. Yours is a different totem. You have no power over us."

"We shall overwhelm you!"

At her side, Mana's grandson spoke. "Repel them," he urged. "We must do as they do, in order to stop them overwhelming us."

In panic, Mana agreed. "Yes, but how? The river is a ford here, rippling over flat stones. They can cross if they want to."

"I think they do not want to," the boy replied. "If our tribes fight, they may lose people – valuable people. Even though they are more than we are, they will shrink back from fighting until the last moment."

Mana knew this assessment to be correct. Killing was most often a deed of last resort, since no tribe wanted to lose members for paltry, avoidable reasons. "What do you think we should do?" she asked.

He took the deer bone flute from his pouch, displaying it. "I will play this," he said. "If they can take our red moon face, we can take their deer bone sounds."

"Play it then."

The boy stood upright, facing the river, the bone at his lips. When he blew into it the wailing sound began, and by moving his fingers he was able to change the quality, in a way that, to her surprise, Mana found pleasant. His sound was more gentle, more soothing than the disquieting noise of the elders on the other side of the river. But, perhaps, their noise was *meant* to disturb. Perhaps the boy had cunning, playing to soothe…

Yet it did not soothe. In a fury, the Deer Bone Tribe shaman raged at them. "You cannot take our sounds from us! Stop playing that flute! It does not belong to you."

"It was a gift freely given," Mana replied. "Ask the granddaughters of your elders, and one will confess."

"Never! Strife comes – and worse."

Hearing this, Mana turned and ran, gesturing for all to follow her.

At the fireside she told them to prepare for blows and killing, though she hoped that eventuality would never arrive. But what could she do? The deed had been done. It was irrevocable. Her grandson had eaten of the deer, the Deer Bone Tribe had played their flutes, then her grandson had played his flute, albeit freely received. Misunderstanding was all that stood between the two tribes, yet it could so easily lead to death.

Mana considered all she had learned as she gazed upon the setting sun. She realised that the boy had used the ploy of their opponent to set up a barricade, one symbol set against the other: red face appropriated against flute. But according to that reading the White Face Tribe were true and the Deer Bone Tribe false, since the flute had been given freely while the shaman had appropriated the red moon under treacherous pretences. Yet, somehow, she had to ignore that fact; she had to quell the desire for vengeance burning amongst her tribe. What mattered was *peace.* Neither man nor woman should perish because of avoidable misunderstanding between tribes.

Somehow, she had to pass her symbol to the Deer Bone Tribe in a way that brought harmony, not strife. In place of a barricade she needed a conduit… a *symbolic* conduit.

At once she grasped the answer to her problem.

Calling her grandson, she asked, "Do you still have those deer bones?"

"Only one."

"Bring it to me. Then fetch bone scraping tools from the hook makers."

Alone, isolated, in a glade near the rock shelters, Mana began her task. The deer bone was broad at one end – perhaps from a shoulder – and one part of it was flat and smooth. Using sharp stone points she drilled, scraped and scratched, so that after a while a sinuous line of dots emerged upon the bone surface. Using the fingers and thumbs of both hands she matched the number of dots with the number of nights between full moons – three sets of fingers and thumbs, minus one thumb.

An equivalence existed between the moon-ordered seasons of the womb and the sky-ordered seasons of the moon. Days between her bleeding matched days between full moons.

Finished, she examined her handiwork. The profound symbols of the moon lay inscribed by her, Mana, the elder of the White Face Tribe, upon a bone held in reverence by the Deer Bone Tribe. In such a way she created a symbolic bridge, handing over her own sacred knowledge by means of the vehicle of the other tribe – a tally stick, which they could keep, a gift freely given, just as the flute had been freely given. And so she hoped peace could be forged.

She sent her grandson to survey the sunrise river and report back.

"The shaman sits upon shingle," the boy declared, "peering at bones lying all around him."

"Then I have my opportunity," she replied. "Tell my sisters to sit quiet. Nobody is to follow me."

"Yes, Mana. I will tell them."

Mana hurried down to the river, where, on the far bank, she saw the black-haired shaman. He glanced up, then, seeing her, stood up.

"Get away from here," he said. "You have done wrong to us."

Mana did not reply as she waded out into the river. The ford was deep in places, but never so deep that she could not pass. Soon she stood upon the muddy bank at the edge of the land of the Deer Bone Tribe.

The shaman approached her, fingering the bones around his neck, as if for comfort. "What are you doing here?" he asked. "Strife will come soon. Go away."

Remaining silent, she handed him the deer bone. He stared: she saw the whites of his eyes. She sensed his astonishment, saw his wonder, felt his awe.

The symbols of her tribe, passed via a twin conduit, from shamanka to shaman.

"There will be peace between us," she said.

He did not reply. Shocked, he turned away, then departed, cradling the inscribed bone as a woman cradles an infant.

That evening as the sun set Mana watched distant lands. In the plains far out from the sunset river, on the very edge of vision, she saw dust in the air, as of the hooves of a thousand beasts. The deer migration may have been late, but it had at last begun.

She smiled. *She* had brought those deer through her act of inscription. Moon wisdom had proved superior to deer wisdom.

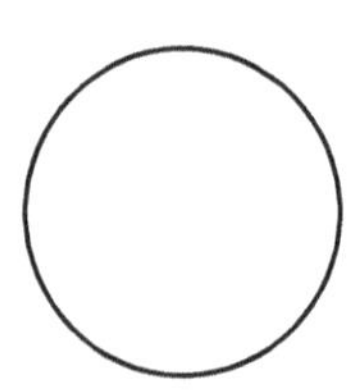

Moonstruck

Pauline E. Dungate

Jefferson looked up at the two who came into his office. One closed the door and took up a position beside it. Rosemary had neglected to say that they wore Air Force uniforms. He frowned, recognising their security insignia. The one who came further into the room was slightly paunchy around the waist, his hair thinning. The other was taller, a decade younger and had her fair hair scrapped back to expose the wine-stain birthmark covering part of her face.

"Colonel Jefferson?" the senior said.

"Just mister, these days."

"Colonel Jefferson, I am Major Ophele, this is Captain Saunders. We are here on official business. Information has come to light that has caused the Department of Defense to reopen an old case."

"How does that relate to me?" Jefferson asked.

"Do you remember Elizabeth Stott?"

The woman had been enough to try anyone's patience, even from the first time he had met her. About the only thing to recommend her was her list of qualifications. She'd been chosen as the lunar geologist to accompany his team to the newly installed moonbase.

Jefferson was punctual to that first briefing meeting with his team but Dr Stott was already there, tablet booted up and fingers tapping the table with impatience. In her forties, her short dark hair emphasised the thinness of her features.

"I was beginning to think I was in the wrong place," she said.

"Not at all, Doctor Stott," Jefferson touched the screen of the tablet on the table in front of him and entered the password it requested before displaying a number of files. He was about to start the conference when the door to the room was thrown open and an unkempt man in his early twenties rushed in.

"Am I late, sorry I'm late? I got side-tracked." He spoke fast, his words falling over each other.

"We haven't started."

"Who are you?" Dr Stott said.

"Charles Doran," he said. "I'm not going."

"So is the point of you being here?" Dr Stott said. It wasn't nasty, just matter of fact.

"You have to know how things work. Really you do." Doran said.

Jefferson raised a hand. "We have a lot to get through. I don't have to remind you that everything is confidential."

That had been his first encounter with Elizabeth Stott. He'd come away from the meeting with the impression of a very rude woman and the knowledge that he was going to have to live in close quarters with her for four months. A prospect he had not relished.

He held Major Ophele's gaze. He said, "Yes, I remember Dr Stott."

"We need to ask you about the incident when she disappeared," Ophele said.

"That was more than twenty years ago. The reports I filed at the time will be more accurate than my memory."

"We need to ascertain the accuracy of those reports."

"Why?"

"Her body has been found."

"That sounds like good news. The file can finally be closed."

"On the contrary. This discovery throws up more questions than it answers. We will need to take a new statement from you."

Jefferson frowned. "You realise I am a civilian now."

"You weren't at the time of the incident. We'd prefer you to come with us voluntarily."

As leader of the expedition he'd been responsible for all the team members and Dr Stott had vanished on his watch. "I'll need to make a few arrangements first."

"Such as?"

"I have a number of meetings and appointments. They will need to be cancelled or rescheduled."

Ophele nodded. "See to it."

Jefferson hadn't expected to be flown to Florida, though it made sense. He knew better than to ask questions during the flight – they wouldn't have been answered anyway. Instead, he tried to relax, searching his memories for the details of the expedition.

Most of the groundwork had been done beforehand. It had taken years. A suitable site had been found close to the boundary between near and far sides. The criteria had been strict. The base would be constructed inside lava tubes making it easier to seal from the vacuum. A deal was struck with the Chinese Government. Together, teams had located an icy asteroid and guided it into moon orbit before nudging it into a collision course. Both countries had the benefit of a water source greater than the supply available under the surface at the poles.

A combination of US Government funds and private enterprise had built the half way station at L1, the place where much of the hardware had been assembled. From there, they went down to the surface, relieving the team that were already working there.

Jefferson landed the shuttle a distance from the entrance into the accommodation. Jefferson turned to the other seven, "This is it, folks. Helmets on, then check your neighbour's seals. Raise your hand when your partner is secure."

A voice came from the back, "We don't need to be treated like infants. We've already practiced more than is necessary."

"It's standard operating procedure, Dr Stott," Jefferson said, keeping his tone mild.

"Fiddle-faddle."

"And I want each of you to respond to your radio in turn." Only when everyone had complied did he instruct O'Sullivan to open the airlock. O'Sullivan and Roma Cho set about unloading supplies, while Jefferson led the others to the airlock leading into their home for the next few months.

There wasn't much to see as most of the base was buried in the crater wall. This was a volcanic crater, not one formed by meteoric impact. The lava tubes had been relatively easy to fit the air-tight linings into. He ushered his team into the airlock. It was a large enough space to take the three rovers. Even with the best will, dust would get in. A deionizing chamber at the far end persuaded most of the dust to fall off their suits as they passed through it into the smaller equalisation chamber. This would only take four at a time in comfort. Jefferson left Sergeant Harrison with the second tranche as he recycled three of them through. From the change in her breathing, he sensed that Dr Stott was getting impatient with the slowness of the process.

The moment they stepped into the living/working quarters the leaving team set out the other way.

Once the task of arranging work and rest space started and Dr Stott was able to concentrate on setting up her laboratory she became less acerbic. She didn't like what she saw as petty rules that overstated the obvious but knew what she was doing – otherwise she wouldn't be part of the mission. Everyone complained about her attitude but they all kept their annoyances low key – to Jefferson's relief. All the team had their own areas of expertise and got on with their jobs. The main source of conflict was the constraint that no-one go outside alone. He noticed that the competition not to accompany Dr Stott was fierce with imaginative reasons being conjured. He went with her on occasion feeling that he couldn't exempt himself from the duty.

They settled into a routine, solving problems as they arose. Then, three months in, Dr Stott disappeared.

When they touched down at the Cape, a car was waiting on the tarmac. Not much had changed except for the design of craft visible. The buildings were very much in the same places and they disembarked outside the Admin offices on the far side from the runway. He was guided to what appeared to be a small conference room and invited to take a seat. Captain Saunders stayed in the room while Ophele went to report. He returned fifteen minutes later with a man braided as a colonel and who introduced himself as Abraham Doyle.

"Thank you for coming, Colonel Jefferson," he said, taking the seat opposite. "I assume Major Ophele has informed you of the circumstances."

"Only that Elizabeth Stott's body has been found. I know nothing other than that."

"How did you get on with Dr Stott?" Doyle asked.

Jefferson chose his words carefully. "I respected her as a scientist. As a person I found her social skills lacking finesse."

"You didn't get on with her?"

"Nobody got on with her. Her attitude was abrasive. I had no choice over her inclusion in the mission. She was well qualified and no-one else of her calibre had the degree of astronaut training she had."

"Did you have to defuse situations between her and the rest of the team?"

"Frequently. She had a tendency to be impatient and assume others know what she wanted without having to explain. She liked things to be done immediately and fast. She was protective about her work and her equipment."

"How did that manifest itself?"

"Some of the team had samples that needed analysing. Most importantly, air and water quality. That was mostly Captain O'Sullivan's responsibility. Dr Stott could be obstructionist when that work needed to be done, claiming to be running her own tests."

"She wasn't?"

"She was aware of the schedules. She also thought Dr Cho was using more water for her hydroponics than necessary. That caused friction."

"Was she? All the water was recycled. Anything else that added to the friction?"

"She could be dismissive of protocol."

"In what way?"

"I don't think she was fully aware of the dangers. She would deride anyone who took time in following procedures. It was most noticeable on expeditions outside. She didn't seem to understand why they had to go in pairs."

"There was always someone with her when she went outside?"

"I insisted on it."

"And she complied?"

"Reluctantly."

"Except for the last time.

"Yes."

There was a month to go before the end of the mission. In many respects, it had been a success. Issues with the machinery working in vacuum conditions had been skilfully rectified, the construction of further inhabitable chambers in a neighbouring lava tube was proceeding well and the pipeline drilled through the crater wall to the ice mass was almost complete. Jefferson had had a couple of amicable meetings with his opposite number at the Chinese base on the far side of the downed cometary body. Dr Stott had agreed to share data with their scientific officer, albeit with caveats. She spent much of the time working on her own in the laboratory space.

Jefferson was working with Diaz entering mapping co-ordinates into the data base after their last trip outside when O'Sullivan asked, "Have you seen Dr Stott, Colonel?"

"Is there a problem?" Jefferson asked.

"She requested an extra-habitat trip this afternoon and she is usually very punctual."

"She's not in the lab?"

"First place I looked, sir."

"Where have you looked, Major?"

"Everywhere in the habitat. Including the impossible places."

"Where is everyone else?"

"Malik and Sergeant Harrison are topside cleaning the solar panels, Cho is in hydroponics and Griffin is checking rations, sir."

"Ask each of them when and where they last saw Dr Stott."

"Yes, sir."

Although he was sure O'Sullivan had done a thorough check – the habitat wasn't that big – Jefferson carried out his own. He found no sign of her either.

"Well?" he asked returning to the main area.

"Cho says she was working on a mineral analysis last night. She assumed she'd risen early to check on its progress. Griffin's been keeping out of her way. Neither Malik or Harrison claim to have seen her since yesterday morning when she demanded that her rover be cleaned."

"Her rover?"

"She always likes to use the same one when she goes extra-habitat."

"The one you'd planned to use today?"

"Yes."

"Is she waiting by it?"

"I'll check." O'Sullivan hurried over to the monitor that tracked all the cameras scattered around the place. "It's not there," he said after a moment.

"You sure?"

"Positive, sir."

Jefferson swore under his breath. How was this able to happen? There were tell-tales which alerted everyone when the outer lock was opened. "O'Sullivan, check that her suit has gone, and find out from Cho what equipment she took. Diaz, I want to know how long ago she left."

"Aye, sir,"

It appeared that Dr Stott had left the habitat more than twelve hours previously, alone. Jefferson was furious and let the rest of them know it. It wasn't just that she had gone out on her own, it was the fact that no-one had noticed that the tell-tale would have shown the outer lock opening and the resultant reduction in air pressure. Harrison and Malik hadn't noticed that one of the rovers was missing when they went topside to clean the solar panels. He forced himself to calm down enough to issue coherent instructions.

"Diaz, find out when her suit was last charged; I want to know how much air she has. Griffin, what is the range of that rover? Malik, try and raise her on the comms. Tell her to return immediately. If she doesn't answer, get a fix on the rover's GPS. Harrison, I want the other two rovers prepped and ready to go, soonest. O'Sullivan, you and I will be the search party. Harrison, you'll be in charge while we're gone."

"What do I do?" Cho asked.

"Check through her notes. See if you can find out what Dr Stott intended to do."

"She won't like that," Cho said.

"Tough. If you can't you get through any encryption she might have put on her tablet, ask Diaz to help you. O'Sullivan, we'll need to take extra air cylinders."

Diaz said, "Sir, I calculate her air supply will be nearing its end unless she took spare."

Griffin said, "All units are accounted for. The rover range will depend on direction. If she heads over the terminator, she'd have only a couple of hours' power."

Jefferson glanced at O'Sullivan. "Load spare batteries, even though they'll slow us down."

"She's got a good head start on us."

"She may already be on her way back."

"Then we will be the reception committee. Any luck raising her, Malik?

"No, sir."

"Let's mount up, Major."

One advantage of the airlessness outside was that everything left tracks in the dust. Granted, the plethora of movement around the entrance to the habitat had churned everything up and the marks left by boots and vehicles overlay each other in a confusion of trails. Malik could only give them a general direction.

Major O'Sullivan finally spotted the trail. It was a straight line heading out of the crater depression and towards the terminator. "What is in this direction?" he asked.

"Nothing of significance. It's not an area designated for survey."

"Then where the hell was she going?"

"It's the wrong direction for the Chinese base," O'Sullivan said.

All they could do was follow the trail. Shadows began to lengthen as they approached the terminator. Dr Stott would have more power, Jefferson realised, as she would have crossed into twilight, then darkness further out than them. "Just my lights," he told O'Sullivan. "You should be able to follow me even in full darkness."

Eventually, they picked out the shape of the third rover. As they got closer, Jefferson frowned. There was no immediate sign of Dr Stott and even hanging back, he could see no footprints leading away. If she had run out of juice, he'd expect her to either stick with the vehicle and hope for rescue, or start making her way back, following her own tracks.

"Wait here," Jefferson said. Taking his flashlight, he switched on his bodycam, dismounted and approached, treading only in the other rover's tracks. He was faced with the impossible. The surface coating of dust was unsullied by boot-prints.

"Colonel Jefferson, the report you made at the time details the search. Do you want to add anything?" Colonel Doyle said.

"No. Satellite imaging couldn't help until dawn returned. That didn't show any tracks in the area other than those made by Major O'Sullivan and myself."

"Do you consider that you made a thorough search?"

"Yes. I even asked the Chinese for help. I was concerned that she would run out of air before we could locate her."

"Did you think to search closer to home?"

Jefferson gestured towards the report. "You can see that we did. I had entertained the unlikely possibility that she had fallen off the rover before it reached a dust free area and it had continued without her until the power ran out."

"Why unlikely?"

"She was a skilled driver, and she could easily have walked back to the base before we even realised she was missing."

"She could have been hurt."

"In that case, I hope we would have spotted her as it was still daytime."

Doyle appeared to study the report, then said, "There were issues between her and other members of your team. Did she antagonise anyone enough for them to want to kill her?"

Jefferson was taken aback by the question. "I don't know." He paused. "I was told her body had been found. Where?"

At Doyle's touch the surface of the table slid aside and a 3D image of the current moonbase appeared floating above it. It was very different from Jefferson's last visit. Where once the shuttle had landed, were a series of domes, their rooves barely showing above the surface. The single array of solar panels on the lip of the crater had grown to arc around half of the rim. If he looked closely Jefferson could just make out the position of the entrance to the original base.

"It has expanded a lot since your time," Doyle said.

"It was more than twenty years ago. So where was the body found?"

The image zoomed in. "The lava tubes that formed the original base are being expanded to accommodate new facilities. This one hadn't been used previously as it was considered too close to the surface and had a crack running along part of the roof. Then, it was considered too difficult to ensure its integrity but with new materials that can be remedied."

The scene moved smoothly through the rock to stop by an area picked out in red. As the imager closed in, it resolved into a space-suited form.

"This is where she was found," Doyle said.

"So she hadn't left the base at all?" Jefferson frowned trying to assess what he was seeing. "I don't remember access to that lava tube. It would have been searched otherwise."

"The only access was the crevasse in the roof."

"Did she slip and fall?"

"That is what I am trying to ascertain. If she did, how did her rover get out onto the plain?"

"How well was her body preserved?"

"Better than expected. Even sealed in the suit there was some decay as the incumbent bacteria get to work but as the suit's systems failed the cold slowed them down and preserved what was left."

"Enough to establish cause of death?"

"Dr Stott was murdered."

Jefferson sat back, shocked. "You have evidence of that?"

"Her suit was compromised."

"The suit fabric has a self-seal property," Jefferson said, "Could it have been damaged when she fell into the crevice?"

"The cut was straight-edged. Forensics also shows a contiguous cut in her torso. At the moment the suggestion is that the body was stuffed in the crevice and her rover was set running to make it look as if she had gone out onto the plain."

"That would mean that one of my team was a murderer."

"You are not above suspicion, Colonel Jefferson."

Jefferson nodded. "From your position that would be so. How do you intend to proceed?"

"By reviewing all the data from your expedition relevant to the incident."

"It is still extant?" Jefferson asked.

"I have had it brought up from storage and transcribed onto machines that can use it."

That was always an issue as the development of technology often rendered systems redundant making retrieval of older data difficult. "What do you wish me to do?" Jefferson asked.

"For the moment, I will assume that you are not complicit. I want you to talk me though some of the procedures as I am not familiar with all the equipment," Doyle said. He changed the 3-D image that still floated between them. Jefferson began to recognise the original base as later layers peeled away. "Photographs show these are the excavation vehicles present on site while you were there."

"More or less. There were two more machines on the other side of the crater where the channel for the cometary mass melt water would be constructed."

The scene swivelled, orientating the view in the opposite direction. The diggers were there. "Where was the shuttle?" Doyle asked.

"At the way station. We didn't expect to see it until change over at the end of our tour."

"So you had no way off if the situation went badly wrong?"

"We had contingency plans." It was easy to be blasé about it at this distance in time but then help would have been critical hours away – from the Chinese base.

At that moment a voice said, "The projection room is ready for you now, sir."

"Thank you, Major. We will be there shortly." To Jefferson, Doyle said, "I want you to walk me through your base."

Entering the projection room gave Jefferson a strange surreal frisson. The total immersion took him back twenty years and he was standing at the entrance of the habitat. He looked down, fully expecting to see a space suit covering his body. Instead, he was still in his civvies. To add to the disconcertion, he didn't have to move, the realistic projection shifted around them. He felt he was the ghost rather than the other way round. He dredged up memories of the codes that allowed entry and they glided inside, Jefferson pointing out the places where equipment was kept and where each member of the team usually worked.

"Now," Doyle said, "I want you to recreate exactly what you did in the time since Dr Stott was last seen."

"I'm not sure I can recall every detail."

"When did you last see her?"

"In her lab space, the evening before she disappeared. We kept Florida time," he added though Doyle probably knew that.

"Show me."

Eerily, the figure of Dr Stott appeared in the area Jefferson indicated.

There had been an argument.

Griffin had complained about the power usage. They were supposed to be scaling back because the lunar night was fast approaching. Dr Stott, though, seemed to be ignoring protocol. In her work space the drain was increasing.

Jefferson stepped through the curtain that separated the area from the rest of the habitat. Lights were blazing and more units than she could possibly be using were lit up. Showing his annoyance at her flouting the rules would be counterproductive. He'd learnt that early. Reasoning didn't always work either but that was the sane approach.

"Dr Stott, I am presuming that you are aware of the time."

"What now?" she sounded waspish. "I'm tired of interference with my work."

"You know that we need to start conserving power forty-eight hours before night-fall."

"Fiddle-faddle."

It was very tempting to go round and pull the plug on all her apparatus. She might listen then. Jefferson took a calming breath before saying. “This is an instruction, not a request. Turn off all items not actively being used.”

She turned sharply to face him. “It is not convenient.”

“It will be less convenient when we are working in the dark. Earthshine cannot replenish the batteries sufficiently for the needs of the base.”

“Cho doesn’t reduce her power usage.”

“Actually she does. Half her specimens are lit to the lunar cycle, the others to an Earth-diurnal pattern.”

“What’s the point of bloody beansprouts?” She’d muttered it under her breath but he’d still heard the comment.

“It is important to find out what crops we can grow in decreased gravity if outposts like these are to be self-sufficient.”

She snorted. A very unattractive sound. “So she roots them up and destroys them! A waste of water.”

Dr Stott had been told this but had obviously chosen not to listen. He said, “Cho needs to assess the uptake of the heavy metals you tell us are in the cometary water.”

“Yes, and that’s another thing. She can’t expect to analyse her samples with my equipment.”

“She knows what she needs to do. I don’t interfere with her work.”

“Then don’t interfere with mine, Colonel.”

“You have half an hour to reduce your power usage. Then Griffin will be instructed to divert power from this area into storage. I hope I have made myself clear.”

“That was the last you saw of her?” Doyle said.

“Yes. I gave Griffin instructions in case she refused to comply, checked on the rest of the habitat and went to bed.”

"Did she comply?"

"No, and when Griffin reduced the power she went to remonstrate with him."

"He told you this?"

"When I came back on duty next morning. He also reported that there had been some issues with the collection system, which is why I detailed Harrison and Malik to clean the solar panels."

"How did she manage to leave the habitat without anyone knowing?"

"That puzzled me as well as there are alerts on all the airlocks. We discovered that the dust had caused the outer lock to malfunction."

"Could it have been tampered with?"

"Possibly. What was Dr Stott stabbed with?"

"At this time all forensics is saying is that it was straight sided and sharp."

Jefferson slowly turned, observing the ghostly habitat occupying the space around him. He said, "You have had access to all the data more recently than me. What do you think happened?"

Doyle smiled then. "You knew she hadn't left the area of the habitat once you found the rover. Who are you protecting?"

Jefferson ran a hand through his hair. "They were all good people. They all had a motive. I didn't ask all the questions I should. I didn't want to know."

"You admit you didn't pursue the facts as rigorously as you could?"

"I guess so."

"Major Ophele has pieced together what he thinks happened. Would it surprise you if several of your team were involved?"

"If it had been suggested at the time, I would have defended them vigorously. At this distance, with your new evidence, maybe not."

"It is unlikely anything could be proved. I'll arrange for you to be flown back to California."

*

Dr Stott had appeared to be in a particularly foul mood. Major O'Sullivan eyed her with caution as she flowed into the communal area. She was dressed for going outside.

"Isn't it a little early for venturing out?" he said.

"No time to waste. I need samples before the light goes."

"There's no-one ready to go with you."

"It's your turn. I checked."

O'Sullivan reined in his annoyance. "Not until afternoon. This is my down time. Wait or find someone else."

She abruptly turned on her heel and strode back up the passage. He hoped she would not wake the Colonel. He was stressed enough without having to lose more sleep. He sipped the apology for coffee. Sergeant Harrison emerged, scanning the area warily.

"I thought I heard her voice," he said.

"She's gone back to her lab."

"She instructed me to dust down 'her' rover, yesterday."

"And you haven't done it?"

Harrison made a rude noise. "Any more of that coffee, sir?"

There was a squeal from the far end of the habitat. O'Sullivan froze, expecting the Colonel to appear. Instead, a distressed Cho stumbled towards them. She stopped at the sight of the two men, swaying on her feet.

"What's wrong?" O'Sullivan asked.

"She – she startled me. I was trimming the plants. She…."

O'Sullivan headed up to hydroponics. Dr Stott was lying on the floor, unmoving. He turned her over. The trimming knife handle was sticking out of her suit. "Fuck," he said as he knelt to feel for a pulse. There was none and no blood either, the suit having sealed around the puncture.

Harrison appeared at his side. "Is she dead?"

"Looks like it." He heard a whimper and glanced over his shoulder at Cho. "I should wake the Colonel."

"Do we have to, sir? He'll take all the blame on himself."

"True. Cho, see if you can find her helmet and gloves."

Not hearing any movement, O'Sullivan turned. Cho was staring at Stott's corpse. "I didn't mean to…." Her voice was a whisper.

"I'll find them," Harrison said. "What are you going to do?" he asked when he returned with Stott's gear.

"Make it look like an accident." He picked the woman up, relatively easy in the low gravity, and carried her to the community room. "She wanted to go outside. We'll let her."

"The cameras and alarms will record us."

"Griffin was complaining about electrical gremlins. Maybe we need a temporary blackout."

"I can do that. This dust has been causing a lot of problems."

O'Sullivan fastened her helmet and gloves before carefully withdrawing the knife. He handed it to Cho. "Wash it and leave it with your others."

The woman stared at it as if she had never seen it before. "She wanted to pull up my plants."

"When?"

"Yesterday. Said they were using her water."

Harrison took the knife from Cho's hand and laid it on the bench. "Come and have some coffee," he said leading her out of the hydroponics area.

Now he had decided on a course of action, O'Sullivan worked efficiently. He dressed for outside and as soon as Harrison blacked out the cameras carried Dr Stott out of the habitat. He'd seen the crevice on the ridge when he'd been working on the solar panels. He'd guessed there was another lava tube below and was satisfied when he stuffed the body into it and it fell.

Harrison fixed the cameras enough to show a figure riding out of the hanger before it want on the blink again. He dismounted and opened the throttle, sending the rover off to go where it willed.

Back inside, Cho hadn't moved from where Harrison had sat her, the coffee untouched in front of her. She was shivering. "I killed her," she said.

"No, you didn't," O'Sullivan told her. "You haven't seen her since last night. She was in her lab working when you turned in."

Cho repeated his words. "She was in her lab working when I turned in."

"Yes. And that's where you'd better go now."

"I won't sleep."

Harrison took the seat next to her. "Roma, do you have any of those pills left that they gave us to help acclimatise to conditions here?"

Roma Cho nodded.

"Take two."

"They give me weird dreams."

"In the morning all you will remember is a weird dream."

She looked at him hopefully. "Should I say goodnight to Dr Stott?"

"Better not. She gets snappy if you disturb her."

O'Sullivan rested a hand on her shoulder. "You look tired, Roma. You have been working too hard. Take a pill and go to sleep."

She smiled wearily. "Yes, sir."

"What if she breaks?" Harrison said as she vanished into the cubicle she shared with Dr Stott.

"Then we both get cashiered."

"It would be worth it."

Jefferson hadn't been as fast asleep as O'Sullivan had thought. He had pieced together most of the events. There was no point admitting it now. Both O'Sullivan and Harrison were long beyond the reach of indictments and Roma Cho had carved out a successful career in plant biotics. He wasn't about to alter that after all these years.

The plane to take him back to Kansas was waiting on the tarmac. Doyle escorted him as far as the steps. The man saluted and said, "Some things buried on the moon should stay buried on the moon."

Gratefully, Jefferson climbed the steps of his ride feeling that chapter was now closed.

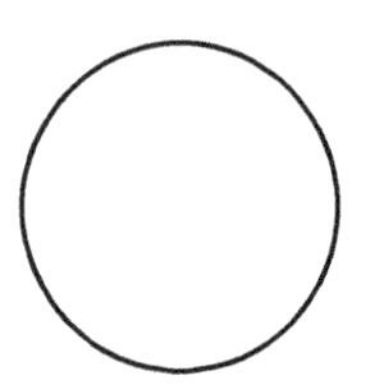

Dissolver

Douglas Thompson

What Eldric Tzysyk had led me to believe was his place of work, turned out to be an auction house. The facial expression of the clerk who greeted me at the door changed, over the space of a minute, from helpfulness to unease as I tried to tell the story of how a tall man with thick black hair and moustache had once invited me in to accompany his piano playing in that very room, telling me it was the office of a scientific institute. How come I remembered all the bizarre objects around that room if I'd never been in there? How could some impostor with a weird name have acquired a key to their door? Such was my pointless conversation with myself, as I walked back down the many flights of warehouse stairs towards the drab old streets below.

My next stop was his home address and his wife, or who I thought was his wife. There also, I was in for a shock, just not quite the one I'd been bracing myself for. Their apartment was inside one of the new multi-storey towers down near the River Clyde. Crossing the car park in late afternoon, I had that feeling of exposure and of being watched which those kind of harsh urban environments almost seem designed to instil. I had phoned first. Maybe Mrs Tzysyk was watching me from behind her curtains above: the scarlet harlot, the other woman, however she might think of me. Then I saw the moon peeping above a low cloud on the horizon and laughed to myself.

Eldric would always seem to be watching me now, because of some of the crazy things he'd told me.

But again, my expectations were to be confounded.

Tzysyk? Mrs Tzysyk? But that's not my name. My name is Novak, Magdalena Novak. But this is all most odd, you must come in and explain. His wife you say? But my dear, I was never Eldric's wife. Is that what he told you? I was his landlady. I merely rented a room to him. Someone back in Warsaw must have given my name and number to him before he came over.

Warsaw? Poland. But I thought he was from Sofia... oh never mind, I must have misunderstood that. But that was the least of it of course. My heart had been thumping, thinking that I was about to have some confessional confrontation with the wife of my disappeared lover. That she was going to break down into self-pitying tears or fly at me in rage with a bread knife in her hand demanding to know how often he'd fucked me and whether he bought me jewellery and called me his little chickadee. You know the sort of thing. Instead of which suddenly there was this: a kind of mirror. I stood before a woman in her early fifties like me, a divorcee by the look of the photographs around the place, with two adult children. Two daughters, while mine were sons. The husband, like mine, had been off the scene for years it seemed. For a bit of extra money, she had rented a room to someone from the old country needing to be helped out for a bit. He'd told her he was a concert pianist. A different story for everyone. *You really didn't have any kind of...* I stammered *...relationship with him? He did tell me he was married to you. Why would he do that? Do you know where he is now?*

Her shrug was as vast as mine, the mirroring potentially infinite.

*

When I first met Eldric, he was, characteristically, fleeing from the rain. I was sitting in a little internet café on Great Western Road, sipping my cappuccino and writing notes in my diary as I watched the rain drizzling down, bouncing off the pavements, and sparkling under the wheels of buses and cars. The door from the street flew open with a gust of wind, and there he was struggling and flapping with an umbrella, furiously, as if every single drop of water might be an existential threat to him personally. But maybe they were.

His accent was subtly foreign, you know how it is. English pronounced just a little too perfectly, suggesting that he'd learned it somewhere else, some international school on neutral territory. I'm sure he implied he was Romanian with a Bulgarian passport, or was it the other way about? Oddly, these sections of my memory of our time together seem to be increasingly unstable, as if written in pencil on yellowing paper, or painted on a canvas insufficiently primed.

What are you running from? – I asked him, uncharacteristically forward, even insolent of me. Then his eyes fixed me, and a smile crept into a corner of his mouth. That small smile of his, barely tolerated on a corner of his lower lip, nonetheless had an immensity about it. As with his eyes, one always felt at the start of a journey, on the threshold of a great secret that might only slowly be revealed.

The rain… he said.

Then you're in the wrong damned city, I laughed. *This is Glasgow.*

Or the wrong planet? He replied, widening his eyes, and tilting his head to one side in apparent loss, slightly mockingly. *This one is 71% water-covered. The human body is about 60% water. A new-born child closer to 80%.*

Now *my* eyes were widened. *You talk like you've been to others!*

With the most astoundingly natural and casual of gestures, he nodded towards my nearly-finished coffee and bought me another one before I had begun to understand that this total stranger was now taking a seat beside me as if he'd known me all my life, as if my slightest objection to this invasion of my private space was simply inconceivable. I should have been horrified. But somehow I was enchanted. *Simple science,* he said, sitting down. *You're a fish out of water, quite literally, you and everyone else. And yet we fear getting soaked in the rain, fear drowning in a river, getting dragged out to sea by a tide on the beach.*

Doesn't it rain where you come from? – I taunted him playfully, then regretted for a moment the note of xenophobia in my choice of words. He looked slightly hurt for a moment, then stroked his black moustache, ran a hand through his thick black hair as if noticing these features of his own appearance for the first time. *Oh yes, but not half as often as here, and not as cold. And not water.*

What? I laughed, thinking I must have misheard him. *Are you a scientist or something?*

He said he worked at the European Institute for Astronomical Research, I think, attached to Glasgow University, an organisation that I would only later find out did not exist. Or maybe I am misremembering the name he called it, or he mispronounced it.

By the time we left the café together, darkness had fallen, the rain had stopped and the moon had come out over Kelvin Bridge. A half-moon I remember, with a beautiful halo of cloud around it. I never knew when Eldric was joking or not. His flights of fantasy were a constant and amusing part of his conversational style. Only in retrospect does that leave me feeling confused about certain things. *Where did you say you were from?* I asked again.

The moon, he said, *the other side of the moon, where my people can hide from all your telescopes and radio waves.*

Your people? I laughed, incredulous.

Yes, he smiled, *your news makes us very sad. But your music is sometimes very beautiful. It is forbidden for most of us to listen to it for too long in case it makes us sorry for you.*

You talk like you're one of the angels! Bending near the earth to touch their harps of gold, as the old hymn goes. Then I remembered that I'd let slip during our conversation that I was a musician.

But you are the angel, Emilianna, you are the one who plays the violin and guitar and sings. Will you rehearse with me, next week?

Where? I asked, taken aback. *You can play too? What instrument?*

We paused together on the old Victorian iron bridge over the river and he pointed up towards the warehouse building on the west bank. *Up there, that is my office, my studio. Why not come visit me next Thursday night and accompany me on the piano?*

I went to Eldric's studio. I pressed the buzzer on the street below although I saw no signage that referred to any Scientific Institute. I would have queried him about that, were I not so gob-smacked when he opened the doors and invited me in. The space was large and full of the most bizarre objects. A furniture auction room or wholesale warehouse for historical curios. I saw stuffed crocodiles and rhinoceros, hundreds of butterflies preserved in glass cases, polished dark wooden armoires and wardrobes, chairs and sofas in a myriad of styles covered in sumptuous fabrics that seemed variously Turkish, Arabic, Louis XIV French, and Victorian Gothic revival. The piano Eldric sat and played at was antique, white-painted wood, with a curious sound as if it was half-celesta or harmonium. The music he made was astonishing but unfortunately I found myself almost incapable of accompanying it to any meaningful extent. Quite where it fitted into the history of western, or indeed eastern, music, I was, and remain to this day, perplexed. Yes it repeated certain motifs occasionally, it was not entirely free-form or twelve-tone, and yet its progress seemed endlessly improvised and invented. I felt for the first time as if music was a language I had hitherto only dreamt that I understood, and that now someone was speaking fluently to me in a dialect that I was at a loss to translate.

Magdalena was incredibly kind and understanding. I got emotional as I told her my story and she poured us both a drink. Although she'd scarcely known Eldric she said, she'd known plenty of other scoundrels like him, back in Bratislava. *But I thought you were from Poland...* I began to counter but she was off on a long reminiscence like a central European freight train that it was impossible to board. She talked, we talked. I was lonely and confused. Maybe she was a bit crazy, sometimes it's hard to tell when there's another language and culture filtering every signal. She was tall for a woman, as tall as Eldric had been for a man, but with icy blonde hair and piercing blue eyes. Her features were strong, almost Amazonian, but there was something incredibly comforting in her manner, as if one might always feel safe with her, as if she would always have the answer to everything, had always been through something similar to the worst of your life experiences and have a practical answer for how to cope with them and get over it. Night was falling by the time I stood and went to the window and suggested I leave, or that Magdalena join me for a farewell walk together down in the park far below. *Oh what a lovely idea, my dear. But look!* She ran her painted fingernails down the window glass with a curious expression of enraptured disgust ...*we couldn't possibly! You can't possibly go just now. It's started raining. You'll get soaked through to the skin, catch your death like a wee drooned rat!* She crooned this last phrase as if hugely proud of her command of Glaswegian idioms and other clichés. She was very persuasive. I stayed.

What do you think he meant when he said those things about the moon? – she asked me.

Oh I don't know. It was just romantic talk perhaps. The moon of love and all that fluff. Forgive me for sounding so cynical and scientific...

Or not scientific enough perhaps, have you thought of that?

No. How so? As I accepted another drink, it occurred to me for the first time how odd the interior design of Magdalena's apartment was, although something had been nagging me about it from the start. Her clothes sense too. You know the cultural differences, even though you don't realise you do. I mean, if you see a woman wearing leather in a British street right now, at this moment in fashion history, you know she's Russian, right? It's crazy, but it's true. Get close enough to overhear her language and you'll be proven right. There's a time lag sometimes, a preference gulf, a fashion divergence, between continents and cultures, despite all our modern chain stores and social media platforms disseminating trends at fifty gigabytes a second or whatever. I lack the stylistic language to fully describe or explain it, but Magdalena and her apartment stood sideways to all that, were outside of time, as if designed by someone nobody had ever heard of nor ever would again.

I mean, if an alien civilisation visited Earth and wanted to observe human affairs, the most logical place for them to station themselves by far would be the far side of the moon, don't you think? A base from which to stage missions, to refuel, without ever being observed.

I never thought of that... I mumbled. *Are you into all that stuff? UFOs and crankery? Eldric wasn't green or grey with tentacles and antennae or anything. He was just a man, an ordinary man. He even... you know, down there... he was like any other.*

Magdalena nodded her head, sagely. *Yes of course. And weren't we just saying that too? How they are all the same?*

*

Not unlike lowland Scots males, Eldric was scared of crying, I recall. But then again, not quite in the way that most Scots males are. Once in a café, he got out a sketchbook and drew me a diagram of what different kinds of human tears looked like under the microscope. He drew tears of grief as very angular, rectilinear things, quite cold and cool looking. Tears of laughter he drew as all globular and chaotic and rounded and bulging. Tears from cutting onions he drew entirely differently: a bit like snowflakes, all circular blossoming shapes, very regular and organic and repetitive, more like natural objects such as leaves and pine cones, devoid of the scrambling effect of human emotions. His point again was that we are mostly water.

Despite his best efforts however, Eldric did sometimes shed tears, although they seemed to hurt him immensely. The sight of people begging or sleeping rough in the streets made him cry, or seeing animals hurt or maltreated by humans. Once he grabbed me and spun me around, held me by the shoulders and looked into my eyes and said: *How is this possible? It is Christmas, people are buying presents for people, things they won't even want, buying huge quantities of food that will make them fat or sick of which they will pour half away, all this in the name of a man who went barefoot and lived like a monk, who preached kindness and compassion. – And yet here everyone is walking past these dejected souls on the pavement in blankets and ignoring them without a modicum of guilt or self-questioning. How is this possible?*

I found it difficult to answer him of course. Had to take him to sit in some dark café where he could dab desperately at each of his tears as if he needed to stop their progress from reaching the table beneath him, as if they would burn his cheeks on the way down.

Another thing that always made Eldric cry, was the moon of course. He said he felt deep down that it was his home, where he really came from, that it was like a memory of the mother he never knew. He said he'd been adopted as a child, spent time in an orphanage. Sometimes his stories seemed to contradict each other, or maybe I didn't listen carefully enough, should have taken more notes at the time. Sometimes he said quite seriously that he longed to return to the moon.

The Victorian architecture of Glasgow also made Eldric cry. He said it made him sad that all the people who had designed it and built it were dead now, that there was no way he could talk to them. We went to museums and libraries for days on end, so that he could pore over old linen manuscripts and black-and-white photographs. Eldric said that the Victorians had understood immortality, that they had thought outside and beyond a single human lifespan, that they understood that the human race was a super-organism like ants or termites. This confused me. *You say we're grand and great and then you say we're like insignificant little ants, I don't understand, isn't that a contradiction?* – I asked.

But why is small insignificant? – He countered. *Your whole earth and everything in it is small when seen from the outer edges of the galaxy. And bees run this place, all the plants that support life. They are the gardeners. They are the most reliable ones who Nature has trusted to guard the entire earth, not you, gaudy, arrogant humankind. You are their immature and unreliable little brothers and sisters therefore. It is the bees who are to be admired and respected, who run the show. Scale is not everything. Do you bow down before whales and elephants? Or perhaps you should.*

I never witnessed Eldric taking a shower or bath of any kind. And yet when we went to bed together his skin seemed devoid of any scent, as if he didn't need to wash, as if he existed already in some state of natural purity. The first time we went into my room, he insisted on leaving the curtains slightly open so that a band of moonlight fell across the floor, the bed and the quilt. It took a long time for him, but when he finally reached orgasm his face grimaced and he seemed to be briefly in genuine pain. I caressed his back, noticing as I did so how my hands passed through the shaft of moonlight landing on his skin, as if I were playing a harp. I thought of that line from the hymn that I'd remembered from our first meeting *of angels bending near the earth to touch their harps of gold.* Eldric's back was pock-marked with a strange and vast array of tiny craters. He said that these were scars of something terrible done to him in the orphanage as a child. I wasn't sure whether to believe him exactly, but I know that whatever the experience he was recalling was; it must have been a source of genuine horror to him, as he wept in my arms.

Afterwards we stood at the bay window together with the lights out, with just blankets wrapped around us, looking up at the full moon. Raindrops began to land on the window and I saw him shiver. *People think there's no water on the moon you know,* he said, as if answering a question that neither I nor anyone else in the room was asking him. *But because of its tilt, there are regions that never receive any direct light from the sun, and there are huge hidden ice craters in those places, more combined than at the Earth's two poles.*

I wish now that I'd asked him how he came by that knowledge, although I doubt he would have answered me other than in his usual mysterious terms. I thought at the time that he was being metaphorical, and the rest of his conversation seemed to confirm this: *I show no emotion most of the time. But so much of me is dark, so much of me is turned away, hidden from you.* At this, he reached out his hand from under his blanket and held my chin, turned my face towards him as if I was a child or his pupil. *You are so trusting. You believe, you think you know that all of me is good, even all the regions that curve away from you, that you cannot see and have never visited. But I need my darkness. On the bright side, the one you see, all emotion, all moisture is instantly evaporated to space, cold, lonely space with all its unanswerable vastness. Gravity, attraction between bodies.* He held me to him, and kissed my forehead softly. *This is what holds the universe together, what stands against the loneliness. Only in the darkness, am I allowed to cry, to be naked and to be seen again in my primal state, my true form, unadorned. But remember, I am an illusion. I have no light of my own. A magic lantern reflecting the sun. It is you, your own shadow and its passing, that animates me. Our peculiar orbit, how I am locked in my relationship to you, this is what preserves my darkness, allows me to retain my secret key, the gift of life. You must never see my other side, for you would only destroy it, as it would destroy you.*

The night I lost Eldric forever, we had planned to get back to my flat earlier. I'll always blame myself I suppose, despite how deeply irrational I know that is. I'm only human. I kept him out too long, walking around the Christmas markets in the city squares, the turning Catherine wheels, the sausage stalls, the families and children wrapped up in scarves and hoods, the Bavarian nativity scenes carved in wood, the spinning cacophony of festival lights. We'd checked the weather reports as usual. We knew that heavy rain was forecast in the evening, but we didn't know about the Underground strike until too late. Deprived of trains we looked for buses, but the pedestrian precinct zones we found ourselves in meant the distance to reach any bus stops was suddenly too far. I encouraged him, taunted him, bullied him in fact, to just run home with his hood and an umbrella up like me. He acquiesced. But there was something wrong. I had gone too far and something had given way inside him. Perhaps it was love itself. I like to think that, although perhaps I am only deluding myself. His emotions were so hard to read for a lot of the time. Love for someone, that moment when we finally abdicate our own selves, our very life, for the well-being of another. When we come to value another life even more than our own. Or maybe he just got tired of living in this world.

I thought at first he was crying. That one of his many obscure and secret sorrows had surfaced again and were taking hold of him, under his hood, in the shade of the umbrella. When we reached Charing Cross and the city grid fell away to reveal the great red and white veins and arteries of the motorway in front of us and below us, I turned to look at him and saw that half of him was gone already and the rest would follow all too soon. Taking his hood down, he gazed towards the stars for one last time as his shoulders, his torso, then his legs, all faded out to nothing under the sizzling onslaught of Glasgow's rain. The last thing I saw, and will always remember, were his sad blue eyes turning back to fix me in one final wistful gaze, before even these disappeared into nothingness and were lost.

I remember looking down to see a curious blue spark of electricity left dancing across the fingertips of my right hand which had been outstretched towards him in pleading valediction. When I looked up again, his anorak, his empty shirt and trousers, had already been caught by the wind, and were sailing off and down towards the ceaseless traffic below, unreachable, impossible evidence of a man who had never been.

I am not a lesbian, nor ever had any inclinations in that direction. And yet, when I woke up in the arms of Magdalena I did not feel any sense of alarm, shame or regret. Only a moderate amount of alcohol had been involved after all. I had known what I was doing. She was just as beautiful as I had remembered finding her in the small hours of the morning, when our mutual sobbing at the cruel perversity of life had given way and resolved itself into the surprising and eternal solace of the human kiss. From which so much else flows of course, if left untrammelled. Well, we did everything else after that, but we didn't trammel.

My sleep was not an undisturbed one however. In it I dreamt I was in some alien landscape. The grass was long and green, and through it invisible horses kept riding towards me, increasingly as if they wanted to threaten and trample me. Just as I began to feel I had mastered this, by watching how the grass was displaced by their galloping hooves, a new threat appeared. Set off by some kind of mini-tornadoes, entire trees began to uproot themselves and come spinning towards me, battering their trunks and branches against me with increasing force. I thought I'd seen a nearby castle on a hill when I'd first entered the dream, but now as I moved through the landscape I looked up again and saw that it was actually made of glass and that it hovered several hundred feet above the ground. And yet, as the dream ended I found I had climbed a long ladder up towards its entrance, where a woman in a white dress, some mythical princess perhaps, was looking at me in a manner full of carnal desire. I saw then that her dress was somehow also a waterfall, white rapids both static and in motion, and began to feel a pleasant sensation in my sex which I sensed that she was somehow causing.

Magdalena seemed a little reluctant at first, said she wanted to prepare breakfast for us both while I washed, but I persuaded her to come into the shower with me. As we kissed in the hot steam, shivering in pleasure as our hands brushed all over each other's skin, she knelt down to kiss my tummy and then to insinuate her mouth into the heart of me, lapping away happily between my legs like a pet cat at a saucer of milk, her hand clutching my shaking thighs. I was scared I was going to fall over, then quite suddenly something changed. As the temperature and pressure of the water from the showerhead had intensified, my eyes had increasingly closed over as the waves of pleasure enveloped me. And thus perhaps, somehow, in the closing moments I missed a critical detail, the vital change. Strangely, even before we had entered the water, and throughout every extremity of our intimacy, I hadn't noticed that Magdalena had no aroma, not the slightest molecule of scent.

Getting my breath back, I looked down and around in bewilderment at the empty shower, empty bathroom, not a trace of my lover of a moment beforehand. Putting on her borrowed dressing gown, I then paced around the entire apartment, even checking inside cupboards, in a continuation of the same vain pursuit.

It had rained heavily again that morning, but by afternoon it had at last dried up. A clear winter evening came on. Approaching sunset, I went to the window and looked out across the city. I felt profoundly lost and yet at the same time strangely comforted. Her fridge was well stocked. I poured myself a gin and tonic with a slice of fresh lemon and left all the lights off, just allowed the whole dusk and ensuing darkness to slowly take me over and fill all the rooms and every recess of my being. Perhaps I had misunderstood my search to find the identity of Eldric Tzysyk. – That it had in fact been, ultimately, a search to find my own identity, my submerged and secret self.

The phone rang at 7pm precisely and Magdalena's answering machine recorded a perplexing automated message from some other machine out there in the wilderness of mirrors:

THIS IS AN AUTOMATED MESSAGE FROM THE EUROPEAN INSTITUTE FOR ASTRONOMICAL RESEARCH FOR MS EMILIANNA VERRECHIO WHO IS CURRENTLY RESIDENT IN THE APARTMENT OF MAGDALENA NOVAK, TO NOTIFY HER THAT THE PROPERTY HAS NOW BEEN SIGNED OVER INTO HER NAME AS HER NEW RESIDENCE.

I wasn't imagining it. I know because I picked each of them up and held them under brighter light in the hall and kitchen; those framed pictures I'd seen around the apartment the day before, which had now somehow changed. Where I thought I'd seen the smiling faces of Magdalena's adult children in various picturesque locations, I now saw that their faces were only ever smooth pink masks, as if painstakingly blanked over in Photoshop. Non-people, ciphers, tailor's dummies. Perhaps my two boys, Adam and Jason, would come and visit me here in time, and their portraits come to reside there.

What is the difference at the end of the day, between one human life and another? Between terrestrial life and alien life even? All pain is the same pain, all love the same impossible longing for some mythical healing of the wound that life leaves upon us each from the moment of birth, and answers, solves at last only with death, that great sewing up of the blue and battered lips of suffering. Silence is the only luxury and the ultimate statement.

Standing at the window of my new home, I watched in awe as the winter moon rose, huge and yellow and full, and slowly rolled like a boulder behind the tombstone of a distant apartment block. In there, within lit domestic scenes, other dark silhouettes moved about, oblivious, unknowing of the cosmic spectacle they were involved in from my unique viewpoint in space. Down below, the streets interlocked and whirred and fizzed with the usual symphony of light, the electricity of blighted hopes.

What is it the moon means to us? It's as if it is lodged in ancestral memory, something our forebears also loved and feared. It's as if it watches us, as if it knows, witnesses our dramas. And occasionally intervenes.

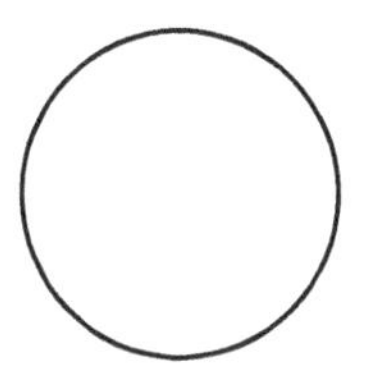

Lunar Gate

Alexander Greer

Collective lunacy had engulfed the world, it seemed, once the chasms on the moon had appeared in a rippling scar across its surface several kilometers long. No satellite could get a good image of the gorge and all attempts came back with large, white spots burned onto the photos as though by a magnifying glass. The Jaw, some called it, others preferred the term 'phenomena' as it seemed more professional, more reasoned or somehow more scientific; though behind closed doors, 'Lunar Gate' was the reigning phrase.

Memories and fears of the last few weeks haunted John as he floated onboard the Unity III; riots, doomsday preachers, even one instance of a suicide cult somewhere in Alaska. He hadn't been able to watch the news in some time, turning away instead to brood on his thoughts. Brooding. Yes, that was the word for it, what he had always done. And now his mind had something important to pick at instead.

He looked at his watch, a digital monstrosity cuffed to his left wrist. 1717 Zulu Time graced its face. Wait. John took another look.

"Matt, what time is it?" he asked, still staring at his watch. "Weren't we supposed to arrive at 1330? It was noon, what, twenty minutes ago?"

Fingers dashing across a small panel to starboard, the second crewman Matt brought up the shuttle's internal clock. As the panel flicked into place, he began to say something and then stopped. The clock face was a collection of sixes across the board.

"What the hell…" Matt began, tapping the clock with his finger. It flickered, then reverted to 1222 after a moment. "What happened?"

"It can't be changed onboard." John said quietly, looking back down at his watch. 1222 read across its face as clear as day. "We need to do another systems-check before descent."

A groan came from the maintenance bay nearby. "Another one? I just ran diagnostics five minutes ago." Pete, the third and last crewman aboard, floated out from the bay with a packet of what was supposed to be pork hanging out of his mouth as he used his hands to navigate the shuttle.

"Just run it, will you?" John said, his voice firm but his mind full of doubt. Pete rolled his eyes, took a bite of his food, and began his diagnostics. "And don't forget the seismic scanner," he added, turning to Matt.

"I've only had a couple weeks with the thing." Matt pointed out. "What can it really tell us about the chasm? The moon's tectonically dead anyway."

"A canyon a few kilometers long just appears on the surface and you still think the moon isn't geologically active?" John observed. "No, something has changed down to the core. We take the scanner."

*

An hour later, once John was satisfied everything was in order, they began their descent. With a silent thud the capsule landed on the lunar surface, dust clouds swirling and drifting into space. John was first out, Matt and Pete following on his heels as he bounced down onto the surface.

"Half a klick East, remember the positioning and use your maps, for Christ's sake," he ordered.

Nodding, the crew began the quick five-hundred-meter trek to the edge of the chasm now marring the surface of the moon. There hadn't been time to load a rover, but the mission was quite clear: 'explore the chasm, report what you find.'

They chatted between the comm systems built into their helmets, idle banter and jokes for the most part. Even John's surly attitude withered during the journey to the chasm.

"Don't listen to Pete, he can't think without eating something at the same time," Matt said, his voice roiling and deep as though he spoke around something filling his mouth.

"Hey! I can stop whenever I want!" Pete responded.

"What? Can't hear you over the crumbs coating your mic," Matt said, unable to keep the laughter out of his voice.

"Why don't you just..." Then they froze, staring, as the maw of the chasm opened before them. John's mouth moved and yet he couldn't speak.

Reflected light, image, and shadow glided across the towering cliffs of the chasm; shiny and smooth, but cracks spiderwebbed across their vast glistening faces as silver shields polished bright with care.

"Mirror, mirror on the wall..." Matt said softly.

"Shut up. We have a job to do. Matt, hook up the rope on that rock there, Pete, I want a scan of the chasm, make it thorough and take your time," John ordered, trying to focus his mind. Reflective surfaces in the depths of the moon, like silver and glass where none could exist. He shook his head, resisting the urge to curse over his mic. Obediently, though slow and distracted, the two crewmen began their work.

That had been why they couldn't see into the chasm; the vast mirrors must have reflected everything. "I can't get a reading." John heard Pete as if from a distance and his eyes couldn't quite seem to focus as though the universe itself had become blurry. He tilted his head from side to side as his sight came into focus once again with Pete shouting that he couldn't scan anything with his signals bouncing off the mirrors.

"Alright, we make do. Give me an optical scan, ten power zoom until you see something of note. We won't have the blind leading the blind, alright?"

Everyone magnified their optical equipment, letting their eyes roam with enhanced vision upon the almost blinding visage of the chasm of mirrors. All of them felt a pressure on their ears that was turning into a thrumming, churning cadence; a tattoo from some primal place in the heart. They muttered, sometimes incoherently to one another, feeling as though intoxicated by the glare of the mirrors that their reflective helmets could not quite mask.

Once satisfied they had seen all to be seen from here, John led the way down the rope, bouncing along the slick smooth faces of millions of stars glistening from canyon walls like cool, deep water that seems to shift with the breath of a breeze unfelt but seen. All the men were becoming gradually more befuddled, their minds finding thought racing away which they could never catch; a sleight of soul that tricks the brain into unseen highways.

In delirium, Pete slipped on his way from the rope, catching his right foot on a ledge and spiraling in slow motion to the pits below. John slid faster, crying out for his friend, but Pete's fall was interrupted as he impacted heavily on a spire of jagged rock made of the same liquid mirrors as the chasm, landing hard on a small shelf below.

John and Matt scrambled down the rope, landing lightly next to Pete. The fall hadn't been too fast, due to the lower gravity, but the crash into the spire had torn the outer layers of his suit.

"He can't stay out here; anything tears that more and he'll be exposed," Matt intoned as if from a manual. John nodded, numb, already unable to focus on what he needed to do. He shook his head, glancing toward the unnatural cliff face next to him where he met a snarling cavern of inky darkness. How he had not noticed the cave that now yawned into the depths, his mind refused to contemplate.

Without looking back at Matt, John hefted the easy weight of his stunned friend and made his way into the cave. What lay beyond, he did not know, but it may be what saves his world from madness.

The moon ticked, like the depths of some infernal celestial-sized clock; it made John nauseous as he felt the tolling of a bell in his soul somewhere, though he couldn't place what that could mean. Like a great big buzzing, the thrumming from earlier now sounded like voices, whispers in the dark of the lunar heart where no human had delved.

"Should we go back? There's nothing in here for us," Matt hissed from somewhere behind. Just then he stopped and looked past John who himself turned to see a great gate, shining in silver radiance standing just beyond the reach of his arm, were he not still carrying Pete. The two conscious men stared at the surface which looked so alike to the moon itself seen from earth in silver glass, boiled in relief with craters like bubbles having burst across its mercury surface.

John reached out his hand, still supporting Pete's legs on his arm, and lightly brushed his fingertips across the craggy plate. An ominous, distant groaning and cracking could be heard within, like the mechanisms of some cosmic clock built of the cores of stars. Voices, clear and soft, could be heard in the thrumming sound pulsing in John's ears, though what they said he could not guess, could not even give a shadow of a guess at the inhuman tones that no natural thing could make. Before he could wrap his intellect around a thought or solution, the gate swung soundlessly open.

Like a deep breath which isn't noticed until faintness and discomfort spur the memory into action, so too did time hold itself at bay while John turned like a somnambulist toward the silhouette of Matt, held against the glowing silver of the mirrors without the cave.

"We can't, John. We gotta go." Said Matt.

Just then, before John could formulate a response, Pete groaned and sat up as best as he could in John's arms, causing the latter to drop his companion's legs in a minor fit of alarm.

"All is made clean under the sun," Pete said, his face invisible behind his helmet though his words held a sonorous, unnatural tone.

John looked at Matt, then returned his eyes to Pete who had begun to sway. They stood this way immobile for some time, though none of them would have been able to recount how long. The voices stirred again, whipped like a wind from the sands of some primordial desert to scour the human heart as John heard them clearly for the first time. "Venture and seek, find the wheels, unlock time," They said, again and again they spoke like sepulchral voices as blood beneath the altar. What horror was in those words, a primordial malice that could not be explained nor denied. John could not describe those voices in any words of man, but he hated them.

Pete staggered backward into the gloom of the gate, John jolting from his fugue to reach an arm out just too late to grab his friend. Pete was gone into the dark, the lights on his suit switched off to disappear the moment he crossed the threshold beyond. John slumped against the cave wall, feeling like he couldn't remember why he was here, his legs refusing to work.

Before the two men could do anything more, the moon shifted from within while the walls creaked like so many million panes of glass snapping all at once. John and Matt staggered for the mouth of the cave, loath to leave Pete but given no other option.

With a groan of glass and stone, the hallways slewed to the side, twisting like a serpent as the two men cast themselves from the maw and began a quick ascent out of the chasm, which was churning and collapsing around them.

"The gate, what was that gate?" Matt asked from above as John had taken the lower position.

John could feel his mind contorting under the constant chanting and cacophony of a moon quaking under unseen forces. "It unlocked something; I don't know what. But..." He trailed off as the two crested the lip of the chasm and looked up into the sky. Without being able to tear their eyes away, a shadow slunk predator-like across the sun, grasping with phantom claws at the bright spark of hope for life.

"Are you seeing that?" John asked, pointing out into space. Matt nodded silently beside him. "We're hallucinating, we have to be; that's not possible." Frozen like a statue, his arm remained raised and unmoving without even a tremble.

"Must have happened a few minutes ago." Matt added, his impassive glare shield over his helmet giving a deeper sense of dread to the note of confusion in his voice. John let his arm drop and the two men finally averted their eyes from the rapidly darkening furnace in the center of their little corner of space.

Briefly, their minds had been cleared by the heartening sight of the sun, but now with its dissolution into ugly, fecund darkness which deepened by the moment, they were once again adrift on a sea of twisted thoughts all struggling to contort the mind and stop the heart.

John turned to lean over the edge of the crumbling chasm as a thundering rose once again from the dead core of the moon, but there was something more, a tint of sorts to the world that no sunshield could stop. Something yellow. Once glowing pale in the warmth of the sun, the moonscape had become dull with gloom, but now a sickly yellow suffused the air and gave John the sensation of breathing through a straw as though the tiny atmosphere he carried with him were thickening. An impossibility within the confines of his suit, but that knowledge did little to dissuade the facts he now faced.

Matt stepped up to John, his gait stumbling and halting as he made his way across the now pestilent tinge of the moon.

"We need to find Pete," he said.

Without speaking, John nodded, his laborious breathing becoming more pronounced as the air thickened to greater effect. Awkwardly, the two stood in silence for a long moment.

John could think of nothing of greater horror than this blind exile to wastes of stone far above the clouds of his home, from whence he could never flee. He knew that now, though with no rationality to follow his thinking as the shuttle was still in space, cared for by those who were not chosen to take the walk on a distant world, and yet he knew it as the truth of his banishment far away.

"Yeah, there has to be another way into the caves, something we can't see from here."

From where he had been standing, head lowered, Matt suddenly started and raised his hand as if trying to catch a thought in midair. "How about the seismic scanner? Could that detect passages underground?"

John almost laughed out loud. "Of course, that should be perfect."

Side by side, they moved among the lunar stones surrounding them, climbing through impact craters with the blundering, hopping step of such low gravity until they returned to the edge of the chasm where they had left their ropes dangling down into tumbled rock. Thick swirls of lunar dust with the consistency of baking flour obscured everything around them, their suit lights unable to penetrate the fog.

"Here, this ridge should be high enough to scan a larger area," Matt said, turning around and motioning to the device attached to his pack. With control returning to his trembling fingers, John removed the tripod-like instrument and began setting it up while Matt unhooked a small power pack from his waist. Practiced and precise, the two men assembled the scanner and had it steadied above the lunar sands.

"Beginning sweep on my mark." John looked at his watch, now affixed into his suit and almost cursed at the nonsensical numbers flashing insanely across its face. "To hell with timing. Begin."

John flipped a switch and the device came to life, whirring silently in the minutely thin atmosphere. Images appeared on the small screen built onto the side of the tripod and a rhythmic thumping could be felt through their boots. "There, see?" Matt pointed to the screen which now showed the hazy outlines of a great number of passages under their feet.

"For God's sake, there's a whole network down there." John cursed and stood, letting his grinding teeth calm him down. "See if you can pinpoint where the chasm entrance was."

Matt obeyed, moving a tiny joystick near the screen to get a better view of the caverns in three-dimensional space.

"There," he said at last, pointing. "If we follow that path up…" His finger traced the waving, crackling lines of tunnels until it came at last to what appeared to be an entrance. "That should take us where we need to go."

They triangulated the position of the entrance, finding it only about a football field away from them and parallel to the chasm itself. A short jaunt led them to their destination, down a long slope into a crater to face the entrance to the caverns. Both men paled behind their helmets and stepped back as the unnatural edifice confronted them.

"This isn't possible. No human could have carved that," John whispered as he gazed upon a portal built of jet-black obsidian, pillars supporting an archway festooned with images of death and madness. Even as they looked at it, they could feel their eyes refusing to focus as the image blurred and seemed to swim in their vision.

"I, I can't keep looking at it," Matt whispered, his eyes twitching unseen.

"Yeah, yeah… We gotta get inside, though. Come on." John grabbed his comrade's arm and plunged into the all-consuming abyss under the moon once more. Even through their insulated suits, they could feel a deep chill invade their bodies, seeping to the depths of their bones to threaten their still hammering hearts. Low and droning, the chanting from earlier returned to plague their minds in twisting chords that could not have been made by human throats.

Boots raising dust, dashing through the dark with only the lights on their shoulders and helmets guiding the way forward, the two men made their way deeper and deeper where the chanting became louder, jarring mind and body with a rhythm not heard in millennia.

"The King… The King is within," Matt muttered, his steps halting as John forced him forward into the dark.

"Shut up." Was all he had in reply, though even this command felt hollow in John's ears. Matt was silent for a time, though if because of the order or something else, John didn't know and didn't ask.

In stark, brilliant light, the darkness of the caverns was seared away by what lay beyond. John and Matt stumbled into a new chamber lit with a wealth of effulgence that threatened to engulf them in white oblivion. John coughed, the chanting had now grown to a fever pitch, and he felt his body throbbing and constricting with every syllable of the buzzing madness that drowned out his thoughts. They stood in a nave of some kind of church to lunacy, carved from the same jet obsidian which glared and reflected the light glowing within like so many hundred mirrors. Even the heavy glare shields on their helmets could not contain the light. John distantly feared what would happen if naked human eyes could gaze upon what he saw. Burned to the skull in an instant, he surmised.

Thousands of skeletal monuments danced along the walls and pillars, corpses hanged from scaffolds and gibbets, some holding what he could only guess was their own flayed skin and crying skyward in their agony. Something in their sculpting gave a deep air of reality, of truly being men who were once alive and now called to heaven for salvation even as they cavorted from the grave.

In the distance, barely perceived through the veil of light and sound, was one figure in sickly yellow hunched over an altar at the far end of the nave. John pushed himself forward, dragging the now muttering and gibbering Matt along behind him. A deliberate movement, a slow turning, and the figure in yellow now faced them.

"Cascade with false hope, the cosmic gate is now unlocked." The hooded head lifted, revealing a mask that John found he could not describe as it shifted and changed even as he looked. "Open the door, find the King and unleash that which was foretold." That voice, that voice from beyond time was familiar to John somewhere in the back of his addled mind.

"Pete, is that you?" he managed as the chanting rose in pitch and volume as though his helmet were not there.

The man in yellow shook as if in silent laughter and returned to his altar. John and Matt staggered closer, finding the altar floating upon a spreading pool of red ooze, crimson blossoms surging through the floor around it. And it was from that ooze that the infernal chanting could be heard. "They cry from beneath the altar," the man in yellow intoned, ignoring John's question. "Witness now the cosmic mechanisms in place before the earth was young."

"The King, the King, the pallid decay of the King," Matt said, collapsing against John. Before he could bring his comrade to his feet, John found himself gazing to the sky to see the stars and lights of the abyss burning in fury above him. How could he see into space from deep below the moon's surface? Even as he watched, the sun was finally and totally engulfed in blackness, the claws of shadow now physical as the star of the solar system faded from view.

A throne carved with a wheel within a wheel upon its back stood next to John, though he didn't remember it being there only a moment before, and as he watched the wheels blinked with a thousand eyes. It watched him as it began to rotate and the moon descended into a thick, poisonous haze before the man in yellow stood before them.

Eldritch madness, pallid horror of the mask which was not a mask, a thousand eyes and a ring within a ring spinning in eternal rotations over all creation. As a sickly, pestilential mist, all image turned to yellow. Yellow, infernal yellow screaming in damnable silence. The moon was silent now. When would this silence cease? It oppressed and devoured John as he gazed into the mask that is not a mask.

"The King lives and all perishes," Matt said before freezing into a statue, black and shiny, upon the surface of the moon.

As John felt his body slip from the bonds of mortality, he beheld a flood of crimson engulf the lunar surface, bathing in the blood of millions the light of the night sky above his doomed world.

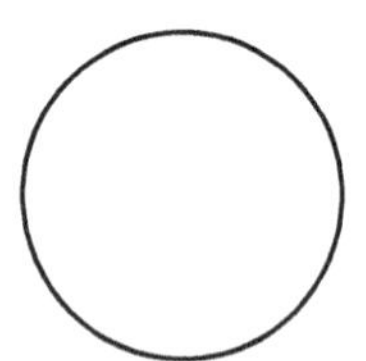

Dream Time's End

Nigel Robert Wilson

"You are late to the Council, Master Leu," the convener complained.

"I have had to come a long way," Leu replied. "The night is shorter at this season."

"Surely the strong illumination of these harvest times allows you a faster journey," the convener chided.

Leu elected not to rise to the complaint as the convener could get cantankerous. The old man had forgotten that the Moon disappeared over the horizon as the harvest began, harassed by foolish young men throwing spears in its direction in the hope it would move along faster. It would not return until tomorrow night for the festival of First Fruits.

"My apologies to the Council," Leu nodded his head, hopefully appeasing this crusty old chief seated on his customary rock.

Leu briefly acknowledged the ring of other seated members with a succession of diplomatic nods. He could sense a large audience assembled in the darkness beyond. It was customary for a large crowd of Ancestors to attend the meetings with Leu Truth-Speaker, the only living contact between the heroic dead and the mundane world of life. Leu suspected many more dwelt in this place above the world of the living, including women looking down on their children. He chose not to speculate as he knew one day he would have all the time needed here on the Moon to learn the whole truth.

"Whilst waiting for your journey to end we have been discussing young Ukr," advised Sigr the youngest of the Council. "Dreamers tell us he distresses the women-folk of the Great Valley. Are you able to tell us more, Master Leu?"

"He is like most young men not quite of age," Leu remarked politely. He had to be careful as both Ukr's grandfathers would be present, lurking in the shades beyond among others. "He has an unfocussed and irresponsible enthusiasm for girls and young women which has proved offensive to neighbourly order."

"It is more than that, isn't it, Leu Truth-Speaker?" Sigr's enquiry implied he was already fully aware of Ukr's behaviour. Leu reflected on the spontaneous dreams that mixed the living with the dead, and the many erstwhile prayers made by the people of the soil to their Ancestors living here up in the sky. There was no prospect for gentle speaking here.

"It is being said that he has raped two girls and still seeks to mate with others outside family consents," Leu replied reluctantly. There, he had said it. The Truth-Speaker had put the human failings of Ukr out into the open for all to know. Now let the uproar commence.

"A rapist!" a shocked voice cried from the dark shadows to the rear of the dusty, grey cavern. "No child of my family would do such a thing!"

The angry assertion rippled across the powdery surface of the cavern floor, lifting the dust into small flurries as if an earthly breeze had whispered across the cratered emptiness. Leu reflected that the Moon was a place of dust, an appropriate place for the dead to dwell.

"It is a word which is being used," Leu persisted in his report. "I am told that in the first instance he threatened some sisters, forcing one to give herself to him to allow the younger ones to escape. Her family demands compensation for the violation. In the other instance the husband of the young bride demands satisfaction through physical contest but is restrained for now by his family which simply demands Ukr's execution."

"This is all nonsense," an old man hobbled forward out of the darkness supported by the mildewed, green copper-tipped spear that he had taken to his grave. "It is jealousy put about by folk keen to disrespect my family."

"Silence, Ikr!" Sigr commanded, standing up to restrain the old man. "The Truth-Speaker is but the messenger. He reports what is being said among our progeny of the soil. Our task is to winnow the truth from the chaff of gossip for the good of all. If wrong has been done, then customary ways are set to resolve them."

"Since when was it customary for the idle and the greedy to bear false witness against the better sort?" Ikr spluttered his indignation.

A noisy, anguished growl came out of the shadows growing in strength as the hurtful implication of the words sunk in. Ikr's arrogance was stirring hostility.

"Ikr," Sigr spoke harshly. "Understand that others here have loyalty with those who have levied the charges against Ukr."

"But they have always borne bad witness against my family," Ikr complained.

"For as long as you lie to protect a rapist from the consequences of his actions then you will continue to suffer bad witness." A deep voice thundered from the dark depths of the cave. It was echoed by a low rumble of respectful voices. "Ikr, your family may feel prosperous as it has the advantage of the best fields but the ways of the tribe are common to us all."

"Who said that?" Ikr screeched, waving his spear about.

"I did, you old fool," a large white-haired old man with a long beard, clad in furs appeared from out of the shadows causing Ikr to cower. It was the shade of Pwl, the Founder Ancestor, ancient beyond naming, scarcely seen at any Council but now insistent on the law. "When we apportioned the land along the Great Valley of the Uz it was agreed that each family was equal and none were above that equality. This is why we Ancestors hold this Council here in the sky to sustain our children in their affairs on the good soil below."

The man stopped speaking for a moment to allow silence to add weight to his words. He then turned to address the Council.

"Dreams allow us to communicate with the people of the soil and them with us, the people of the air. They also speak to us in their prayers, but we have only Leu Truth-Speaker to convey actuality to us. Our children have prospered long from our advice and judgements so have little reason for jealous squabbles. Ukr must face the judgement of the Grand Council among the living when it reconvenes at the end of the harvest."

Such words from Pwl, the Founder possessed the necessary charisma to soothe emotions. The grand old man nodded to Leu and walked back into the shadows, the darkness separating respectfully before him. The ensuing silence showed the last word on this topic had been spoken.

"We asked you here, Leu Truth-Speaker, to discuss the harvest." After a suitable pause the convenor was taking back control of the Council with a more positive tone to his voice. "How does it progress?"

"The wheat is ripe in the fields and the reapers cry in sorrowful regret to its spirit as they cut it down," Leu replied. "The first sheaves have dried in the fields and the grain is being ground for baking the loaves of First Fruit tomorrow when the Moon is restored. So far all goes well along the Great Valley of the Uz."

"We look forward to the joyful odour of baking bread," the convener remarked. "It pleases us to know the Moon ensures your nights continue dry and fertile."

"The people of the soil are grateful for your interventions," Leu responded allowing his voice to echo gratitude. "The warmth of the sun and softness of the rain in due season have helped as well. We hope for a generous bounty."

"It is distressing to learn that despite this prosperity rebellious youth is engendering bad feeling," the convener returned to the earlier matter. "I can remember being young myself and obdurate to my father, but he cuffed me firmly and I never regretted it. I hope by the time the singing and dancing is done that these unpleasant matters are resolved."

"If you decree it, Father, then it will." Leu bowed in placation. "I must now leave as I have to return by morning."

"You are dismissed, Truth-Speaker."

Leu turned to hurry back to the branch of the World Tree that hung over the face of the Moon. The barren lunar landscape always impressed him with its timeless majesty. He had been coming here for years, ever since he became the shaman for the people of the Great Valley. It never failed to remind him of the immortality of the tribes, the fertility of the land, the gentle beauty of the Moon and the warming powers of the Sun. How these massive entities combined to work together, forming one productive unity, humbled him. There was a great providence in the universe. The tribes were the children of all these things and the Ancestors their assurance of eternal life.

Aided by the low gravity, Leu clambered onto the nearest bough, pushing aside the leaves and the twigs to grip the rough, homely surface of the bark which would lead him back down towards the Great Valley and its tribes for whom he was responsible to the Ancestors. As he descended, the central trunk of the World Tree became thicker, the branches denser, allowing a faster and safer progress. After a couple of hours, he arrived breathless at the top of his ladder. Carefully he crawled backwards onto the topmost rungs to begin slowly stepping downwards. After a long while he looked down to see the layered rock above his cave inside which his sleeping body lay recumbent under his blue cloak close to the cave mouth. He was nearly home. He relaxed.

*

Leu woke up with a jolt as the sun was rising in the sky. The dull ache of his withered right leg reminded him that he was back in the world of the living where he was lame. He enjoyed the wanderings of his spirit as in the places where he journeyed he was a complete man rather than this part-broken creature hobbling along with a crutch. Yet this crippling difference had marked him out from childhood as a Truth-Speaker incapable of deceit.

Carefully, Leu raised himself on his left leg to grip the crutch he had left leaning against the cave wall last evening. He was hungry and a smell of oats boiling in watered milk beckoned from down the hill, below the trees that defined the boundary of his sacred domain. He slung his cloak about him to hobble down the path to the enclosure of the priests and the bards.

"Was it a good meeting, Master Leu?" Anwn, the chief judge, asked cheerfully as Leu settled down to break his fast before the cook's fire.

"There is concern about Ukr and his friends," Leu reported as he pushed his bone spoon into the wooden bowl of porridge. "The rest was routine for the time of year."

"How much concern?"

"Pwl, the Founder Ancestor, was concerned."

"Ouch! This could get tough."

"I am sorry to place this trouble on you, Anwn," Leu was apologetic. "Ikr spoke harshly in his grandson's defence. It stirred deep emotions. There will be many troubled dreams and angry prayers before the harvest is done."

"On top of which Akr, son of Ikr has asserted membership of the Council," Anwn advised. "Combined with the behaviour of his son and his friends there will be difficulties before much more time is spent."

"Then it will probably start tonight at the festival," Leu reflected as after First Fruits the entire focus of the tribes would be on bringing in the harvest.

"That would be contrary to custom," Anwn emphasised looking Leu sternly in the face as if to deny any disturbance before it happened.

"I don't think Ukr cares about custom," Leu spoke gently, puzzling at Anwn's strange denial. "His begetters appear to support him." Was something going on which could not be spoken about?

Leu finished his breakfast, bowed courteously to the judge and the priests to hobble down the hill to where the fire would be lit to bake the first loaves of the new harvest. Preparations were well advanced. The limestone fireplace had been laid in slabs and stacks of wood made ready for burning. Only the loaves were missing as these were being kneaded by selected women in their homes to be brought to the fire later on.

Since this was the last holiday for a couple of months, a group of young males had congregated at the boundary of the festival site loitering and observing, their thoughts intent on the arrival of the wooden barrels of beer. Leu regretted that excessive drunkenness had become a feature of recent festivals. It was as if some of the people had forgotten the purpose of the seasonal ceremonies. It was right to be intoxicated at times of festival but not until moon-rise and never to the point of incapability.

The distance of last night's journey had left Leu tired. The prospect of another long night caused him to return to his cave to rest until Moon-rise later in the day. He relaxed at the mouth of his cave enjoying the solitude, watching the birds busy in their own affairs among the trees whilst in the distance came the rising, joyful sound of people assembling for the festival. By late afternoon a glance into the sky showed the curved, silver line of the rising Moon. The Ancestors had arrived.

Leu hobbled down to the ceremonial fires to watch as the heat first caused the loaves to rise and then bake into firm rounds. Each loaf was lifted from the fires by the bakers and given to the churning crowd as each member of every family tried to consume at least a morsel of the new harvest. To the rear there was a familiar racket as inebriated men sought ownership of the barrels of beer, only to be castigated by the supervising priests.

Leu mingled among the friendly courtesy of the crowd, hailing friends and admiring the children of distant cousins until darkness fell, torches were lit and the real carousing began. The women and children retreated as the men formed circles and began to talk as they drank. At first there were jokes, the good humour of festival, then there began the discussions. Leu always listened to these as they informed him of the daily experience and concerns of ordinary people which often led to debates at the Grand Council. Suddenly the issue of Ukr and his family erupted into the conversation.

"This youth has no discipline," one man hazarded. "He even tried to give me orders! What happened to equality, I asked him? Who does he think he is?"

"He has no concern for others than the gang around him," another sympathised.

"I feel sorry for the families who have been violated." This expression of solidarity caused a widespread murmur of sympathy.

"Silence!" a single, angry voice interrupted.

Everyone jumped. It was Ukr pushing his way towards the front of the group. Suddenly the crowd surged as the original circle scattered away from the light of the fires into the darkness to avoid Ukr's angry eyes picking them out. This dramatic movement drew in a wider audience to encircle Ukr who was holding a copper-tipped spear. Leu recognised it. It was the same spear Ikr had waved on the Moon last night. Leu stepped forward to confront Ukr.

"It is forbidden to bring weapons to the festival," Leu began. "Besides I know that spear, it was buried with your grandsire. Have you robbed his grave?"

"Pah!" Ukr snorted as a few of his companions assembled in a tight knot behind him. "They call you the Truth-Speaker but you tell lies to fool the people."

"I speak with our Ancestors," Leu replied indignantly.

"You tell people stories you make up in your cave, you idle cripple." Ukr laughed and raised his voice. "You tell us our Ancestors are living on the Moon. What piffle! They are in their graves, here in the soil. You say they live with an old man with a long white beard. Utter drivel! Why is it with you that the Moon is so important, when it is the Sun that has all the power and splendour?"

This sequence of insults was designed to upset Leu and it did. It wasn't just him either, there was a discontented rumble of voices from the crowd. They did not like what Ukr was saying and how he was saying it, but none would intervene directly as he held a weapon. Leu wondered where Anwn and his priests had got to.

"Why have you stolen that spear from your grandfather's grave," Leu retorted, trying to keep calm. "It is taboo to violate the remains of the dead."

"He came to me in a dream," Ukr jeered. "You know all about dreams, don't you? He told me I could have it. He said it was time this Great Valley had just the one leader, not a cacophony of councillors who, in following the whim of a stumbling shaman, talk too long whilst doing absolutely nothing. All of this was in a dream, Truth-Speaker! I have to be making this up, mustn't I?"

"Why did you bring the spear here, where it is forbidden?" Leu remarked coldly, ignoring Ukr's puerile insults.

"I brought it here to kill you," Ukr screamed as he suddenly thrust the spear point forward at Leu.

Leu was quick and spun on his strong left leg away from the spear thrust, allowing his crutch to deflect the blow upwards away from him. As he recovered his balance he saw Ukr calculating another thrust. Around them was uproar as men called upon Ukr to stop, but they had not come ready for conflict so were reluctant to intervene.

Ukr's next thrust was more directly aimed. Once again Leu twisted his body away from the spear but this time the sharpened copper tip caught in his blue cloak, ripping the skin of his stomach causing a hideously sharp pain and an unquenchable effusion of blood. Leu staggered. He had no idea if the wound was serious but he still felt strong enough to hold his ground. Ukr came at him again, but Leu used his crutch backed by all his strength to hit first. He knocked the spear out of Ukr's hands.

This did not stop Ukr. His left hand reached to his belt to draw a heavy stone-headed axe, which he slipped into his right hand. Accompanied by a high-pitched scream, his blow came overarm aimed directly at Leu's head. Leu smashed the padded armpit end of his crutch into Ukr's face. Ukr choked mid-scream and dropped the axe. Empowered by the desire to live, Leu swiftly stooped, picked up the axe and with all his strength slammed its heavy head into the back of stumbling Ukr's skull. Leu heard the cracking of bone and at that moment knew he had killed Ukr.

Briefly, all the noise around them stopped. Ukr's gang looked aghast at Leu who just stood there covered in his own blood staring at the corpse of Ukr. Leu knew he had broken the taboo all shamans had to honour. He had killed. Even if he survived the bleeding wound in his belly he knew he was finished. He dropped the axe and limped away, leaving his crutch behind.

"Anwn," he cried out, hoping to find the judge. "Where are you?"

There was no answer.

"Are you alright?" A man separated from the crowd to ask him anxiously. Leu felt too unwell to answer. He expected to die.

"Where are the priests?" Leu mumbled more to himself than anyone else as he broke away from the people and the fires into the surrounding darkness lit only by a sliver of the Moon and the many stars.

He staggered up the track to the compound of the priests. Nobody was there.

"Anwn, it is Leu. I need help!" Leu shouted again but to no avail. Where were the priests? They had to intervene, to calm things down, to recover Ukr's body and hopefully bind Leu's wound.

Leu stumbled further up the hill. He crawled through the line of trees that defined the boundary of his territory. He found his bed at the front of the cave and lay down on it. By now the wound appeared to have stopped bleeding. He ran his hand along its torn, ragged line and sensed the flesh where it had been penetrated. Maybe all he had to do was sleep and waken to a new day in the morning when all would be restored to normality. He knew this was a false hope.

As he lay on his back looking up into the sky he saw the shining edge of the Moon whose two sharp points reminded him of Ukr's spear cutting the skin of his stomach. Leu shuddered. Suddenly he knew how to fix his problem. He had to visit the Moon and speak with Pwl, the Founder Ancestor, the man with the long white beard that Ukr had denied. In the eye of his mind Leu began to assemble the ladder by which he would make this journey. The repetitive nature of this exercise sent him into a trance.

Leu suddenly woke from this trance clambering up the broad trunk of the World Tree. He was going to the Moon but had somehow missed the ladder section of his journey. His body felt good. He touched his stomach which was free of any cut or scar and both his legs were strong. All around him was the deep darkness of the space in between the Great Valley and the Moon, illuminated by clusters of stars. As he climbed further he found he was passing through what appeared to be a snow storm. Small flakes of matter were falling from the Moon down through the leaves and branches of the World Tree.

Fascinated, Leu grabbed one as it passed. It wasn't snow and it wasn't ash. What was it? Leu squeezed it with his hand. It screamed. It was alive. Shocked, Leu let it go to watch it slowly drift downward with its many fellows alongside the trunk of the World Tree. Just what was going on?

Leu tumbled from the branch closest to the surface on the Moon. The deep, thick dust and the light gravity gave him a gentle reception. The familiar landscape that was around the cave of the Ancestors was welcoming as usual. In his heart, Leu was troubled. He now felt uncomfortable as if he had somehow become a fraud. He realised that before he died Ukr had upset him with his words.

Leu now felt doubt and that was feeding him with anxiety. He knew then he had come here to reassure himself that all would continue as before.

Only it wasn't. The Council place was empty. The twelve stones the councillors sat upon were still there but their occupants were missing along with the dark mass of spectators. Leu rationalised this to himself. This wasn't an allotted time for a Council. He had come here unexpectedly so everyone would be about their other Ancestral duties.

"Welcome, Truth-Speaker," a voice declared behind him.

Leu turned to see Pwl, the Founder Ancestor, standing tall and proud in his long animal furs, his huge white beard spread across his vast chest reaching down as far as his navel.

"Greetings, Father," Leu muttered, relieved that there was someone here to greet him.

"What have you come here for?" The words were spoken with some surprise.

"I come looking for advice," Leu spoke hurriedly.

"I fear you may be too late for that," the old man replied looking intensely at Leu. "Matters have changed greatly since your last visit."

"But that was only last night." Leu was puzzled by the remark.

"For you, perhaps. For us, it was a long time."

"What has happened?"

"A collective failure of imagination has dispersed us."

"How come?" Leu's disappointment made the question come out aggressively.

"Don't get grumpy at me," Pwl replied equally forcibly but with a wry smile on his face. "You won't know this but as people of the air, the tribal Ancestors have no substance so can only exist where the people of the soil expect them to be. Now that the priests have ordained that the Ancestors sleep in their graves our community on the Moon has ceased to exist."

"Were they the snow that fell past me as I climbed the World Tree?" Leu suddenly understood why that snowflake had squealed.

"Indeed," Pwl replied with a note of regret in his voice. "They have all gone back to the Great Valley to hang around in cemeteries, cracks in the rock and among fissures in the trees. Rather than communicate through dreams, they will whisper as ghosts and wail as phantoms in the vain hope that some priestly pretender will give them the time of night."

"You blame the priests for that?" Leu was suddenly aware that this might have been why Anwn had failed to hear him. Had he been betrayed by men he considered his friends?

"I think you understand now, Truth-Speaker," Pwl looked Leu directly in the face. "Ukr was supposed to kill you to make a clean sweep of the old traditions. You have rather upset those plans for now but I expect they will catch up with your mortal remains by morning."

"What will happen to me?" Leu asked fearfully.

"You can go back and lurk by your grave for eternity, or you can allow your imagination to improve you."

"How can that happen?" Leu sounded puzzled.

"Since I was in my mother's womb my imagination flowed with the Moon," Pwl began. "In those distant times we gathered and hunted for our food. We were no farmers as the tribes are today, but we knew that when the Moon waxed fat both the animal herds and the fruits of the forest were generous to us. We accepted the Moon as our mentor and guide, sending the souls of our dead here to keep improving the strength of our people."

"I understand the purpose of the Moon but what can you and I do here when all the others have left?" Leu continued in his confusion.

"I had hoped that the imaginative power of our species could use the Moon as a gateway to the stars, but that idea is now defunct for the time being," Pwl sounded annoyed. "I will have to stay here as the people of the soil say they need a man in the moon, an old patriarch on a cloud or a ruler in heaven they can all pretend to like now that in their arrogance they have chosen to deny their obvious equality. Foolishly they have taken to worshipping themselves but need another to reassure them this is the best thing to do."

"But what will happen to me?" Leu begged.

"I may not reach the stars, but you can, Truth-Speaker."

"What, me?" Leu gestured to himself then pointed up into the firmament. "Go there?"

"Why not?" Pwl replied. "You have been travelling regularly between the Great Valley and the Moon for many years. I accept the stars are further but they are not beyond your capability. Get dreaming, my friend."

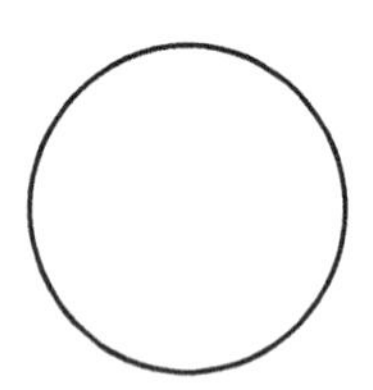

The Empties

Gary Budgen

I lived in Mansfield House, which everyone called the Block. It was an old London County Council low rise, opposite Peckham Rye Common. It was three storeys with a balcony walkway leading to the front doors of the flats. I think there were a few thousand people left in London now, clustered around the odd focal point. Ours was the local corner shop run by Mehmet and his cousin. Mehmet had carried on operating the shop as though nothing had happened. He stacked the shelves and you went in and got just what you wanted. He even carried on taking money for a while till everyone ran out of cash. Once a week he and his cousin would drive off to one of the distribution points where religious groups, who'd refused to ascend, gave out supplies.

I waited by the shop for the van to come. Brian Lang was there too and he was, as always, carrying a plastic bag full of empty bottles. I had my rucksack to put a few things in for myself and to take up to the roof of the Block for Mr Margoles. When the van came back Mehmet's cousin opened its back doors and started to hand stuff out. Mehmet shouted something in Turkish. I don't think he liked the stuff going straight from the back of the van to us.

"I'll just put the empties here," said Brian and placed the clattering bag by the shop door. Then he went to peer into the back of the van to see what was there. Mehmet's cousin nodded and gave him two bottles of wine.

When I had my stuff I went to sleep through the afternoon. About an hour after dusk I made up a flask of tea by boiling water on a camp stove. Then I mixed some tinned tomatoes with Quorn slices and heated these and put them in a tub. I carried everything up the stairwell on a tray to the third, topmost, storey of the Block then to the end where there was a door that gave access to the stairs to the roof. Up on the roof Mr Margoles was at his telescope. As I came out of the dormer at the top of the stairs he looked up at me.

"Ah, Gideon," he said, "fine night tonight."

There was a bit of a nip in the air but he didn't mean the weather. He meant for using the telescope.

"See anything?"

From below voices rose; there was the shouting of a woman's voice.

You don't know, you don't know.

The Langs had probably been drinking all day.

Shut up. Shut up.

"In answer to your question," said Mr Margoles, "yes, I have seen something. I think they are beginning to build on the surface."

"Build. Build what?"

This was new. We had watched over the weeks as the greenery had begun to spread. Faster than any natural growth. The resolution of the telescope had been able to make out vast tracts of what must have been fully-grown trees. Presumably the super rapid progression from seedlings to shrubs had been at first invisible. Now large areas of the lunar maria were tinged with a deep green that was becoming visible to the naked eye.

"Structures are beginning to appear around the edges of some of the mascons."

The mascons were where it had all started.

Suddenly Mrs Lang's voice rang out, an enraged desperate edge to it.

"Why don't you understand? Why don't you understand?"

It shattered the silence of the night.

"You think we should do something?" I asked.

Mr Margoles had gone back to looking through the telescope but he looked up again. Then he took the thermos flask from me.

"Oh I don't think so," he said, "We all have to deal with things in our own way. Now, perhaps you have brought me something to eat. How kind."

Mehmet and his cousin came up onto the roof. But not the Langs. They would carry on drinking and soon it would grow quiet in there, some particular stage of what they did. Mr Margoles explained to Mehmet about the appearance of structures.

"It might be some kind of signal," I suggested.

"Yeah," said Mehmet. "Perhaps they build a big message we can see from Earth. Big finger telling us to piss off."

He laughed and then spoke rapidly in Turkish and his cousin laughed too. I snorted politely. Mr Margoles said nothing. I didn't really think it could be a signal. There had been the messages and nothing more. It was soon after the reports about the mascons that the messages began to appear. You might be reading a book or newspaper and words would stand out, demand your attention. Apparently it was almost impossible to ignore them. Reports were hazy for obvious reasons because soon after someone got a message their portal would appear. It was only their portal, no one else could use it. It might be the door to the kitchen, beyond the curtain of a changing room, into a cupboard. Whatever it was, the person who went through it disappeared.

More and more messages came: print, radio, TV. The messages varied but reports from the religious people who'd not succumbed showed variations on a common theme.

Come to the Moon.

All those with souls are welcome.

That's why those of us who never received a message, who were never called, knew that we were the people without souls.

"Big finger," Mehmet was saying, still laughing.

"It must be significant that the structures are near the mascons," I said.

We were all experts on the mascons though most people had never heard of them until a few months ago. Scientists had known since nineteen sixty-eight when the Luna-10 orbiter showed oddities due to what was called a roughness in the moon's gravity. A later satellite launched by Apollo 16 was supposed to have stayed around the Moon for eighteen months but the orbit fluctuated between thirty miles down to six, back again, before it crashed into the Moon's surface after thirty-five days.

In turned out that there were these gravitational anomalies, places where the gravity was much stronger than the rest of the Moon. Mass concentrations or mascons.

Then they'd begun to change, minor variations and then a massive increase in gravity. There was wild talk about a runaway effect and a gravity acceleration going towards the infinite. A black hole on the Moon. There was panic and talk of the end of the world but then the messages had come.

"I like the Moon, when it just the Moon," said Mehmet.

We sat on garden chairs and drank the raki he'd brought up.

Before everything had changed I'd never have done things like this. I spoke to the people around the Block but that was it. I'd been like that since I was little. Never liking to be around crowds. I had lived in the Block all my life and never went very far except my walks when it was getting dark and there were less people around

Once mum had taken me to the West End. To Hamleys. She kept telling me about how wonderful it was, all the toys you could ever imagine. All the way there on the bus I clung to her. There were so many people everywhere and then, in the toyshop, it was so full I felt I couldn't breathe. Children running around filling every space so that I couldn't move without coming near someone. I think I started to scream. I might have screamed all the way home.

*

Third quarter. Even to the naked eye the Moon swelled with a green tinge above us. There were the dark regular areas Mr Margoles said were buildings amid the wider spread of forest.

One night we were on the roof as usual and Brian came up. He didn't want to look through the telescope though, just sat drinking from a bottle of Thunderbird wine.

"The detail is quite captivating," Mr Margoles said to him.

"I'll pass."

"You can see a lot more now the Moon is nearer."

"How can the Moon be nearer, wouldn't there be earthquakes or floods or something?"

His voice was slurred.

"I'm just relating what I observe," said Mr Margoles.

"What makes you an expert?"

"Now, Mr Lang," began Mr Margoles.

But Brian had had too much Thunderbird. He stood, swaying.

"You don't know anything really, do you? You always try and come across as so wise. Mr Bloody Wise. But you don't know anything more than the rest of us, do you?"

He took a few steps towards Mr Margoles.

"Brian."

It was Mrs Lang. She had come up without anyone noticing.

She stood there in a grimy dressing gown, her hair not brushed. She was not like I remembered her from before, when she was always so neat and trim. Even though she was over fifty there had always been something glamorous about her. Her daughter Sally was the same. I used to get shy seeing Sally about the Block. Even more shy than I had been in general before the world became emptier.

"Come home, Brian. I think that's enough for the night."

He took another step towards Mr Margoles, bottle swinging in his hand.

"What do you know?" he mumbled. "You haven't lost anything like we have."

"Brian."

He turned and went with her. Maybe soon it would be her upset and him trying to be calming. I had known them all my life but now I found it easier to talk to Mr Margoles even though he wasn't even from the Block. I hadn't known him before. I'd found him in the street after I'd been walking over the Rye, which is what everyone called Peckham Rye Common.

There had been a group of people further down the road, not people I know. Mr Margoles had looked sad.

"Can you help me, young man?"

"What do you want?"

The group of people were watching us.

"I'm looking for a place to stay."

There were lots of abandoned places to stay but I knew he meant something different.

"This is our Block." I said.

As we made our way over I saw the group of people walking away.

Clouds over the waning crescent. Then a new moon, a great darkness above us. Mehmet and his cousin came back from a run with an empty van. The religious group hadn't turned up to the distribution point.

"They fucking gone up," he said, "to Moon."

I suppose we'd always assumed they would resist. We knew it was very difficult to because when the messages had come people went quickly, compelled. But the religious people had faith. They'd told Mehmet about it.

Brian was coming towards the shop with his bag of empties.

"What's going on?"

"No food. No booze." said Mehmet. "We have to go out and search places. All of us. Can't do it all by myself with my cousin."

All of us, apart from Mrs Lang, gathered together. I went out with Mr Margoles, Brian calling after us to get wine, get spirits.

We ignored him but as we were walking towards Asda I thought I'd speak to Mr Margoles about it.

"Brian, Mr Lang that is, seems angrier all the time."

"Well, it can't be easy for him and his wife. I understand their daughter went on ahead of them."

"Ahead of them? You mean you think they could still get a message, still go."

"Oh yes. I think the changes we are seeing must augur something momentous, don't you, dear boy? The structures, the forest, surely they indicate that. We might not have been ready for the full transition, therefore this is all in the way of a kind of halfway house, a preparation."

I wondered how long he had known this.

"And we can all go?"

"Yes."

"Even though we don't have souls."

"Perhaps we just needed a little longer to nurture them. Yes, I think something marvellous is being prepared."

I thought of all that had happened. Of all the people who had gone because they had received messages, of the world as it was now, which was in many ways a more comfortable world for me.

"I don't think I'm ready."

"You will be," he said, and patted my arm.

On Rye Lane, as we approached the supermarket, I saw other people ahead. It was a group of men and women and they stood and watched us for a while. I thought that one of them might have nodded at us and Mr Margoles nodded back. I realised that some of them were the ones I'd seen when I found Mr Margoles.

"Are they your friends?"

"Mere acquaintances."

In the supermarket we took different aisles. Mr Margoles to tinned foods while I said I would go to the far side to get some drink for the Langs. I had a trolley because we'd decided to fill one each and push them back to the Block. There had been others here before us but there was still lots of the cheaper wine like Thunderbird and little cans of ready-mixed vodka and tonic. I piled them all in and then thought I'd go down to the magazine rack to see if there was anything worth reading.

There was a kid's buggy in the aisle as a copy of *History Today* caught my eye. I made straight for it and then gagged at the sudden smell.

I think Mr Margoles must have been calling for some time.

"What is it?" he was saying.

He pulled me back.

"They left her there," I said. She had been wearing pink, a little beanie hat on with her name on it, Abigail.

"Come on, dear boy."

We were outside in the bright sunlight. Mr Margoles was propping me up. For some reason he was holding a bunch of white shirts in their plastic packaging.

"Someone just left her. Got a message and just went through their portal. How can we be the ones without souls?"

For once Mr Margoles didn't have an answer.

After the new Moon the waxing crescent, forward to the first quarter. Visibility a little better. The Moon shone green dotted with the black shapes of the new structures. It blossomed enormous above, as though it might envelop us.

On the first really clear night Mr Margoles knocked on my door and I said I would come up to the roof. I was being polite because after the supermarket I didn't really want to think about what it all might mean.

On the roof I looked across the city towards the tower blocks further into London. In the night there was the odd light now, candles, paraffin lamps and electric torches, whatever people used now there was no mains.

"Come and have a look," Mr Margoles said.

I didn't want to upset him.

"You see, you see," he said. He was excited.

I think I saw, yes, I think I did, after that initial moment of adjustment, the dark of my own eyelashes obscuring everything. But I couldn't look for long. Couldn't bear it and I was shaking afterwards.

I stood up.

"I'm a bit tired, Mr Margoles," I said.

"Really?"

I was already walking away, getting off the roof.

"Is everything all right?"

I went down to my floor and then out onto the balcony. Brian was outside his flat, smoking a cigarette. He glanced at me then carried on looking down into the courtyard.

"Been up there with him, have you?"

He flicked the cigarette and it made a bright arc as it fell.

"Yes," I said.

He picked up a bottle from the floor. Drank. Rested it on the top of the concrete balustrade.

"You shouldn't listen to him," he said, "he's full of shit. Pompous bastard. What does he know?"

"I've looked through the telescope."

But I was sure now I hadn't seen what Mr Margoles had seen.

Brian turned to me, his eyes wide, too much white, too empty. He reached out as though to grab me but didn't. He took another drink.

"How can any of it be true? How can our Sally have a soul and we don't? How can we give birth and bring up someone with a soul without us having a soul?"

"I don't know."

All I knew was that something had happened. Something had taken them all away, the loved ones, the families and friends of people like him.

"I don't know."

He lifted his beer and drained the bottle. Looked at it.

"It always seems so hopeful when it's full. You have the evening ahead of you, nice little drink. Then before you know it's gone. You've argued, all the good feeling has drained away."

Then he tossed the bottle over the balustrade where it smashed on the courtyard below.

For the full moon there was going to be a party. Mr Margoles arranged it all. I didn't think it was necessarily a good idea but I didn't say anything.

I hadn't seen as much of him. I went back to going for walks on my own. Trying once again the freedom of being alone. I went out in daytime now, over the Rye, in the ornamental gardens where the little river ran, the swing park where there were no children, where the only sound might be the clinking of the swing chain in the wind or creak of the boards of the roundabout.

Once I saw Mr Margoles on Rye Lane talking to those other people he knew but I went away quickly.

I'd be tired by the evening, enough to sleep, to be inside and away from the Moon, the diseased eye that was zooming in on us. I imagined the Moon as it was supposed to be, a colour that can't be fixed by easy words, not silver, not grey, a softer colour than one, warmer than the other. Most of all the emptiness of that landscape, the great rise of the peaks on craters' edges and the sweep of the lowlands of Serenity, Tranquillity. Storms.

I had been so caught up in the change that I hadn't realised how much I missed the Moon, the real Moon, whose gentle desolation had always been a comfort to us below it.

On the day of the party Mr Margoles knocked on my door but I didn't answer. He called through the letterbox.

"I do hope you're coming tonight, Gideon."

I said nothing.

"It's so close now. The detail through the telescope is incredible."

Later that morning I went over to Mehmet's shop to see what I could get for breakfast. There was no one at the counter but I could hear them out in the back so I went through into the little back yard. There were plastic bags against every wall, some had fallen spilling their contents of empty bottles and cans.

"Mr Lang," said Mehmet, "I take them from him. He fucking think there's still recycling or something?"

Mehmet's cousin picked up a bag, clattering in his hand. He put it down again.

"I tell him not to bring any more bags, no bottles, no cans," said Mehmet, "Then we can use yard to store things. Do big collections and not have to go out so often."

He shook his head and we all went back into the shop.

"You help me take stuff up to the roof tonight," he said to me.

Everyone was there. Brian Lang because there was plenty of booze. Mrs Lang with him. They both sat around a small garden table.

Mr Margoles stood at the telescope wearing a new white shirt. He greeted me and Mehmet as we came out onto the roof.

I said hello to everyone and helped Mehmet to lay out plates and arrange the packets of crackers, crisps, Turkish stuffed vine leaves from a can and other stuff we'd brought, all on a plastering table. Mehmet's cousin stood at the edge of the roof by the little perimeter wall looking out as the Moon rose.

"Bring me that bottle of Thunderbird," Brian called over to me.

I took it over.

"Would you like anything, Mrs Lang?" I asked.

"Gideon, come and see," Mr Margoles called.

"In a minute," I said and went back to the plastering table. Mr Margoles was back looking through the telescope, distracted from bothering the rest of us.

But soon enough he started.

"We'll begin soon," he announced.

"What?" said Brian and guffawed.

Mehmet's cousin said something and laughed too.

"Ah," said Mr Margoles, "Here we are."

People. Other people, began to come out onto the roof. It was the first time I had seen them so close up, the ones that Mr Margoles had been with, when I first met him and other times. There were men and women of various ages, but they seemed to be all the same because they were all wearing white shirts.

"Please," announced Mr Margoles, "let us welcome our friends. Let all gather round to make ready."

"What is this?" I said because I couldn't help myself. I didn't want there to be other people here.

"I think I might leave," I heard Mrs Lang say.

The white shirts were coming forward, fanning out to fill the roof. There were more of them than I imagined.

"Please," said Mrs Lang, "would you mind moving out of the way?"

"Mrs Lang, you must stay," Mr Margoles' voice came over the heads of the crowd. "This is for you too, Mrs Lang. And your husband. This is for all of us. Behold."

I saw his hand above the heads of the white shirts, pointing at the sky.

The Moon was nearer, much nearer. It was as though he'd conjured it, larger than the sun, the metallic green light like a death ray seeking us all out.

"We are the ones who will no longer be left behind."

He was standing on something, a stool or chair. I couldn't see because the white shirts were crowded around him.

"I have seen the place they have prepared for us, the place that will displace the emptiness we have been left with. Come, come see."

The white shirts parted to make a space around him and the telescope and then one peered through it for perhaps ten seconds. Then moved away to let another. As this went on, one after the other, Mr Margoles carried on talking.

"Do you see the place that is waiting? The minarets and ceremonial arches, towers and spires. The great city nestled within the foliage of the wonderful garden. We will walk in those groves and arcades, bathed in earthlight…"

"I want to see."

It was Mrs Lang. And as she came forward the white shirts fell away to make a space for her. She wasn't swaying, not drunk but there was something about the way she moved that showed she wasn't entirely in control. On autopilot.

I wanted to tell her to stop.

Mr Lang had got to his feet. Bottle in hand he tried to get to her but the white shirts closed around her, blocking his way. He began to swear and Mehmet joined in, bursts of Turkish punctuated with fuck… fuck.

Then Mrs Lang called out.

"It's all right. Brian. It's all right. Come and see."

The white shirts let him through. Everything became calm and I glanced up at the Moon for a second. Quickly looked away.

"...all will be received there," Mr Margoles was saying, "to join those who have gone before us, to be in the place they have prepared for us. The place where we will at last be at peace..."

I could see Brian Lang looking into the telescope. If I moved quickly I could get there. I could smash it.

Because I too had seen. It was true that there were buildings amidst the forests of the Moon but what I had seen was a collection of ruins, a cemetery where the teeming dead roamed around unwilling to be buried. All those who had gone there wandered like wraiths. They were empty vessels filled with diseased light. The thought of being among them, trapped and enclosed by their presence, terrified me.

"Is she really there?" I heard Mr Lang say, and the white shirts began to murmur, to say names, different names, over and over.

I felt the Moon light on me. If I looked up I would see the gravestones and mausoleums of the departed. I knew what I should do. Run forward and hurl myself at Mr Margoles, push him off the roof, watch as he arced through the air and shattered on the courtyard below.

"Won't you join us?"

He was standing next to me. The roof felt too packed, the crowd doing what it always did to me, hemming me in, making it difficult to breathe. I edged back a little but I couldn't go any further because all there was behind was the low wall, the drop.

Some of the white shirts were looking at me, turning away from where they had been watching the Langs. Their eyes fixed me and the weight of the coming Moon pressed down on my head.

"Leave me alone," I said.

"You really are very important to me," said Mr Margoles.

"I'm nothing."

He smiled at that.

"You see, I understand why the others were not called. Mehmet and his cousin clinging to the ritual of the shop. Mr and

Mrs Lang depending on each other in their misery. All the people here have a reason. But why you, dear boy?"

"I don't want to go there. I don't want to go to the Moon."

"It hasn't been the Moon for quite some time now. Not exactly. The mascons have collapsed to a point of singularity. Whatever caused it has come for us."

I would have to push past him, push through the crowd, then I could run out, out of the Block and over to the Rye, be in the open.

"There's no escape now. Why won't you accept that?"

A murmur from the crowd that began to rise, everyone was looking up to the sky and Mr Margoles stepped back from me and looked up too.

"It's here," he said, softly so only I might have heard. Then declaiming loudly: "It's here."

The throbbing vibrated through my body. The light washed me, rotten like overripe fruit. Caught in this light the crowd held their arms aloft to greet it. A look of joy in their faces. Then I saw Mehmet's cousin who looked confused for a moment until he too raised his arms high to welcome the Moon.

I didn't know if they were being filled or being emptied.

That was when I leapt from the roof.

I thought I was alone in the days after that, deposited safely on the Earth by the passing Moon I had run, not knowing where I was going, away from the Block and everything I had ever truly known.

Without the Moon the nights were darker but the passage of days and nights was much shorter as the spin of the Earth grew quicker, unhindered. Everywhere the abundances of nature, which had begun to creep back when most of the people had gone, grew even wilder, plant life sprouting from every crack in the road, every patch of earth in a yard and railway embankment.

I don't know how much time passed. It was difficult to tell now but I could go anywhere I wanted without encountering a crowd. Without meeting anyone. When I tried to think about all those who had gone I just found myself thinking about years ago, about mum, and how a heart attack had taken her through a portal all of her own too.

I crossed a bridge over the still surface of the Thames and eventually found what I'd been looking for. I wandered through the aisles picking from the shelves the teddy bears and model cars, dollies and action figures, Lego sets and Airfix kits. It really was the most wonderful toy shop in the world. Then, as I passed a window, I saw something in the shop opposite, on the other side of Regent Street. It might have been a man or a woman. I can't be sure. We stood and stared at each other for a while.

Then they disappeared into the interior and were gone.

I stood by the window and waited. Without the Moon, Venus rose as the brightest object of the night, then the other stars came. The sky wasn't empty at all.

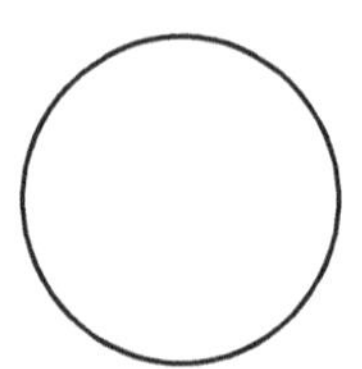

Moonface

Elana Gomel

The woman disappeared into the side alley so quickly that the edge of her mantle whipped around the crumbling bricks like a black tongue licking away the residue of shadows. I stood staring after her until Vadim tugged on my arm, steering me into a puddle of silvery light. I knew that I was breaking the protocol but there was something so perversely alluring about that hunched, shapeless silhouette that I allowed myself another microsccond of wonder before following him.

I had not seen a woman's face in ten days. Or ten thousand years, depending on how you counted.

The town sprawled around us in a chiaroscuro of black and white: a maze of tangled passages, a field of swaying shadows. The crooked little alleyways were fronted by blind walls of brick and stone. Unexpected plazas sported spiky iron contraptions. They may have been works of art, or pedestrian traffic dividers, or idols. I had tried to ask Vadim but as always, he avoided a straight answer though I had no doubt he understood the question. Their language had not deviated much from Standard English, which made me suspect that ten thousand years may be an exaggeration. But another reason suggested that it was a wild undercounting. The reason hung above the peaks of gabled roofs, flooding the town with lifeless radiance.

I was no astronomer, so I could not calculate how much bigger was the visible face of this Moon from the tepid little circle of my Iowa nights. But it was huge. The mottled sphere seemed to be within my reach. I remembered a drawing in a book I used to read to Aidan: a child balancing a smiling Moon on his fingertips. But there was nothing whimsical or lighthearted about the massive body above me. It hovered in the sky like a leaden balloon about to crash down and obliterate that mean little town below.

"They start soon," Vadim said. His pronunciation was a little strange, words running into each other with a fluidity I associated with languages like Russian. But the grammar remained the same. How was it possible? Linguistic drift was fast; I would not be able to understand Old English. So was it just a couple of hundred years? But how long would it have taken for the Moon to spiral so close to the Earth's surface? Surely longer than that. I looked up, searching for the familiar spots on the pockmarked surface and caught Vadim's scowl. I had already been told that staring at the face of the Goddess was very bad form.

Another contradiction: moon worship on the one hand; disinclination to talk about it on the other. It seemed to me there was an undertone of caution and even disgust in the way they approached the subject.

We came out of the maze into a larger plaza. It was surrounded by blank whitewashed walls painted dove-gray by moonlight. Around its circumference were those black iron things. From close up they looked like coat-racks gone wild and sprouting a multitude of thorny arms. In the middle was a wide open space, already filling with people. Men.

I towered above them. That was another thing that had changed: these people were small and undernourished, sallow-skinned and thin-limbed. They did not look capable of physical violence and I was glad of that. When I had emerged from the pod I had fearful fantasies of stumbling into an apocalypse: being engulfed by raging flames, trampled by rampaging mobs, or caught in the middle of a race war. What I had seen so far seemed to indicate a peaceful, if technologically backward and quietly starving, community. Except, of course, for their treatment of women.

Vadim led me to a knot of people that, he explained, was his family "shadow", which I took for a group noun. It was comprised of a very old man, bent and gnarled by arthritis; a couple of younger males approximately the age of Vadim; and a gaggle of boys. No women. Not for the first time, I tried to get it straight.

"Are these your brothers?" I asked Vadim, pointing to the men who eyed me curiously and a little fearfully, whispering in reedy voices. He nodded.

"Valerian, Vitaly and Vernon. We were born in the same cycle."

"No sisters?"

He gazed at me blankly. One of the boys burst into giggles and was shushed by a stern look from the patriarch of the family.

The ceremony started as the Moon cleared the top of the town's tallest building, which was about three stories high. It hung in the ashen sky like an overripe fruit about to fall off the bough, bloated with fermenting juice. The worship was not very impressive as such things go: a chant led by another old man in a silver-embroidered stole and dutifully repeated first by the elder of each family and then by the rest; a genuflecting that went around the plaza like waves of corn swaying in the wind; and long, apparently meditative, silences. The chant was in English but so distorted by a singsong inflection that I only caught occasional words. Unsurprisingly chief among them was "Moon". I let myself drift, trying to convince myself that this was some bizarre dream.

After Krista had left me, taking our son with her, I went through a bad patch. I drank too much; I burned through my savings with internet gambling; and so when I was offered that job, I took it eagerly. The job was connected to NASA and European Space Agency but there was nothing heroic about it. They were testing a new hibernation system for long spaceflight. Basically all I had to do was to get into a high-tech pod and close my eyes. The recruiter tried to convince me that there was more to it than that but I did not care. It paid the bills. The first couple of trials went so easily that I was getting bored. The third trial ended with me waking up parched, blades of silver light slashing through the dusty dark of the room, and the pod tilted and splintered. I got out and went in search of water. When I stumbled into the street and saw the monstrous yellow orb glaring at me from the sky, I forgot about my thirst.

Vadim found me and took me home. Like most of them, he lived alone in a stonewalled apartment in the town that had been clearly built to accommodate a much larger population. I found out later that men with young sons banded together to share childcare, especially if they belonged to the same "shadow". Where the women lived I had no idea.

The ceremony ended but the crowd did not disperse. I felt tension building up in the air. Men whispered; children fretted. The silver-stole-garbed oldster walked through the throng, parting it like Moses the Red Sea. The people squeezed to the sides forming a path. And a line of veiled, mantled figures emerged from one of the buildings around the plaza and glided through this path.

My breath caught in my throat. I had seen burka-wearers but this was something else. The mantles – painted black by the moonlight though their real color might be different – fell around their hidden bodies in overlapping petals of stiff fabric, trails spreading and dragging along like squirming leeches or blind worms attached to the host. The mantles were so heavy and many-layered that it was impossible to gauge the shape and size of their wearers. They all looked like walking lumps of darkness: too big, too formless, too hunched-up. Their fronts were additionally draped with sheets of gauze. They might just as well have been blindfolded. And yet they kept distance from each other and progressed through the hushed crowd of men without stumbling or touching the onlookers. One by one, they disappeared into the gaping mouth of a large doorway.

And only then did the men, myself included, release their pent-up breath.

I looked at Vadim. His forehead was bathed in sweat.

Then and there I decided I needed to talk to a woman. Face to face.

I had been a good husband, or so I believed. I had never been unfaithful. I let Krista handle our family finances. And if I loved my son more than I loved my wife, wasn't it only natural?

When she walked out during one of my tours of duty, leaving behind a recorded message that basically said she did not love me anymore, I freaked out. I found them staying with Krista's mother. She was not trying to hide from me; just figuring out what to do next. Our meeting consisted of yelling on my side and stilted answers on hers. No, I had done nothing wrong. Yes, she would let me see Aidan; and no, she would not relinquish custody. At some point I realized she did not see me, just as I had not seen her for a long time. We were just two stock characters going through a hackneyed script not of our writing. And when I saw my son's frightened eyes as he peered into the room, startled by my shouting, I knew I had lost my family.

The People of the Moon, as they called themselves, had families: fathers, brothers, sons, uncles and nephews. But how could a family exist without a mother? I had read about extreme forms of gender segregation in certain cultures – the purdah, the gynaeceum – but this was far more extreme. Wherever the women were kept, it was in a different part of the town altogether. And I saw several men with babies in slings, feeding them with chewed-up bread mush and cow milk from a bottle. It looked as if the mothers were not even allowed to care for their newborns.

Talking to Vadim was useless: his narrow eyes would sink even deeper into his scrunched-up face and he would turn away, muttering something incomprehensible. I decided to explore on my own. Initially it seemed easy to do. Despite my standing out like a sore thumb, I was allowed to wander. The men were busy during the day, toiling in the paltry little fields that surrounded the town. Food was scarce and unappetizing; technology almost non-existent. It was hard to believe they had built this sprawling settlement. I was beginning to believe the People of the Moon were squatters.

The Moon was visible during daytime as a ghostly white disk floating in the cerulean blue. At least the sunshine erased the dead-man's face that I fancied I saw on her surface. I could not decide whether the markings were different from what they used to be or simply more detailed because of her proximity to the Earth. I had never paid much attention to our satellite. But now she was as obtrusive as an unwanted guest at a party. She scowled down at me at sunset, peering above the horizon. She diluted the night with her morbid radiance. And during the day she spied on me: a cataract-filmed eye in the sky.

I quickly discovered that there were limits to my freedom of movement. I could roam in the central part of town. But when I tried to go further, a posse of young men materialized out of thin air and politely but firmly escorted me back.

The town center was sparsely populated, mostly by men without children, and there was nothing interesting there. The town seemed ancient because of its bare-bones architecture but actually was not. The walls were sound and bearing traces of paint that seemed to have been scraped off brick and mortar. I remembered sci-fi movies and books about primitive tribes living in civilization's ruins. But there was no sign of lost technology: no dust-choked power outlets in the walls or rotting cables snaking in the basements. I went back to my pod and found it gone, the room as bare as the rest of them. I confronted Vadim, demanding to know what had happened to the pod. He pretended he did not understand.

The only signs of manufacturing were those spiky iron contraptions. I examined them minutely but still could not decide what they were for. They looked like bizarre statues: dead iron trees bearing long sharp thorns. No two were exactly alike. They did not connect to anything and did nothing, as far as I could tell. I got some dirty looks when I tried to move one of them but nobody tried to stop me.

But it was different when I tried to walk through the large doorway into which the procession of veiled women had disappeared on the night of the Moon ceremony. It was blocked by a heavy wooden door, iron-bound and solidly made. It had an actual lock. I tried to open it when the door swung by itself.

Standing at the entrance was the old man I had seen officiating at the ceremony. In bright daylight, his face looked grooved and fissured like a drought-stricken field. He was not wearing his fancy stole.

His toothless mouth worked in frenzy as he yelled something and banged the door in my face.

The Moon was finally waning. When she was full, the streets were more crowded at night than at daytime: men hanging about, talking in low tones and falling silent when I approached, drinking fizzy oat brew from crude tankards. Children were out in force, darting through the silvery alleys like minnows. It was difficult to engage in clandestine exploration. I decided to wait for the dark of the Moon. Vadim's apartment had a stock of crude candles and some matches. I was confident I could find my way around.

One morning when Vadim had gone to the fields, I followed my usual aimless route through the part of the town that was free to me until I came to another one of those plazas. The iron tree standing in its center was bigger than most: a tangle of barbs like an Iron Maiden turned inside out. And hanging on one of its thorns was… something.

I approached and picked up the gauzy thing. It was moist and warm, unpleasantly clinging to my fingertips. I was reminded of the Korean sheet masks Krista had used to improve her skin-tone: a crude approximation of a face with holes for eyes and mouth, made of tissue and permeated with some magic formula. I used to laugh at the way it made her look: like a fetus with a cowl. It was just one of those marriage things I regretted having said and done.

Was somebody using sheet masks in this far future where the Moon threatened to crash into the Earth? The thing was mushroom-pale, wet and thick, and its underside was dappled with wormy protrusions. The eyeholes were surrounded by ragged flaps. It was revolting. I dropped it and went away, rubbing my hand on my scuffed jeans.

Next day I found more of them. The iron trees now looked like actual tress in bloom, festooned with drooping, dripping scraps of whitish tissue. At least it was clear now what the spiky stands were for, even though I was no closer to understanding their strange blossoms. They smelled terrible: a warm, organic stench like a gangrenous wound. The pavement below was wet with their gluey runoff.

Next day Vadim came back early from the fields and conspicuously locked the door of the apartment, which he had never done before.

"You are staying in tonight," he said flatly.

Tonight was the dark of the Moon.

We ate together. He shared his scant ration of unleavened bread, bitter cheese and weak beer with me as he always did. It occurred to me that he did not have to do this; did not have to feed the clueless giant who had blundered into his life uninvited. Having been in the Army, I could appreciate the goodness of men, their simple brotherhood. For a moment I felt guilty about the sacrilege I was contemplating.

But what about the women? How could anything justify these veil-swathed prisoners?

I waited until Vadim fell asleep in the next room. His snoring was always surprisingly loud for such a small fellow. I gathered my candles and matches. I took the flimsy door off the hinges with no difficulty at all.

The darkness felt as thick and suffocating as tar. I realized that I had gotten used to the lunar radiance that made nights easy to navigate. Even when gibbous, the enormous orb provided enough illumination to see one's way. Now, though, the Moon was dark, a hungry hole in the star-sown sky. There were no streetlights and the windows were black. I was apprehensive about lighting my candle prematurely and drawing attention to myself. I made my way to the square largely by touch.

The air was thick with an unclean stench, like old blood and rotting offal. I stumbled into one of the iron trees and inadvertently grasped a handful of masks hanging from its thorns. They liquefied into a thick mess that stuck to my fingers.

Finally I reached the plaza where the women had walked on the night of the full Moon. And there I saw I had no need of my candle.

The plaza was brightly illuminated by hundreds of lit candles placed around its circumference and stuck on the iron tree in the middle. And surrounding it were the women.

They stood still, facing the tree – or so I thought because with these hulking shapes it was impossible to tell back from front. The tree was blooming with bloodless and fleshy masks. The older ones lay under it in rotten drifts but the fresh ones were draped around its thorns. A tree of faces.

Yes, faces, because in the candlelight I saw that the eyeholes were not empty. A multitude of glittering balls, dark like sloe-berries, observed me, rolling in the drooping skin-folds. Shapeless mouths twitched and mumbled.

I rushed forward, seized one of the veiled figures, and turned her around. I realized now what I should have realized long ago – they were as tall as me or taller, far bigger than the diminutive males. But I did not care. I tore at the layers of veils. They were filthy, stiff with secretions. But my horror gave me strength as I ripped the dirty fabric away.

And was confronted with – nothingness.

She had no face. A moist expanse of raw flesh, leprous and pale, indistinctly mottled with random squiggles of shadows. Even if she wanted to answer my frantic questions, she had no mouth to speak with.

But there was a voice in the hush – a slurping, liquid sound, but articulate enough.

It was one of the faces hanging on the tree. Without the underlying bone structure it was impossible to tell whether it was young or old, beautiful or ugly. It was just a rag of shed skin.

"You will be killed. They will kill you."

The other creatures – I no longer thought of them as women – lifted their veils simultaneously. Most were like the one I had uncovered – faceless. But there was one whose face was still half-attached to her flesh, hanging askew like a poorly applied bandage. She ripped it off with a wet sound and draped it on the tree.

"Who are you?" I cried.

"Women."

"No!"

"We wax and wane. We bear babies. Isn't it enough?"

"No!" I yelled. "Women are human beings! You are not!"

One of them lifted her arm and I saw that it was just a cudgel of raw flesh, fingers fused and bleeding. Before she could touch me with it, I pushed her away. She fell into a clutch of her fellows. The commotion slowed them down as I ran away, falling and crawling through the dark, skinning my hands and feet on the rough pavement. Iron thorns snagged on my clothes and bit into my flesh.

Vadim waited for me at the entrance to the apartment.

"You saw." It was not a question.

"What are they?"

"Women."

"What? You are crazy!"

"They become human enough when the Moon is full. This is when their faces look… well… they are attached… and they look…"

"Human enough to fuck!" I finished. "What are you, people? How can you?"

"What would you have us do?" he yelled. "Go extinct? We are the only ones left."

"Left from what?"

"From the disaster of 2032," he said calmly. "Fifteen years ago. Yes, Sergeant Eric Miller, it has only been fifteen years since your stupid pod malfunctioned and locked you in. Well, you were lucky. You missed the Coming of the Moon."

The fact that he knew my name and rank was less horrifying than the date. Fifteen years. Aidan would be eighteen now. Krista forty-five.

"What happened to women?"

"We don't know. Nobody knows. One day we woke up and the Moon was hanging in the sky like a rotten apple, so close that it seemed we could touch it. Only there was nobody fool enough to try. No planes, no cars, no fucking internet. I was ten. I looked for my Mom. She wasn't there."

"Your father?"

"Never had one."

So this was how they survived – banding together, making a community the best they could. And breeding with creatures who shed their faces like snakes shed skin. Reproduction – the strongest drive of all.

"Where are we? It can't be Earth. This town…"

"Looks pretty well cleaned out, doesn't it? All disappeared – plastic, electronics, books. We make do with what's left."

"So what is it? A glitch in spacetime? An alien invasion?"

He shrugged.

"That thing… it said I will be killed."

Vadim nodded somberly.

"Looking at a moonface is taboo. The punishment for breaking it…"

"Death," I finished. "Fine. Wouldn't be the first time. I served in Afghanistan. But I won't be here for long. I'm leaving."

I went back into the apartment and packed a couple of candles and a loaf of bread. There was nothing else to take.

Vadim looked at me as I laced my boots.
"Where are you going?" he asked.
"I'm going to find my wife."

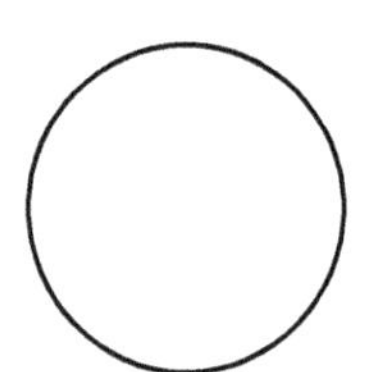

Between the Librations

Anna Fagundes Martino

Libration: an apparent or real oscillation of the Moon, by which parts near the edge of the disc that are often not visible from the Earth sometimes come into view.

His full name was Patrick Fitzgerald Long Island and it was always easy to spot him in a crowd: it's not like there are many five feet eleven albino men around the campus.

If he were a woman, you'd be tempted to employ words like *diaphanous* around him, even though there was nothing gossamer-like about him: he was all hard angles, broad shoulders and deep voice, round eyes like polished pewter that commanded attention. He was the sort of man that knew he was observed at all times – and he basked on it, extremely comfortable to be seen in broad daylight.

"I'm a Moon Child, but I prefer the cockcrow to the nightfall," he'd say to me as we walked side by side. That was when we were still in the strange ritual of dating, playing the rules according to his rulebook and not mine.

"What do you mean, you're a Moon Child?"

"My star sign. Don't they have that expression in Brazil? Those who are born under Cancer are often called Moon Children. And I'm two times a Moon Child: I have both my Sun and my Moon in Cancer. I'm the sort of bastard that cries at weddings even if I don't know the happy couple."

"You believe in Astrology?"

"It's not a matter of belief. I know how to speak that idiom and I profit from what it can teach me. It's a man-made language like all the others, and it communicates things like all man-made languages."

"But surely you don't believe in stars guiding our fate and things like that. It's ludricous!"

"The word is *ludicrous*, Tainá. And no, it isn't ludicrous at all. It's only a matter of comprehending that we can only communicate certain things through certain idioms. And sometimes we are ill-equipped for the task. Consider the butterfly. It has five cone cells in each of its eyes. A cone cell translates the light we see into colours. Do you know how many of those cells do we happen to have? Three. A butterfly can see more colours than you will ever know in your life. How's that for perspective?"

"And you're telling me astrology is like having such cone cells, is that it?"

"No, I'm telling you that there might be a language in the stars that astrologers and astronomers cannot decode on their own. Of course, I don't believe the stars can direct our fate. But there might be something in there that people can only hint at, because we lack the proper cone cells or something. It's all in what you can convey from the message."

I assumed Long Island was a scientist because he was always at the laboratory compound. He was always chatting with the mathematicians, hanging around with the astronomers, helping out the Computer Science BA students and the like. He had a tight-knit family in the laboratories, the way he had a tight-knit family at the university chaplaincy and the local faculty rugby team. The nerds and the geeks of the Chemical and Astronomical brotherhood respected him, sought his opinion and his praise. So, what was his major? What was his line of studies?

To my surprise, I discovered he was a scientist – a social scientist. He had an MA and a PhD in Linguistic Studies. He taught Varieties of English to the undergrads while conducting a post-doc research in Sociolinguistics. What the hell was he doing in the Astronomy laboratory, of all places?

You asked that to anyone in the lab, and the answer would be always, "Oh, Long Island belongs here, you know. He's our secret weapon on the Selene project."

"But how can a glorified English teacher help with that?" I asked.

But nobody would answer me, not with words: they'd just shrug and go into radio silence. I wasn't supposed to be in on the joke. I wasn't one of them, not yet.

Selene was one project about which people spoke in whispers, afraid to raise their voices lest it'd sound like utter madness to anyone outside the Academia: a real human colony on the Moon. A dream shared and put into motion by the countries that made up the European Space Agency and which my university, among many others in the continent, was helping to foster.

I was there at the project's launch party, and so was Long Island – the only non-STEM person apart from the waiters and kitchen staff, probably. He was fêted by the professors and the scientists, but it takes one to know one: in spite of his smile, he was uncomfortable as he was paraded around like a novelty item. It was the same way I was introduced to other people at the Chemistry compound. It was because of my dreadlocks, my humble origins and my acrid accent. We were the odd ones out, and the professors couldn't help strutting us to show just how progressive they were, how open to new ideas they proclaimed themselves to be.

Later that night, I found Long Island smoking outside the party tent, hidden in the shadows of our nearby copse. Picturesque, I'd think, if it wasn't for the fact he looked as if he was having the worst bout of cramps ever registered in the books.

"You need help?" He stared at me with stark surprise. He looked almost ermine white under the pale Moon glow, his eyes even more greyish than before. Why was he wearing a hat and gloves? It wasn't even that cold outside, and I'd know. "I mean, should I call a doctor? An ambulance? Something?"

"No need. It's going to end soon. It's just... " He forced himself to smile. "I'm on a bit of a neap tide, you know. Not my sparkling self, tonight. I am Patrick, by the way," he said as he extended a trembling hand.

"I'm Tainá," I said as I took his hand. The tremors felt strange. Like putting your hand over the bonnet of a car to feel the motor running. "And I am calling you a cab."

I took him to his bedsit. Thick blackout curtains smelling of dust hid the windows; there was a Roma flag, green and blue with the Red Wheel, pinned on a wall. Miniatures of astronauts and reproductions of space pictures – the Pale Blue Dot, the first step on the Moon – littered the shelves over the bed. He winced as he hid under the covers, cold sweat gluing his hair to his brow. "I hate when she does this," he murmured. "And just when I need to be my best! Just when I need to do my job."

"Can I help you with anything?"

"I don't think you can tell the Moon to shut up."

"No, I don't think so," I tried to laugh it off. I thought he was drunk, or that the pain was making him speak in riddles.

"Then there's nothing you can do. But thanks for asking. Not everyone seems to notice me, in spite of the obvious war colours... What's your name again?"

"It's Tainá."

"Beautiful. It sparkles when you speak. Is it Greek?"

"Tupi. Brazilian indigenous language. It means 'morning star', and nobody knows how to spell it here in Britain."

He smiled again, amused with the titbit I'd told him, and that was how it began for us. It was unavoidable, like the tides or the phases of the Moon: Long Island always brought you to his atmosphere, whether you liked it or not.

The Selene Project visitors started to show up at our campus a couple of weeks after my first meeting with Long Island. Astronaut candidates from all corners of Europe, men and women with all sorts of accents, skin colours and technical backgrounds – Army brats and Computer Science PhDs, biologists and engineers, all very fit and with the proper stars in their perfect 20/20 vision eyes. They were the best their nations could produce in terms of physical and mental abilities, and they knew it: theirs was the hope to fulfil the dreams of countless generations and actually get to live on the Moon for three months, if everything worked according to the plans.

And the only reason these future astronauts came to our corner of the world?

An albino sociologist.

Long Island was received in our compound with the red-carpet treatment. He'd greet the candidates with a wide, candid smile and then the work would begin. One would expect locked doors and soundproof rooms for that, but he'd simply take long walks around the university lake with one candidate at a time. Like a wandering priest hearing the last confession from a hardened gangster, the potential astronauts talked and talked while carefully hidden security guards kept everyone else away. And, like a priest, Long Island keep quiet about what he heard, confessing his own thoughts to the top brass at the ESA war room at the Dean's office.

Everyone in the lab behaved as if they hadn't seen those strange gatherings, as if they didn't know that future astronauts were among us. As if they didn't know what Long Island was doing to the men and women that came and went – in good measure because nobody really knew what he was doing and there wasn't a soul that would tell us why the sociolinguist seemed to be the most important man on campus all of a sudden.

Long Island wouldn't talk to me about it, either. "Too many NDAs going around, I'd say. And it's not like you'd believe me if I told you," he said over beers at the Uni pub. We were still dating, no expectations of fidelity or exclusivity, nothing with a proper title. "Suffice to say nobody will ever know why I was there, and that's why I took the job."

"You make it sound like it's the worst thing in the world."

"It's not the worst thing in the world, but it's certainly not nice either. I hate breaking people's hearts and I certainly don't like robbing them of their dreams."

"Robbing their dreams? Patrick, what the hell are you doing?" I choked on my drink. He ignored me as only a British person could, looking elsewhere and pretending he didn't hear me. "Should I ask the Moon, then?" I said in a mocking tone. "Since you were so fond of her? Perhaps she'll tell me."

"Perhaps," he replied, still not looking at me. "She'd tell you a lot about me. Not nice things, I bet."

"Oh, what would she say?"

"How much of an ungrateful brat I am, never following her instructions. Every child leaves the nest, but I am not allowed that freedom." He took a deep breath and looked at me. "So don't ask her, or you will never kiss me again. I won't stand it. I am more than fond of you now. It would break my heart to see you go because of this."

"Is that supposed to be a declaration?"

"Ask me again when I'm not drinking," he said as he raised his half-empty glass.

*

The Moon, it is said, rules the lives of women: our menstrual cycles usually match the waxing and waning of the satellite above us. What I found observing my silvery male specimen was that the Moon ruled Long Island as well.

During the Full Moon, he became as needy as a feverish toddler, desperate for any crumbs of attention he could grasp. You'd see him late at night at the library bringing tea for all the PhD students who couldn't sleep unless they finished their work, or rescuing someone who drank one pint too many at the pub.

But these good deeds were for strangers that did not know how much he craved their attention. Those he knew suffered when the Moon began to show up in the sky, because the other known behaviour of a toddler is to throw tantrums... And the academic equivalent of throwing the toys out of the pram was to correct the students' papers with beady eyes and an extra sharp pen.

It was during the Full Moon that my problems pronouncing words in English became nails to the chalkboard to him. The only time he'd informed me about it, he did it loud enough, with the same vocabulary he'd use to eviscerate his students' papers. It was because of these words that Long Island learned how rich Brazilian Portuguese could sound when one is angry enough, and how red an albino face could get when a furious Brazilian woman slapped it with enough potency.

When that happened, the palm of my hand vibrated as if I had hit a metal sheet. And he looked at me not in anger, but plain mortification as he winced, sitting down at his bed.

"Whatever is wrong with you?" I asked, still scared about the vibrations in my skin. I thought he didn't understand what I said, because of my accent and my discontent coating the words. But he did understand: It took me a couple of minutes to figure out the mortification in his eyes was aimed at him, not at the situation, not at me.

And then, his eyes turned to a black and white picture I trained myself not to see in the bedsit: a tall, dark-haired and dark-eyed man in front of a churchyard in a Sun-drenched country. He had the same sharp features I saw in Long Island. I tried to imagine what it would be like if Patrick had inherited that colouring. Would people gravitate towards him if he had blue-black hair and black eyes?

"Do you remember when I told you about the butterflies?" He began to speak with a voice as firm as weak porridge. "How they can see more colours than us?"

"What does this…?"

"This is your answer. I can hear more than anyone you know. I can hear things you would never ever understand. Not because you lack the intelligence, but because you lack the proper equipment. The ESA needs to know whether the candidates have this liability."

"Fine, and you can tell if they have this equipment just by taking them for a walk around the lake."

"Yes, I can. It takes one to know one, isn't it what they say? It's horrible to be able to hear things at this frequency. The Moon is cruel."

"Why would it be cruel? It's just a piece of rock floating in space."

"And you should be glad that you think that. If you could hear what I hear, you wouldn't be so smug."

Of course my first reaction was to say *you're mad*. But something struck a chord. The European Union Space Agency wouldn't leave such an important task such as the choosing of astronauts in the hands of a mad person. The university wouldn't risk its respectability in the hands of a mad person. There are limits to what charm and charisma can do, after all – in my field of work, there's only so much room for lunacy.

"Won't you tell me I am insane to my face? I'd prefer that you did, Tainá. Who the fuck can listen to the Moon, after all?"

"I'd rather ask you what it speaks," I said at last. That was not the answer he expected to hear, and it showed. "Supposing you have the cone cells to hear the Moon and I don't, I reckon I must take your word for it. What does it speak? Is it painful?"

"It can drive a man insane. It nearly drives me insane, rest assured." He walked towards the window and opened the curtains as he spoke. The light of the Moon crept in and he stood there, his hair as bright as hot metal, and his eyes were like moon stones in silver sockets.

The satellite's pallid glow brought that on him: there wasn't another word to use but diaphanous, with his ermine white skin as clear and as bright as a Paschal Moon. He didn't become anything; he didn't turn into a strange creature, a pale werewolf, or a zombie or what have you. If anything, he became more himself: as if someone found at last the missing puzzle pieces and the whole mesmerizing picture emerged in front of my eyes.

"Come", he closed the curtains, "let's take a walk outside. The two of us and the bitch above our heads."

And walk we did – round the students' digs and the road towards the lake at the edge of the university grounds, and then back. For a while, we didn't speak, and it was OK. I think it was a heavy novelty for him to find the right words out.

"It's so fucking implausible, it might as well have come from a fairy tale", he finally spoke up. "I'm *gitano*. Spanish Roma. I know I don't look like it nor do I sound like it, but I am born of a Calé father and a Roma mother. Two different tribes, two different customs, their marriage would never be valid. Well, the Roma woman could hear the Moon. It ran in her blood. And the Moon, it seems, agreed to help her get the man, with a little caveat. She'd have to give up her firstborn to it if she wanted the marriage to proceed."

"Give up the infant to whom? To the Moon? How ludricous."

"For the last time, the word is *ludicrous*, Tainá," he sighed. "And yes, ludicrous indeed: what would the Moon do with a baby? Who would cradle it when it cried? My blood mother could be considered insane by 'ordinary' people, but let's not question that. If she was mad, then what does that make me?" He stopped to catch his breath. "Anyway, the wedding took place. And when I was born... Well, suffice to say my blood father took offense at my appearance. I was proof of her cuckolding."

"Nonsense! Albinism is a genetic disease; it has nothing to do with –"

"Well, I am not an albino, love", he shrugged. "I am full-blooded *gitano* and I am his son, but... Remember what I told you. The deal? The Moon wanted her payment. I am who I am – and my mother was murdered – because I'm a bloody tithe." He took a deep breath, trying to calm himself down. "A British family was camping nearby and they saw a bundle by the side of the road: A bundle that cried and cried in the spot where my blood father left me to die. My luck: scientists, the two of them. They gave me my surname and my accent, my education and my vocabulary. I am theirs. I will always be theirs. But I am also *gitano*. And I am its child," he pointed at the skies, "and fat lot of good it ever did to me. People always take offense at my colour. I force them to like me. Kill them with kindness. Sometimes it works. Most of the time it doesn't."

"Did you ever see them again? I mean, anyone from your blood family."

"Oh, yes. And how I wish I didn't. My blood father found me when I was an adult. I decided to visit the mountain where my life began. Imagine the surprise to see him a dark-skinned man coming up to me calling me *hijo*!" Long Island stopped, choking on a sob.

"Did he ask for your forgiveness?"

"No. Why would he? In his mind, he had done the right thing. He had been lied to. His honour had been sullied. I remember I told him he was a murderer, and that he'd better leave me alone unless he wanted the police on his tracks. He said he'd welcome the police. It'd make a nice change from the Moon. It spoke to him, he said, every night it was visible in the skies. It told him about me."

"What did she say?"

"It said he'd never be free. You can hide from men, but you cannot hide from the Moon. And it said that I would live. It would guide my steps to be sure I'd live through whatever came my way. As mothers do." Long Island looked up and smirked, as if he remembered a private joke between him and the rock floating above us. "The *gitano* came to ask not for forgiveness, but for me to lift the curse from him."

"And did you?"

"I would if I could. But it's not a curse. Just like having albinism is not a curse. It's something you are born with. Some mistake it for schizophrenia. NASA and the ESA, lucky me, know what's up. Once they managed to get their men on the Moon, they started hiring people like me to tune their astronauts… They found out the librations made them act funny. And that's how I landed this job. I can discover who can hear it – and then I teach them to tune it out. Mere humans can ignore it if they work hard enough."

"And of course the public cannot know that."

"Of course not! It'd be ludicrous! Like saying they choose the astronauts according to their star sign." He sighed, lowering his head. "People expect astronauts to be scientific and cold-blooded, but they are human. Humans come with snags. They come with defects and handicaps. And people want us to find life in other planets, but they would be terrified to find out what exactly is there to learn. If they could hear what I hear… They'd stop asking those silly questions. They'd look elsewhere."

His pewter-coloured eyes again stared at the heavens. "She wants to know why I can't go with the astronauts. Now that Selene station is going to be constructed, why can't I go with them? What's stopping me now? She's been browbeating me. I took this job, so I could better understand her, so I could see if worshipping her like this, I'd shut her up."

"But you can't simply show up at the launching pad as if you were to pick the inner-city bus!"

"I could. I'm that good at convincing people. And the ESA could do with someone like me up there, smoothing the ruffled feathers as the months went by. They have hinted as much. I am fit enough to survive the journey."

"Then why don't you go?"

"Because I don't want to," he turned to me with weary eyes. "Because I want to stay here, and because I am fond of the way Earth's gravity shapes your steps, Tainá. I like your librations, you see. And the way you sparkle when you speak."

"Did you tell her that?"

"Of course not."

"What's the worst that can happen if you tell her?"

"I don't know. I never answered back at her. What if I stop hearing her? It's my job, you know. It's why people put up with me. If I lose that, who will I be?"

"You'll be Patrick Fitzgerald Long Island, PhD: A *gitano* with a Home Counties accent. A passable fly-half with a taste for pale ale, who uses Astronomy terms to compliment a woman expecting her to understand it. So you have strange eardrums and less melanin than most, what of it?"

He stared at me as if he had seen gold in the cracks of my skin; as if it had never occurred to him that someone would want him for himself and not for his strange connection with worlds beyond our own. He closed his eyes and turned his face to the Moon, letting the pale glow wash over him.

Patrick didn't speak another word as we returned to his bedsit, walking hand in hand for the first time. It was as if he was trying to prove a point – not to me, but to himself. Praying, perhaps, that the affection we shared – that he now dared to enjoy out in the open – was a constant source and not something that ebbed like the tides, according to the light reflected upon its surface.

We moved to Paris when the Selene colony was at last established; that's where the ESA headquarters are. He quit the university to work full-time with the agency, monitoring the astronauts, hearing their travelogues and matching their words with the words from the satellite. It's harsh work, but he enjoys it – it gives him a purpose for his gift and nobody makes questions.

What the Moon tells him, I still don't know. I take the librations as they come, showing or hiding his surface, as constant and bright as we can make it in a world that treats people like us as strange little animals.

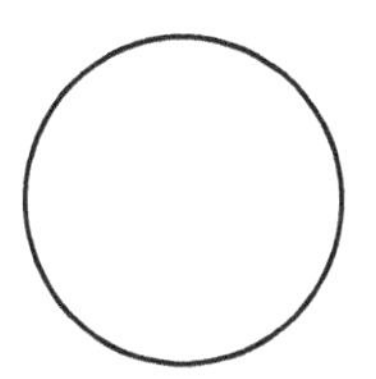

To Sharpen, Spin

Charles Wilkinson

Arthur prays that his father will come home drunk. In the flat above the shop, the workscreen, with its burden of unsolved equations, has been switched off. The room is tiny: just enough space for a bed and a small desk, its surface trapped in a noose of yellow light. The boy is approaching the end of adolescence. As he walks to a window overlooking the lamp-polished cobbles of the Old High Street, he stoops to avoid banging his head on the wooden beams. He's grown so quickly that he is not completely in control of his elongated limbs. Above the pitched roofs and mansard windows of the shops opposite his father's business, the lower half of the night sky has a dusty orange glow. The city is daubed, slashed and throbbing with luminescence: high rise flats bleached to match the full moon; fantastical, multi-storied corporate offices – some in the shape of everyday objects, one a giant parcel wrapped up with glimmering walkways, a great bow on its roof pulsating with pink. There are the flares of mini-crafts sent to augment defence systems; a space bus carrying miners to Mars and beyond.

Arthur knows the Old High Street is an anachronism, the last area in the city left where shopping is an art form for pedestrians. A dying race, the off-line retailers live above their shops. The boy's friends can hardly credit that his home is in a building with no lift; they have trouble too with his forename; most of theirs have been taken from the periodic table. And in spite of his height he is story-tale quaint, a gawky prince from an almost forgotten legend.

A creak on the landing followed by a tap on the door and then his mother's nervous white face and anxious, pale blue eyes peering in. Arthur's quick, gangling himself across the carpet to forestall further incursions.

"Is your father back?"

"No."

"Is he out on business or …"

They're both hoping that he will have been in one of the drinking dens in the basements of the high rises near the city centre, or even in a legal bar at the one of the better hotels.

Alcohol makes him less censorious, seems to blunt the violence that's always present, a naked blade waiting to cut, whenever he's sober. Arthur's mother has long claimed that this quirk is proof of an essentially kind nature. It's the world's moods that are mirrored in his brutality. She sometimes cites a tag about 'wine' and 'truth', still current though even the name of the language in which it was coined is half forgotten.

"He said he was going to a club, I think."

"Go down to the barrier, will you? Ask them what time they're shutting the gates."

He's about to protest when he realises that this errand will mean the end of algebra for the evening. He reaches for a peg. Now that he's decided, he welcomes the prospect of night air, an escape from his cramped room.

"Okay," he says, struggling with his overcoat like a snake attempting to wriggle back into its skin.

"Don't stay long. Just go down to the barrier, check the times. Then come right back."

"Fine."

Outside, the street is empty. A few of the shops are shuttered, but most have front windows that are still lit up, illuminating displays of shoes hand-crafted from genuine leather, their shine slippery; silk ties and handkerchiefs; the glimmering barrels of shotguns, manikins attired in hunting tweeds. The barriers at either end of the Old High Street are visible. Security is tight. Arthur's not sure why his mother is so insistent that he return promptly; they live in one of the few safe areas of the city, and there are no bars, or even a restaurant, for him to visit. Doubtless it is all part of her escalating neurosis.

He goes towards the barrier that is closest to the city centre. A light's on in the guard house and he can see the silhouette of the watchman, who's holding a cup of tea. Someone will be on duty until midnight, most often much later, if there are events that are expected to run late. Arthur taps on a pane and the watchman slides the lower half up. It's not a man he's seen before.

"Do you know where …? My mother said to let you know my father's still out."

"And which one would he be?"

"Galen Kelso."

"What's his shop?"

"The Case of Knives."

The man consults a screen. "He should be back by now. According to this, he was going for a drink and the bars have been shut for over an hour."

For a moment, there's a silence between them. They both know that the drinking dens serve until the early morning.

"What time does the barrier shut tonight?"

It's then that they hear a shuffling of feet on the far side of the guard house. The man glances at what must be Arthur's father on the screen. "This could be him now."

There's a clunk as the lock on the steel door between the house and the barrier is released. Then Galen Keslo stumbles through. "It's not right," he announces, to no one in particular.

Arthur catches his arm and steers his father away from the guard house. "Why are you so late? Mother's been …"

"It's the moon, it shouldn't be like that."

As they pass under a street light, the boy sees that his father's face, which on such an occasion would normally have been pudgy with alcoholic affability, is stricken with fear.

"Like what?"

"She'll only get worse … with all this …?"

He seems about to stumble, but the boy tightens his grip. And who is 'she'? The moon or Arthur's mother?

"Tell me about it when we're back home."

His father's trying to weave away from him as he points at the night sky.

"Can't you … can't you see it?"

"What?"

"The moon, what's happening to it?"

How is he supposed to respond to this? He catches his father's arm and tugs him forward. At least the street is empty and there are no witnesses to these ravings. When his father falls silent, Arthur glances up. It's true the moon appears larger than usual; its surface is bright, as if electroplated with silver, etched with grey maria. No doubt it is closer to the earth tonight. What's the term? A super moon.

The street has never seemed so long, but now they're almost back. The knives are glinting in the shop window. As Arthur searches in his pocket for the key, his father waves at the moon. At first his movements seem almost a salutation, but as his son tries to pull him inside, they become urgent, as though he is exhorting the moon to leave at once, lest it break the morning sun's monopoly of light.

As Arthur passes his mother's door, he hears her crying. He stops for a moment. No sound of his father's voice, which is unsurprising; for over a month his parents have had separate bedrooms. He reaches towards the door handle, but then glances at his watch. If he doesn't hurry, he will miss the school bus and face the perils of public transport. His father is already up and rearranging knives with carved wooden handles, which have possibly been designed for a ceremonial purpose. The man's eyes appear to have been prodded deep into their sockets: his features are narrow, as if his bones and skin have shrunk during the process of drying out. Arthur decides to risk a sentence or two. He knows the signs: his father will be too hung over to shout.

"Mother's upset again. She's crying."

His father looks up. There are black bags beneath his eyes. He hasn't shaved and his skin is preternaturally pale.

"Forget it. She's going through a phase."

The voice is phlegm-thickened, rasping. Arthur nods and goes out quickly.

Outside, a cold easterly sharpens his face. The wintry glitter, the frost still visible under the eaves, combines with a residual image of the knives. The day has an edge to it.

He hoicks his bag high on his shoulders and thrusts his hands deep into his overcoat pockets. The cloud is high and level, with a metallic sheen. Will the sun be trapped for eternity?

For the last two months, it's been worse between his parents than ever before. His father's forbidden his mother to leave the house. On many occasions he's taxed her with taking a lover. Someone is visiting the house while he is out drinking. He's sure of it. There's an unfamiliar fragrance, not feminine; a beard oil or an expensive deodorant designed to allure. He has been known to check the waste for hastily discarded flowers. Arthur's been assigned the role of evening watchman. He's to listen out for the door bell or subtler signals: a gentle tapping or nonchalant whistling out on the street, the clack of the letter box as a clandestine message is delivered. His mother is not to use the computer in his father's bedroom.

Arthur's through the barrier and out on the main road waiting for the StudyHub bus. A few of his classmates are already there, stamping on the pavement, their breath grey-white and efflorescent. One of the High Street's armed guards is present and will wait until they've boarded. The bus arrives. It's already more than half full with students who've been picked up in the suburbs. The duty lecturer, strap-hanging close to the door, ushers in the newcomers. As Arthur wriggles through the throng, he catches a fragment of a conversation.

"Have you heard about the moon?"

"What about it?"

"They're saying there's something wrong with it."

"Don't talk rot!"

The pressure of passengers behind him pushes Arthur down the aisle before he can identify the speakers. As he settles himself into the one spare seat near the back, he wonders if he has misheard. Is there another word rhyming with 'moon' that would make sense in the context? He rhymes through the alphabet. Certainly not 'spoon' … could 'tune' be a possibility?

As they leave the centre, they take a detour. Arthur has a glimpse of a street corner reduced to rubble, no doubt by a rocket attack or a stray missile. He tries to remember what stood there before, but can only conjure up a vague recollection of a mid-twentieth century apartment block, an unattractive period piece with small windows and balconies that appeared not to have been designed for use. Attacking such a target seems more than ordinarily pointless, but no doubt it was all about maintaining proper levels of uncertainty; the notion that there can be no return to normality while the demands of the anti-government, whoever they happened to be this month, were not being met.

As always, Arthur feels a wash of relief as soon as the bus reaches the StudyHub, with its state of the art air defence systems. The monthly seminar took place the previous week and so he will be working by himself in the comforting silence of his carrel.

At lunchtime, he sees a boy whom he has privately designated as a 'friend'. With so much of the timetable allocated to auto-tuition and no interest in sporting activities, he has developed few close relationships. He struggles to remember names and faces, even in his own year group.

"Hi, Argon," he says, picking up a tray and joining the queue.

"Oh, it's you again."

"Have you heard… that there's something… not quite right about the moon."

"What's that supposed to mean? Are you asking me if there's been another mining disaster?"

"No… not exactly."

"Well, what then?"

His friend does not appear to be in the mood for him today.

"Oh, it's nothing… just that I heard. But I might have got it wrong."

Argon looks at him levelly, but says nothing.

Once they've been served, Arthur puts his tray on the first vacant table, but his friend, if that is what he is, walks straight on and finds a window seat on the far side of the room. *Just because he doesn't want to sit with me today,* Arthur argues with himself, *it doesn't mean we're not on perfectly good terms.* But now Argon is talking to two girls. After a moment, all three of them stare across the room at him, their expressions indecipherable. Then they begin to talk amongst themselves.

Arthur finishes his meal and returns to the carrel. There's half an hour for free composition. He logs on and begins to write:

The full moon, profligate with light,
as if refusing to go through her phases,
tugs black desire with the pull of tides.

The malign influence of the moon on Arthur's mother? That must be what his father was talking about. He couldn't have been referring to the moon itself. And what about the poem? It will have to reach an acceptable level if he's to add it to his portfolio. He deletes 'black' and writes 'dark'. He tries to add to what he has written, but the moon seems metaphor proof. A scythe, a coin, a sickle, a scimitar, he can't find a fresh image. He connects to the internet and types in 'moon'. His search is blocked. He tries 'sun' and gets through at once.

The worst kinds of customer arrive in the evenings. On Saturday mornings well-dressed women buy sets of knives, which are clearly intended for use in the kitchen. No one buys a single knife unless it's of antiquarian interest. Arthur helps his father on the weekends. It's best not to be alone after dark. Even in summer men come in wearing heavy coats, caps pulled down over their foreheads. There are knives for special occasions, which his father keeps in locked drawers. In the months when there are riots or on days when the weather is ripe for killings, strangers wearing gloves try to sell his father knives, which are always too clean, with every print and trace of blood wiped off.

Custom has been slow and his father's been abnormally restless. Three times Arthur's been sent upstairs to check on his mother. Once he's been told to mind the shop when his father hears movements in the room above and goes to check. There's been no mention of the moon, for the night sky has been obscured by cloud for more than a week now. Is his father convinced that meteorological conditions mask an unaccountable waxing, a strange fullness, as if the satellite has been fattening itself on the desires of its worshippers? Or perhaps he believes it's moving out of its orbit and coming towards the earth, preparing for the moment when it can kiss every wife it likes through the windows. According to the calendar, it must be waning by now.

At dusk, the door opens and a man in a brown hooded jacket that makes him look like a member of a mendicant order comes in. He's wearing a face mask even though the High Street is one of the least polluted parts of the city. He's ill at ease, glancing at innocuous cases of cutlery, although it's obvious he's come to buy something sharper.

"Arthur, just go and check on your mother again."

His father's taking the keys to the locked cabinets out of a drawer behind the counter. In a minute, they'll be old-fashioned zombie knives, blades for an abattoir, and the ones with long handles, suitable for sacrifices, all displayed on the table in the back. Arthur knows that his father never likes him to see these; after all, some of them are of doubtful legality.

One of the light bulbs on the staircase has gone out, but the door to the flat is open. As Arthur goes up, the wall on his right-hand side appears less solid than usual, almost porous, open to the shadows that shift over its surface and then disappear. Perhaps a faint draught from above is moving the light slightly. When he's almost at the top, there's a flitting, white and tenuous, more like something forming than solidly present. It's there for an instant and gone by the time he's on the landing. He peers around. No apparent explanation. It's as though he's glimpsed the white flesh of his mother's imaginary lover.

It's a relief to be away from the shop. He goes into the kitchen and switches on the kettle. His father won't want him to return at once; it's the right moment to extend his errand. He will look everywhere he knows his mother isn't, before going to the bedroom, where she is bound to be.

Once he's finished, he makes his way to his mother's room at the end of the corridor, which not so long before had been set aside for visitors; a theoretical use since none were ever invited. His father still has the master suite. He's about to knock when he hears the rustle of sheets, the sound of first one voice, his mother's – the softest of whispers; then another, barely audible yet the tone somehow recognisably deeper. He tells himself it's impossible that anyone should be in there. The only access is through the shop; all the windows face the street.

"Who's there?"

She's aware of his presence, even though his approach had seemed silent, without so much as a single telltale creak.

"It's only me."

He opens the door. She's sitting in a chair that has been placed so it overlooks the window, the one from which she's been accused of waving at passers-by. The bed has been made up and there are, of course, no signs of any of her lovers. In the past few months, she has ceased to brush or arrange her hair, so it now hangs, lank and matted, down to her shoulders. Deprived of sunlight, her skin is sickly, moving towards greater transparency.

"Shouldn't you be helping your father?"

It's terrible how she will always take her tormentor's part, in spite of his treatment of her.

"He's got a special customer."

"Oh?"

"The sort he likes to talk to in private."

Losing interest, she turns to the window. She seems to be staring, not at the forbidden street but at the sky.

"Is there anything I can get you… a cup of…"

"No, no." She's impatient, as if he's interrupted a critical task. Then after a pause: "Do you think there will be a clear sky tonight?"

"I didn't hear the forecast. Why do you… ask?"

"It would be wonderful to see the moon."

For a moment, her sallow features are illuminated with longing. It's as if she believes that only the moon in an unclouded sky can make her desires fully manifest, her imaginary lovers becoming more than tricks of light playing on the counterpane or glimpsed for a second at the top of the stairs.

*

The bus breaks down when they are less than a mile away from the StudyHub. The guards, both heavily armed, instruct them to get out and walk. The first principal of survival in the city is movement. To remain beached at the side of the road is to invite the type of scavengers who feed on the wounded. It's a fine day, the first for weeks. The pavements are glazed with early morning frost. The crackle of gunfire is reassuringly remote and appears to be coming with the breeze from an outer suburb somewhere to the west. Arthur is walking alongside Argon, who may or may not be his friend today. It's Arthur who breaks the silence between them.

"What is that they want?"

"Who?"

"The anti-government lot?"

"Their demands keep changing, probably because they're an alliance of different factions. I think it's what they're against that's more important."

"And what's their position on the moon?"

Since it became apparent that Arthur's previous comments about the moon were not a sign of incipient insanity, Argon's been less aloof.

"I don't think they've made a statement on the subject."

Arthur recalled that his father had expressed his fears about the moon earlier than most; not more than a week afterwards, reports of people with similar anxieties became widespread. There were rumours that years of exploitation by mining companies had damaged the moon, the most imaginative claimed that its orbit had been affected as a result, a few predicted that it would come closer to the earth; others said that it was either moving quicker or slower. A religious cult asserted that despoiling the moon had upset the hidden ancient order governing the universe. Only the immediate cessation of mining could prevent escalating disorder, above and below. Government scientists assured the public that none of the observable changes were without precedent. The rumours had been bruited about by anti-government agents.

"And what do you believe?"

"The moon's doing exactly what it's always done. Of course, there will be alterations; we've known that for centuries. But they will take place over millennia."

"And so this is a kind of… hysteria?"

"The fact there's no single theory that commands assent suggests we make our own moons. Everyone's perceptions are at variance. We create the moons we deserve."

In the morning seminar, there's an undercurrent of unease. The day has continued cloudlessly, the unblemished sky is both welcome and feared. Their spirits rise with the fine weather but are tempered, first with apprehension, later with moon-terror. Once Arthur's back on auto-learn his anxiety abates. It helps that so many of the afternoon's tasks are abstract then mathematical and algebraic. Once he's completed these he has some coding to do.

It's not dark when he leaves the StudyHub campus. The days are moving slowly in the direction of spring. As he walks out of the main gates and towards the bus stop, he notices that many of the students are staring upwards. For a second, with fragments of code still running through his mind, he's nonplussed. Then he understands: the sky's still cloudless; the moon is sure to be visible tonight.

By the time, he's back on the Old High Street, it's nightfall. Most of the shops have already shut. His father's is one of the few that stays open late. The owner of the Italian café brings in his A sign and the last of the chairs. The street lamps are on, but there's something about the milky luminosity that implies other sources of light.

To Arthur's surprise, the entrance to the shop is shut. It's unlike his father to close so early. Fortunately he has a key. As soon as he's inside, he hears an unfamiliar sound, as if something's rotating. Not the low rumble of a washing-machine or tumble dryer.

This noise is higher, almost musical, yet counterpointed by harsher and higher notes. There's a sense of one surface being applied to another. He switches on the light and calls out for his mother; then, a moment later, for his father. As he climbs the staircase, a naked man, his skin aberrantly white, flickers across the landing. Arthur stands still. Although the figure moved quickly, he is certain it's not his father. He hurries down the corridor to his mother's room. Three men, their pale faces one on top of the other, as if they have been carved onto a totem pole, crane round. Their mouths are letterbox large and one has a huge, lolling tongue.

He runs back down the passage. Once he's near his father's room the noise worsens; it's as if something's being prepared for war. A metallic shriek. He pushes through. His father's standing by an open window. The moon could be outside or just inside. It's spinning so fast its grey craters have been subsumed in a silver blur. His father holds the long knife to its edge: a whetstone cry, metal sharpening on rock. The second he takes the blade away, the moon stops.

The door opens. An abnormally small man with a tiny round head, his worn face textured like biscuit, slips in. Although he's bald, he has a straggling goatee. His body is that of a baby, the skin pudgy and lustrous – as if with afterbirth. He's naked apart from a pair of tight black underpants, which accentuate his enormous sex, its contours as hard and knotted as the bole of an ancient tree. Lashless, his eyes suggest unblinking erotomania. His mouth protrudes, ready to suck. After watching the moon for a moment, he leaves as quietly as he entered.

"Have you seen them," his father says, more to the knife than his son. "You come with me. There's cutting to be done."

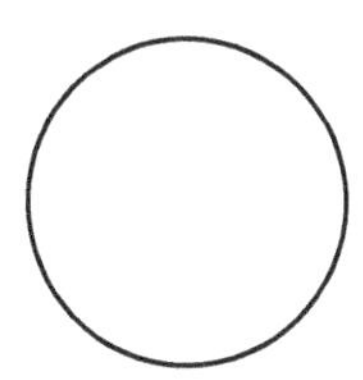

The Great Lunar Expedition

Thomas Alun Badlan

Thursday December 17th 1838

Great Astronomical Expedition to the Lunar Surface.

Made by Sir John Herschel L.L.D. and company.

From The Edinburgh Journal of Science.

When last our journal reached the headlines in the New York Sun, in August 1835, we reported the astounding discoveries brought about by Sir Herschel's innovative new telescope. Correspondence from around the world expressed both wonder and bewilderment. Some among the theological and scientific disciplines have accused those tireless workers at the Cape of Good Hope of crimes of the most heinous sort: blasphemy against God and ridiculing Newtonian models of the heavens. Others have claimed that the reports are little more than conspiracy to increase newspaper sales or defraud the public for nefarious endeavours. This so called 'Great Moon Hoax' hypothesis can only be described as slanderous against the good name of Sir Herschel, whose character is beyond reproach.

These are the facts: the telescope built at the Cape of Good Hope by Sir Herschel and his amanuensis Dr Andrew Grant, whose entirely new principle allows a vastly increased magnification, was able to solve or amend a great number of astronomical conundrums plaguing natural philosophers since before Copernicus.

Their greatest works, however, came when the telescope was aimed at the closest and most familiar heavenly sphere: our moon. Here was discovered not an inhospitable landscape that many had theorised, but a lush and vibrant world akin to our own. There was not only a plethora of flora – including trees, grasses, flowers and fruits – but also fauna. Many readers will be aware of the bipedal tailless beavers and the so-called unicorn goat but Herschel's greatest announcement was the race of human-like beings designated 'vespertilio-homo', the man-bats. These flying people have shown mankind that intelligent life can also propagate itself beyond our own small world.

While many would expect Sir Herschel to rest on his laurels and continue to explore the solar system, we can instead now reveal that the lunar discoveries have spurred him on to the next and ultimate leap into the unknown. With the help of friend and companion Lieutenant Drummond of the Royal Engineers, the last three years have been spent designing, constructing and testing a revolution in transportation technology. The machine – part balloon, part steam conveyance and named for her Royal Majesty Queen Victoria – departed from the Cape of Good Hope in January. Aboard was, of course, Sir Herschel and Dr Grant alongside Lieutenant Drummond and several members of the Royal Engineers acting as crew. A platoon of Fusiliers from the 7th Regiment of Foot were also aboard, commanded by Captain Henry Mitchell Jones, a decorated veteran of the Napoleonic Wars.

The balloon's canvas bag, oblong in shape, is reinforced with a lightweight aluminium frame. Beneath is the gondola, shaped like the hull of a battleship and made airtight and insulated to protect against the non-existent atmosphere and sub-zero temperatures expected beyond Earth. Large boiler-powered turbines constructed beneath the gondola provide propulsion expected at up to 75 miles per hour in favourable conditions. Also aboard was a revised and miniature version of the telescope that had made the entire venture possible. According to Sir Herschel's mathematical computations the expedition was expected to reach the fringes of lunar atmosphere three weeks after departure.

Dr Grant and Lieutenant Drummond's rigorous testing and mathematical equations proved equal to the challenge ahead. Even with the weight of twenty-five fully grown men and all of their personal belongings, expedition equipment, food and water, fuel and oxygen, the *Victoria* lifted buoyantly when released from its tethers. Drummond redistributed the ballast and sent the *Victoria* floating upward.

In awe, the expedition was soon among the clouds. Towns and cities had become indistinct specks against the vast irregular line where land met sea. Dr Grant estimated their altitude to be four thousand feet and rising which must have been somewhat akin to divinity, looking down upon your creation.

After several hours of ascent the cloud cover thinned and the temperature dropped. Readings from the external barometers showed that the atmosphere outside was exceptionally thin, beyond the tolerance for any perhaps save the rugged primitive tribes of the Himalayas. If Sir Herschel felt any trepidation at this stage of the journey he did not offer sign. He addressed the crew in that moment:

"Gentlemen, we here are only at the beginning of the greatest expedition in the history of the human race. No others will have gone further than us, or will have discovered more. I cannot promise you a safe or easy journey, but you, as learned men of science, industry and duty are more than equal to the task. May the good Lord watch over us and bring us safely back to Earth so that we may relay our discoveries for the benefit of all."

Later, beyond the Earth's atmosphere and its gravitational reach, the crew reported floating free as though suffused with helium! Even the steadfast men of the Fusiliers were rendered helpless and floundering.

The *Victoria* held up remarkably well under its maiden voyage, though its turbines were frequently frozen solid by ice particulate build-up. One of the Engineers was forced to go outside of the ship in an adapted, pressurised diving bell to clear them. Lieutenant Drummond spent the most time outside the *Victoria* and reported a sense of astounding calm and serenity while alone in the heavens. Indeed many of crew spoke of a great wonderment, of looking back on the retreating world and finding all things rendered in a more realistic perspective. Even Sir John, as stoic and philosophically minded man as ever born, marvelled for the unprecedented discoveries he and the *Victoria's* crew were undertaking…

Locke put down his pen and stepped away from the desk. It was all so frustrating. He paced the study while trying to decide how he wanted to continue. Outside the hansom cabs traced their way down Chambers Street.

The original articles had proven too successful. Had been a runaway sensation in fact. Benjamin Day, his editor, had been pleased. It had led to a drastic increase of sales of the New York Sun. Richard Adam Locke had never really cared for his employer's circulation figures. His motivations were pure. He had wanted to ridicule. Far too long he had sat silent as all manner of outlandish claims had found their way to print. None of it backed up by scientific rigour. The charlatan, the self-proclaimed 'Christian Philosopher', Thomas Dick, had even gone so far as to claim that the solar system contained over forty-one trillion inhabitants! Such ridiculous nonsense. He had sought to show the world that they were frauds. Except the Sun articles had worked too well, had become popular and, worse, believed. His writings had even been dramatized at the Bowery Theatre in the Lower East Side, an unwelcome surprise, since he had benefited none from such performances.

So now he was penning this follow up. Sir Herschel, a real and notable scientific figure, was now travelling through space in a flying contraption. Would this be enough to show people that they should apply critical thinking to the things they were reading? Would anything?

Locke sat back at the desk. It was growing late. The lamplighters were at work and soon New York would be a sea of twinkling stars to rival the heavens. He plucked the pen from its receptacle.

*

...The journey continued apace. the crew diligently attending to their duties. Sir Herschel and Dr Grant spent hours cataloguing and observing the lunar surface. Without the Earth's weather as potential obstacle they were able to work uninterrupted.

The proposed landing site for the *Victoria* was the 'Valley of the Unicorn' midway between the seas of Mare Faecunditatis and Mare Nectaris. It was thought by Sir Herschel and Captain Mitchell-Jones to be the safest point for landing, avoiding the rugged basalt mountains to the north and the Vespertilio-homo civilisation to the south. It was decided by Sir Herschel to avoid a repetition of disastrous contacts with savage peoples of deepest Africa by avoiding direct exposure. Though several animal and plant specimens were to be captured, harvested or shot, Sir Herschel was firm in his convictions that Earth-Lunar relations were not to resort to bloodshed.

And so on the 7th of February, 1838, the *Victoria* reached the lunar atmosphere and began its slow descent. During the previous three days Sir Herschel had been observing a vast cloud formation moving across the lunar surface. Though invisible from the naked eye on an Earthly vantage point, the clouds spread, lightning rippling within. It soon overtook the proposed landing site beside Mare Nectaris. There was a short debate over an alternate landing site but the storm's size soon rendered any suggestions impossible. What's more the moon's gravitational reach, though not as mighty as the Earth's, had already begun to Impact upon the *Victoria,* dragging down the vessel. All strapped themselves into restraints and prepared for a difficult landing. The storm below was of immense strength, a hurricane, mostly comprised of dust swirling in tempestuous eddies. The *Victoria's* hull was viciously assaulted and all attempts by Lieutenant Drummond to control their descent proved futile.

The *Victoria* struck land at 11:04 GMT. None were killed, though there were several minor injuries. The *Victoria* took the brunt of the crash. Her keel cracked along the starboard line and both turbines were badly smashed. The balloon also deflated entirely after several punctures, leaving only the skeletal frame askew.

It was, it goes without saying, a much more violent and devastating landing than the one Herschel had been hoping. Still, there had always been this possibility and there were contingencies. The first was for Lieutenant Drummond and the Royal Engineers to repair and reconstruct the *Victoria,* spare parts and tools having been stored aboard, as well as enough noble gases to lift the vessel free of the surface…

Locke sighed and sat back. One of the secretaries had brought him a cup of tea and it sat untouched and cooled before him. His latest articles had taken on an air of the serial adventure, the kind of grand fantasies conjured up by Mary Shelley and her ilk. This was the hope, that as the tale grew more outlandish the reader would become incensed that anyone would be so brazen. Who would ever accept a tale of men visiting other worlds or encountering strange creatures from the heavenly spheres?

The newspaper had never offered to print a retraction of what they were now calling the Great Moon Hoax. All reports had suggested that the real Sir John Herschel was greatly amused at his name being lent to such a wildly popular flight of fancy. And yet many still believed and still listened to the hokum offered from all the other self-proclaimed experts. Would this make them scoff? Would this stem the tide?

While some lesser men might have despaired at their predicament, Sir John Herschel was not one of panic or doubt. Instead he set the crew to work. After a day's work assessing the *Victoria's* damage, Drummond reported to Sir Herschel: the *Victoria* was salvageable.

It would certainly take a significant amount of time to repair and ready the ship for launch and so Sir Herschel announced he would take the crew out for an expedition.

The ship's barometers suggested an atmosphere thinner than that of Earth, but not quite enough for altitude sickness. Any concerns of toxins or poisons in the lunar atmosphere were quickly dispelled after the *Victoria's* hull was breached. Indeed many of the crew had already been outside of the vessel to assess damage or simply to secure the perimeter. It was Sir Herschel who took the first steps on the moon's surface, declaring to Dr Grant that: 'No man can conjure words for such an august occasion.'

Soon Sir Herschel and his party were heading off into the unknown; the earlier storm had proved to be ferocious but short-lived. The Royal Engineers and half of the Fusiliers would remain behind to rebuild and defend the *Victoria.*

The expedition journeyed south-easterly, heading toward the inland sea of Mare Faecunditatis that stretched out along the red sandbanks of the 'Valley of the Unicorns'. The storm had blown the *Victoria* considerably off course, adding potential days of extra travel. Almost immediately the queerness of the moon's surface was revealed.

Firstly; a lack of transition between day and night. The moon is tidally locked to the Earth, due to the cosmic providence that the moon takes twenty-seven days to both orbit the Earth and spin on its axis. The expedition would witness no sunrises or sunsets. The Earth however, hung in a translucent sky, acting much as a moon in a more terrestrial vista. It was a sobering moment for Sir Herschel and company, to look up and see all of humanity's achievements, mistakes and possibilities.

Secondly; an abundance of insect life. Invisible even from Sir Herschel's mighty telescope, now on the surface a plethora of small creatures emerged; flying, crawling and hopping. There were too many species to count, though thankfully none proved to be of the biting or stinging disposition. The science team, with astounding ease, managed to capture several live specimens, including a variety of glowing butterfly with transparent wings.

The day was thoroughly pleasant, with a swift, dry wind coming in from the east. A vast plain stretched out in all directions, featureless but for waist high yellowing grasses. Far to the north, through a haze, was a line of red-hued mountains, snow capped and proud as any Earthbound peak.

Over a low rise the party encountered a herd of the oft cited lunar Buffalo. Unbelievably larger than their Earth counterparts, the beasts snorted and stomped across the land, stripping every patch of grass within reach. The party observed the herd, which numbered in the hundreds, for almost several hours. Sketches were taken, along with a few so called photographs using the daguerreotype process. Once the herd was a safe distance away footprints were measured, and hair samples collected.

The expedition moved on, camping within a sheltered oasis of trees with wide overhanging foliage and red cucumber shaped fruit. After one fearless Fusilier, spurred on by his fellows, took a bite of the dangling fruit and not only failed to expire, but also expressed delight, many of the party partook of their first Lunar foodstuff.

Though there was no night forthcoming the group pitched their tents, started kerosene stoves for a meal and set a watch.

After a good seven hours of rest the party packed up camp and continued their journey south, further and further from the *Victoria.* Dry grass plains began to give way to gentle low hills.

Compasses had already proven useless on the moon, possibly due to a temperamental magnetic field, was Sir Herschel's hypothesis. Instead the expedition navigated solely by the position of the sun and Earth in the lunar sky and by amended and improved lunar cartography by map making luminaries such as Tycho, Riccioli and Blunt.

Several lunar water birds and cranes flew overhead. Captain Mitchell-Jones' men shot a few specimens to be catalogued by the science team. Time and time again they were astounded by the similarities between the Lunar species and their Earth-based counterparts, as though God's grand design had been translated across the universe.

It took two further days to reach the inland sea of Mare Faecunditatis. The shore was littered with geometric crystal formations the likes of which had been visible as towering clusters several miles to the east. The geologists among the science team took samples while Sir Herschel and Dr Grant visited a nearby settlement of small, windowless mud huts. These structures, having already been observed by Sir Herschel's telescope back on Earth, were constructed by the bipedal, tailless beaver-like species. Sir Herschel reported evidence of recent habitation, including embers in several fire pits. There were no signs of the creatures themselves, suggesting that they fled at the first sight of human appearance, perhaps to the sea. Several collected artefacts proved them no simple creatures, but a developing intellect, a primitive tool-maker like early man...

All of the creatures were birthed from his imagination. In hindsight Locke had realised his imagination was quite limited. The lunar animals had proven to be slightly altered copies of more familiar beasts. Afterward a writer friend, chastising, had cited the platypus, an animal only discovered in the Australian colonies a decade or two ago. It was a ridiculous specimen; duck-billed, egg-laying, mammalian and amphibian, initially rejected by the Royal Society of London as a forgery. A missed opportunity perhaps. Still, Locke felt his finest imaginings were the vespertilio-homo. Mankind had a peculiar and, in Locke's opinion, misguided and unobtainable dream of flight. People were often throwing themselves from tall cliffs or buildings in homemade contraptions hoping to take to the air like birds. Locke knew deep down that this was mankind's greatest folly. The best flying machines created were balloons and they were dangerous, fickle things, killing most occupants that dared grace them. The man-bats were simultaneously an outlandish narrative flourish and his own cutting barbs at man's hubris.

...The seafront village exhausted, the expedition continued its journey south. Every hour presented some new wonder, a miraculous beast, or unusual topographical detail. The land was gentle and thus far no significant danger had presented itself.

The Man-bat approached the expedition as they passed through an area pockmarked by impact craters. Captain Mitchell-Jones had his men ready their rifles but Sir Herschel quickly ordered them to stand down.

It swooped over the group, causing all to crouch low. Perhaps unafraid of humanity, or believing the men were some kind of hitherto undiscovered wingless cousin. Vespertilio-homo proved to be only superficially human. They were of extremely limited stature but very graceful and adept at gliding through the air with only occasional flaps of wide leathery wings.

That was when the Fusilier's rifle shot rang out, panicked at the proximity of the creature. The man-bat's wing tore at the shoulder and it fell hard into a small crater. While Captain Mitchell-Jones disciplined the man, Sir Herschel and Dr Grant approached the fallen. The creature's grey fur was slick with dark blood and it was panting softly, appraising them with large bright eyes. It appeared as peaceful and placid as the telescopic observations had promised. With preternatural trust the man-bat allowed Dr Grant to dress its damaged wing. A few times it tried to fly off, but seemed incapable. After some conference Sir Herschel decided to quickly escort the wounded man-bat back to its people in the hopes that they might be able to render assistance.

Two Fusiliers were sent back to the *Victoria* to report on recent events while the rest quickened their pace toward the vespertilio-homo civilisation carrying the man-bat between them on a makeshift stretcher.

Scientific curiosity was abandoned in the relentless march south, the party took only short rest breaks and the man-bat did not resist, seeming to understand that the expedition was trying to help it. It offered a few cooing words but as no human ear had ever heard such sounds they were therefore unintelligible. It took a little offered water, but refused all foods, even those strange red moon fruits.

Three days travel later the expedition first caught sight of the gargantuan sapphire temple built into a crevice of an immense cliff. Above its layered columns was the angled architecture of curved metal representing flames wreathed around a mirrored sphere shining in the sunlight. The valley itself was a paradise akin to biblical Eden; high waterfalls cascading into a wide, slow river, with lush forests on both banks and gently grazing creatures moving across flowering meadows. Above the temple's yellow roof and tiered pillars were specks of darting vespertilio-homo.

Captain Mitchell-Jones cautioned against approaching the temple unarmed, but Sir Herschel disagreed, declaring he wanted to right a wrong. Much of the expedition's equipment, including the Fusilier's weaponry, was left beneath the twisted trunks of a forest of yew-like trees. Then, as one, Sir Herschel and co walked into the valley and the heart of Lunar civilisation…

A spike of violence was sure to whet the appetite of the article's readership. There was a part of Richard Adam Locke that just wanted to tell a fantastical story. Except that was at least part of the motivations of

Thomas Dick and his fellows. Timothy Dwight's Plurality of Worlds was particularly dangerous as it supposed that a merciful God would not suffer a barren empty universe, when the Earth was so bountiful, again without anything beyond wishful thinking. Yes, they desired adulation from the masses. Locke had actively shied away from such temptations. He sought to expose, not wallow in the morass of public attention. There were real discoveries to be made. There was no gain in wrapping up pure imaginings in the trappings of the scientific. He had no problem with speculative writers like Edgar Allan Poe, whose intentions were not to defraud but illuminate. The Christian Philosopher had a following of great reach but his work of so-called natural theology was nothing but crude speculation. It was dangerous to both rational religion as well as inductive science.

It was the small hours of the morning. Locke stifled a yawn. This was not the first time he had remained the only soul in the office. He was aware of his reputation as an eccentric, even obsessive. Still, the image was set and by the time he walked home it would already be close to daybreak. He continued instead.

...The man-bats welcomed the party without any outward sign of hostility. A few flew down and peered quizzically between the Fusiliers carrying their wounded kin. One of the higher order, taller and darker furred, gestured for them to follow. The valley was a pleasant place, the waters slow and glistening as vespertilio-homo children splashed and bathed. Rows of pointed conifer-like trees flanked a path up toward the temple while swarms of man-bats darted and dived. The grasses here were neatly manicured by freely wandering herds of lunar sheep and unicorn goats.

They passed into the temple through a wide high door built in an impressive black stone archway. Inside the temple was a sort of priest or cleric, also of the superior race, wearing an outlandish headdress of inlaid feathers and glasswork beads. The interior was grand, large enough for the worshippers to fly within its halls and perch on ledges and platforms built into the walls. They assembled now as the Fusiliers placed the injured fellow on a stone dais. The Priest or Chief stepped forward and examined its wing and spoke again in that song-like language. Several others approached and began to tend to the poor creature.

While this unfolded Sir Herschel, identified as leader by the natives, was showered with gifts, including fruits, sweet smelling incenses and perfumes in finely crafted glass vials, and intricate gold and silver workings. Sir Herschel accepted these gifts hesitantly and only when it seemed refusal would offend. Sir Heschel offered his own late father's pocket watch in response to such hospitality, eager to foster a cordial relationship.

The expedition was led to another chamber and offered a place of high honour at a banquet table beside the man-bat chief. A huge variety of lunar foods were presented in long deep trays. All the men ate and drank their fill, at first tentatively and then eagerly, as befitting their weary disposition after many days hard journey.

Afterwards they were offered chambers filled with comfortable pillows and silken drapery. While the scientists and fusiliers made themselves comfortable, Sir Herschel and Dr Grant explored the temple proper. On the roof Sir Herschel and Dr Grant surveyed this astounding new world. Above, the Earth hung like a disk, at once majestic and insignificant. A few man-bats landed and drew their attention toward the north. There a dark shape hung, making steady progress in their direction. It was the *Victoria...*

How to end such a tale? Locke had, at first, veered toward the melodramatic. He imaged a subterranean race of vicious beasts whose prey was the gentle man-bats. Perhaps the Fusiliers would make a heroic stand against a bloodthirsty horde of lunar savages until the expedition could board the repaired Victoria and make their desperate escape? Locke pushed these concepts aside, exciting though they would be. The truth was he could not quite find a satisfying end for his romp. He did not want to resort to vulgar conflict, but it seemed anticlimactic to simply have Sir Herschel and the Victoria return home.

He already knew that Benjamin was reluctant to publish further material on the fantastical discoveries of Sir Herschel. It was not only legal action from Sir Herschel that concerned him, but that the public might turn against his newspaper should the truth emerge. Right now his articles were a curio, a light bit of fun that some had believed. If they kept pushing, that good-nature might evaporate.

Locke put down the pen. Outside the moon was still bright in the inky black. The stars might be banished by the gas lamps, but the moon refused to be evicted. He took a moment to imagine Sir Herschel and his intrepid band up there, encountering all manner of astonishing sights.

...The man-bats guided the *Victoria* to the roof of the temple where Sir Herschel greeted Lieutenant Drummond and congratulated him on a job well done. Drummond reported another approaching storm, this time from the southern hemisphere. There were still several days before it arrived, but Sir Herschel was unwilling to take chances with the expedition's success and safety. Once the crew were aboard and equipment and provisions stored the *Victoria* lifted. The hold was full of specimens, as well as artefacts both geological and anthropological. As Lieutenant Drummond steered them upward all the crew watched the lunar landscape retreat and fall beneath cloud cover. The man-bats followed them for a long time, before turning back for home. It seemed to Sir Herschel a sort of honour guard. Dr Grant remarked that despite one initial blunder, lunar-earth relations were off to an excellent start. Sir Herschel, aiming his telescope back toward the Earth could only agree.

The return journey was uneventful. Apart from a few weakened sections of the gondola's hull, which Lieutenant Drummond expertly patched, there were no issues.

The *Victoria* returned to the Earth three weeks later on April 30th, landing much more successfully in the vicinity of East Africa, around Lake Tanganyika. Sir Herschel and crew quickly returned to the Cape of Good Hope, where Sir Herschel booked passage back to England to report his findings to the Royal Society. That debriefing resulted in this report and shall now be distributed throughout the civilised world, so that all of humankind can better comprehend its place within God's limitless universe.

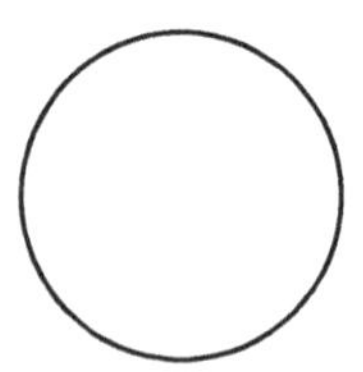

The Eye of God

Adrian Chamberlin

Full Earth. Perigee.

An iridescent blue and green gem, far more precious than those hewn from the lunar rock face, awaited them on the completion of their ascent. The climb was one of darkness: the flares from miners' arc cutters on the lower level became distant sparks, and only the flashing blue streaks from the solar collectors on the rim of the blasted cliff, four hundred feet above the base, marked the journey's end.

Depending on the time of lunar day and the cycle of the moon, the cosmic jewel of the planet greeted the returning miners – or mocked them. Unlike the rare minerals at the base of the mine, this jewel was unobtainable.

You had me once. You'll never have me again. Think of what you've lost. Usually, it was only the new miners who hesitated at the elevator's threshold, a weighted boot hovering over the two-inch gap between the access gate and the catwalk leading to the airlock and safety. The older hands barely noticed it, or had forced themselves to ignore it. You could always tell the new guys by their strange, back-bent-backward postures as the elevator disgorged its travellers, the result of trying to lift eyes to the heavens in a rigid minesuit with limited vision.

The older hands… yeah, that's what I am. But not like *them.* The thought of having a mindset that could block out the cosmic jewel had horrified him. So he swore that at every shift end, just before the elevator pulled the three-man crew from sublunar darkness, he would spend a few moments gazing at the planet. No hurry to bring out the crystals to the cataloguers eagerly waiting at the other end of the catwalk, with their scanners hooked up to the current electronic catalogue and its promises of shares and bonuses… no. Let the others claim his credit. Let them waste it on the digital fleshpots and ersatz alcohol in the overpopulated colony laughingly called 'home'. If they couldn't see what he saw, that was their problem. Fifteen years he'd managed it. He would do so until his last day.

The irony – and indeed cruelty – of the twelve-hour shifts spent digging for the lunar minerals they'd been assured were the rarest and most beautiful humanity had ever discovered paled into insignificance compared to the cerulean and ivory that festooned the home planet. A double irony: the blue and white masked anything brown. A blue planet indeed, with the majority of its land reclaimed by the seas.

But still, it was home. It had given him life.

And he had given life to it. Life that probably no longer cared or even knew about him…

A rueful smile reflected in his faceplate, became a twisted, inhuman leer and the beads of condensed sweat blurred momentarily. He sniffed, winced at the amplified sound from the helmet speakers and waited for the mocking banter from his shift mates' suit comms. Everyone moaned about the inability to pick your nose or puke last night's overindulged beer, spit out thick gobbets of phlegm in the helmet, but no man – *no man* – dared admit to the inability to wipe away tears.

Strangely, there were no jeers. No wind-ups. The rhythmic breathing from the two men stood before him stopped, and they did not move onto the gantry when the elevator gate opened. Their wedge-shaped helmets obscured his view of the airless sky, but it was clear that something had happened to make even these hardened men take notice of their home world.

The sweat trickling down his back turned cold. He blinked away the blurriness and raised gloved hands to push against the men's shoulders; they stepped aside, parted like curtains opening on a stage show.

The earthly gem was corrupted. A perfect black disc obscured the centre, consigned one eighth of the Earth's surface to darkness. Around it, the oceans' blue had darkened, become indigo. The spirals and whorls of the planet's cloud cover had retreated as if forced away, hiding from the encroaching darkness.

A huge, alien eyeball. Staring, unblinking, at half-living men on a lifeless moon.

"The eye of God stares down at a dead world. Does He weep? Or are there no more tears to shed?"

It's a cruel joke. The Tears of God is an appropriate name for the cataclysmic floods but they show no signs of abating; if they are from a heavenly source the god behind them has no shortage of tears. And yet today is different. The only time I can remember that black storm clouds haven't crowded the sky, the first time since childhood I've felt the sun's warmth on my face. Earlier, the scent of apple blossom filled the air; a harbinger of summer and a reminder of what was so prevalent in this corner of England. That itself is a cruel irony, now that the sun is going to disappear.

Water has returned Glastonbury's environs to the swamps and marshes that – if you believe such things, as she once did – greeted Joseph of Arimathea and his holy cargo over two thousand years ago. The isle of Avalon, surrounded by floodwater, as it once was, and now is.

But now the Tor appears defeated; the ruined, roofless tower of what was once St Michael's Church is listing, like Pisa's did before the River Arno rose to consume it. The hill is marshy and full of sinkholes; ascending the Tor from the stolen patrol boat was like wading through the shelled craters of a waterlogged battleground.

She stands in the archway of the ancient tower, her green dress tattered and torn, her perished Wellington boots abandoned as she shuffles blackened and swollen feet on the sodden grass. Oblivious to the pain from her gangrenous legs, she raises her palms to the skies and the slow moving black disc that slides toward the sun. Her silver hair loses its lustre in the encroaching midday darkness, becomes the grey of lunar dust.

"We have men on the moon right now, digging for minerals. Why are they not here? Helping to rebuild our coastal defences, reclaim the lands, rather than overstuffing the pockets of fat corporations who look further outward for new worlds to plunder? And *this* is a sign of God's displeasure!"

Men on the moon. I wince, feeling once more the guilt of not caring if my father still lives or has died up there. Does she care? Did she hope for his death, or does she hold hope still?

And me? Does her madness allow any memory of me, any thought of the adult I'd become?

Her audience is pitifully small. They're only here to seek high ground, feed on the few sheep and cows that were stranded before the last deluge. Sullen plumes of smoke dribble from the openings of the yurts and camping tents, but there is little smell of beef or lamb. One skeletal old man had emerged when she began her tirade; he sits beside me, cross-legged, and gnaws listlessly on a femur that has not come from a cow or sheep, and has long lost its meat. His eyes are as vacant as the bone, its marrow long gone. He doesn't even take interest in the unzipping of my rucksack and the prospect of food.

Of course, there's no food. Just the one thing I've kept with me all these long years.

All those years of searching for her. My childhood's a memory as distant as my community service years in the Dry Zones with my foster parents. They wept when I left, feared for my safety, but they understood a child's desire to find his roots.

I didn't need to scour the water lands of Britain for her. When I heard the report of the eclipse I knew she'd be here. I glance to the southwest slope and the stolen dinghy at anchor; it's slipped its mooring and is heading out to the inland sea the town of Glastonbury's become.

Doesn't matter. I suspected this was a one-way trip.

Her eyes shine as they alight on me. They gleam with religious fervour. Or madness. And yet they don't recognise me. Have I changed so much since boyhood? Or does she see all of humanity as the same – tired, beaten, pathetic and unworthy of salvation?

She used to, according to Dad. Even before the floods there were railings against capitalism and corporate rape of the planet. The petitions, the demonstrations I was dragged along to. Other ten year olds back then wore designer T-shirts and knock-off trainers; I can't remember not wearing a yellow Hi-Viz with some ecological message beyond my understanding, handing out leaflets.

No leaflets now. The message had been ignored. She has a new one now. Abandoned her pagan gods for a more recent one.

Just after she and Dad split, and the waters rose. Who could believe in the benevolence of pagan gods after that – when the very Earth itself used its powers to destroy all life?

The shadows lengthen; the ruined tower casts a dark pall over her and the brightness of her eyes diminishes. Her face takes the pallor of a corpse. Grey slug-like things mark her dance; the feet they come from ooze black blood.

The tent dwellers greet the darkness with resignation. Few had been energised with the sun's burning of the clouds, believing it a trick of false hope from a cosmic comedian who had long since left the stage of this world. They retreat sullenly into their canvas shelters.

She doesn't seem concerned by the disappearance of her audience. I doubt she was speaking to them anyway, so wrapped up is she in her own world. But she's aware of my presence now. She narrows her eyes.

If she doesn't recognise me, surely she'll know the one thing that kept her and Dad together in the happier years. I've carried it so far, and for so long. And now's the chance to show it to her, in the light of a conjoined sun and moon.

A crystal which is nothing compared to what is being mined on the moon. But a crystal which has immeasurably more value. From the rucksack, I take the heirloom. I extend my fingers and palms in an attempt to create the semblance of a blossom, the magic trick my grandmother performed which would reveal the crystal at the hand-flower's heart.

A second moon appears in the sky above the drowned world.

Relieved laughter, with metallic echoes, bellowed through the suit comms. A relief he neither felt nor shared.

"Bloody hell. Never thought I'd see a solar eclipse on the other side! Looks pretty shite, though."

"More than you know. Looks like our ol' homeland's grown itself a big asshole! Back in the day, there was talk of space tourism, people paying big bucks to see an eclipse on the moon. They'da wanted their money back, and who'd blame 'em?"

It wasn't the first time he'd seen the moon shadow the sun. It had its own magnificence, another facet of cosmic wonder exemplified by this special jewel in the heavens, and he hoped his rookie shift mates' mocking of it was the normal banter that masked their own despair at never going back to Earth. He'd seen – and heard – it all before. But this time he felt anger.

This time, instead of holding his tongue and allowing the jibes and jeers to wash over him, he spoke. The vehemence of his words, the anger amplified in his helmet comms, almost surprised him.

"You don't have to be religious to see it as a sign! Darkness over the world, the sun blotted out by the *very thing we're raping.*"

"Eh? Jesus, man! That's coming it a bit –" The speaker found himself twisted by his companion's arms; no longer exhausted by the arduous shift they clasped his shoulders and powered him to the edge of the gantry, forcing him to his knees. His back bent, his faceplate filled now with nothing but the lunar sky and the darkening globe.

"My wife was right. We don't deserve to survive as a species if we're going to use our technology to plunder other worlds rather than save the one that gave us life." His vision was no longer blurred by tears; scarlet flared at the edges of his faceplate and the blue planet became pink. His suit's kneepads were no protection against the fragments of ungraded gemstones on the elevator floor; they dug into his kneecaps, didn't pierce the suit material but imparted pain. Righteous pain that purified and justified his rage. The man knelt before him was a symptom of all that was wrong with his species: living for today and the false promise of bonuses he would never spend while richer men got even richer in their gated, floating cities.

"Our bosses will look after themselves when the off-world colonies are complete. D'you really think they're going to share their luxuries with us? *That's* all that awaits us! Life in darkness, digging more holes on other dead worlds until we create one that swallows us all!" Another shake of his captive, hands on the helmet aiming the faceplate to the pink planet. The gantry trembled and dust trails floated, thin tendrils of this dead satellite's ghost.

"She was right. She was right and was ignored, laughed at! *And no one laughed more than me!*"

His suit comms filled with echoes of his rage, then laughter. It was his own laughter, from years before, when he left her.

It was her laughter now, bitter and resigned rather than mocking. And the blackness in the Earth grew larger, fatter, greedily swallowing the planet and even the distant stars, and the helmet lights joined them to plunge him into darkness.

The family heirloom: a tennis ball-sized crystal, a milky-white sphere with uneven dimples and craters in daylight that turn a fiery orange when held to the lancing beams of the full moon.

No one knew where it had come from, or who had been the original owner. Whether it had been cut and polished into this perfect sphere or had come from another world, another time, in this form. There were stories of it coming from the stars before the first settlers colonised the land around the Tor and made it habitable; other tales spoke of it appearing from one of the numerous wells in pre-Christian Glastonbury, a gift from the moon goddess or the lord of the underworld.

Each matriarch who passed the stone down to the next generation told a different tale of its origins, but each had the same message: this is a symbol of the harmony within the Earth and the cosmos. The light of the sun, the deathly glow of the moon, and the earthly colours of our home planet. All are one.

The trick I have learned from those who went before: making the crystal appear from nowhere to a child's coos and gasping smiles – now it's greeted with laughter.

It's the laughter of recognition, bitter and resigned. She recognises me now.

The tent people are forgotten. Even the cosmic spectacle is mere background to our reunion.

In midday darkness we approach. Midnight at noon has taken the Somerset Levels; the tarnished silver disc of the sun is obliterated by a black sphere that turns the once-mystic landscape into a shadowland where dreams of Gaia's eternal renewal seem as fanciful and childish as the legends of King Arthur waking from his Avalon sleep or the healing powers of the Holy Grail. A ruined, dangerously listing church tower atop a natural geological formation perilously compromised by the floodwaters caused by humanity's greed and short-sightedness – that's all this is.

Even the wonderful prospect of reuniting with my mother, which has kept me going all these years, has lost any trace of magic. And yet…

The sphere is iridescent. There are faint tendrils of green which impart light to the sapphire and ivory. This is no magic; the lines of fuchsite are what give it its light. Even so, in this darkness cast upon the ancient land by the moon which carries my father and the perverted last quest of humanity's scientific and engineering ingenuity, this globe is the only light. My heart is in my mouth and sweat beads my forehead, yet the light from the crystal gives me hope.

"The wedding gift from Gran. *Your* mum," I say as I approach the shadowed archway where my mother awaits. "A time when you believed in magic…and love."

I hold it to her; its luminescence bathes her face in green and blue. For a moment the wrinkles and dirt-crusted lines in her forehead vanish, and she is young again, smiling serenely as she watches me play with the crystal sphere her mother has been bequeathed from generations of Glastonbury women before her.

And then her face darkens, her wizened hands are claws that seize the globe; the shadows of her fury blots out even the light from her mother's crystal. The gift has been accepted, but not in the spirit offered.

I stand, stunned, as she clutches it to her breast, the remnants of her fingernails cracking and snapping as they try to break the surface. She looks up, and her expression is one of bewilderment and hurt.

"How could you?" The voice has lost its stridency, its mad prophet's hectoring. It is broken and lost; a little girl's, returning to childhood.

I don't know what to say. I wasn't sure what reaction I'd receive seeing her again, but I haven't prepared for this. *Dad, why can't you be here?*

A brief flare from above; the eclipse has entered its second diamond ring stage, signifying the moon's occultation of the sun is coming to an end. She follows my gaze and her eyes fill. The tears are slow to fall; her eyeballs have been so dry the tear ducts are slow to reopen.

"A wedding ring…" she whispers. "I always dreamed of a diamond ring on my wedding day, not *this*. But Mum said there was no need for diamonds. The real jewels are in the heavens; the ones below the ground should remain where they are…"

She is lost, hurt, confused; I'm once again the awkward child attempting to comfort a mother crying on the sofa when the door slams shut by a departing father, stifling his own tears because he has to be the man of the house now, inwardly screaming because he has no words to soothe her pain and is trying so hard to be strong, *so hard* for them both… and the tears run down my cheeks.

My arms open to embrace her. She steps back, her toeless feet making wet sucking sounds in the swampy ground. Even within the ruined church tower the earth beneath our feet is a quagmire. A strange luminescence emanates from the stones, the crescent sun above imparting a pink hue to the granite. The light within the crystal my mother clutches to her chest is more pronounced. Green, blue and ivory in the midst of scarlet-hued darkness.

Held by my mother, who now smiles at me with the warmth and love she had long believed to have vanished from this world – and herself. It is radiant.

It is ephemeral. It lasts as long as it takes for the first stones from the crumbling battlements to fall into the site of our reunion. The ground swallows the first two as easily as the moon swallowed the sun; then brown craters horizontally streaked with chalk begin to appear. The smell of ancient, sodden earth and the stench of long dead things fill the air as the final, inescapable chasm blossoms and takes us to join them.

More blocks of granite follow us, pounding into our bodies, tearing and crushing flesh and bone, and a sound like shattering glass accompanies my mother's screams. Whether from physical pain or the anguish of the family crystal destroyed in her embrace I don't know.

Yet the glow from the heirloom remains undimmed. The light of the sun and the moon illuminate our descent into the bowels of the Earth.

Consciousness returned the moment his fall began. The suit's electronics were shot; the helmet lights were extinguished, the comms were dead, and he fell in a world of silent, solitary blackness. The rippling blue arcs from the solar collectors turned the escaping oxygen from his severed airlines into a gravity-free waterfall of shimmering sapphire, accompanied by the mocking cerulean and ivory sphere with its attendant stars that steadily diminished in size.

The technical specs from the daily health and safety briefings were just words, meaningless. Little atmosphere and no wind resistance... no terminal velocity, yet still a fatal drop if one fell, unimpeded, to the base of the quarry shaft a kilometre beneath the lunar surface... by then he'd be travelling at over a hundred and twenty miles per hour.

He had less than thirty seconds before the descent ended... and if the fall didn't kill him, the bolt from the third miner's arc cutter into his oxygen tank meant his time was up. His oxygen would run out long before his body landed, assuming any outcrops of the mine shaft didn't rip into his suit. Any breath in his lungs would be expelled with the force of the impact.

It didn't matter.

He felt no panic, no despair at the prospect of imminent death. Not even anger at what his shift mates had done. He'd asked for it, really; they were simple, young men, acting to save one of their own from an old timer who'd gone mental.

He wasn't the first. He wouldn't be the last.

Strange. It felt the way one would fall in a dream: surreal, disconnected, with the certainty one would wake before the impact. Should his life not be slipping before his eyes? It all seemed so long ago and so far away, the time measured in eons, not the fifteen years he left his wife and child; the distance in light years, not the mere two hundred and thirty-thousand-odd miles between moon and Earth.

He was still breathing. He was still falling. He mentally counted to thirty… yet still he fell.

Darkness in his field of vision. Surely he should see the base of the crater, lit by the arc cutters of the current shift's miners? The headlights of the transport crawlers reflecting in the fragments of the silvery ore?

Something appeared. He thought it was the partially-occulted Earth, this tennis-ball sized gem. The colours were the same, the iridescent blues and whites and partial greens, but the black disc had shrunk. Became smaller with each heartbeat.

A pinprick of a pupil, then nothing. Not a speck of darkness corrupted the brilliant sphere before him. The sapphire and ivory swirled, intermingled, became one dazzling, blinding, unearthly incandescence.

I shouldn't be able to see this, he thought. *No living man should. It's the light of gods and…*

The light reached out to him. Swallowed him until the darkness retreated. He felt no heat, his suit did not crumple and burn, his flesh did not smoulder, his eyeballs did not boil and explode.

And in the centre of the impossible light, the sphere that birthed it cracked. Fractured, fragmented, fell to pieces as though pounded by an avalanche of sharp-edged rocks – he had glimpses, intimations, of tumbling granite blocks, carved and dressed and undoubtedly the handiwork of humans – and the light dimmed.

This too became human. It was the smile of a woman, as bright and loving as the day he first met her, and the tears that marked their parting were forgotten, no longer even a memory.

The earth relinquishes me. It feels like I'm being forced out, vomited like a poisonous piece of meat. Even the mud and chalk are reluctant to cling to my body; only the flood water remains, soaking my jeans and sweater. The same waters that had soaked me prior to my ascent of the Tor.

When I look behind me and stare at the subsided earth and the collapsed walls of the tower, lining the oval crater in perfectly formed symmetrical recurved bows I think of birth.

Birth? Ridiculous. *Death.* I remember the walls tumbling, the blocks crushing my body. I remember my mother –

Mum! I clamber to my feet, stand on unbroken legs above the wreckage of a site sacred to both pagan and Christian. The earth has set, become hardened by the sun, and nothing will come from –

The sun. I'm aware of the warmth on my face, sense the vapours of condensing water rise from my body. Across the Somerset Levels, more vapour steams into the cloudless, azure sky. Like ghosts, souls released from physical torment, finding peace – and life – at last. For a moment, my mother's death and my rebirth are forgotten.

I stare into the sky and gasp at the brilliance of the sun. The moon is no longer visible. I squeeze my eyes shut, and the afterimage burned into my retinas shows a perfect sphere glowing with the fires of life; a small pinprick of black centres it, the absolute darkness of death miniscule yet ever-present. An eye, watching over its new creation.

A glint, a shimmer of blue and white in the corner of my eye. Something else has emerged from the womb of the Tor. I stare at the heirloom, the unbroken crystal on its earthen bed. I wonder whether to take it or leave it.

The tent dwellers have emerged, blinking in this new sunlight. Tears mingle with smiles. Perhaps those tears will fade, dry in the sun and become nothing but memory.

Perhaps. I glance again at the crystal. The dark, staring pupil in its centre, blacker than blindness, fades, becomes smaller, indistinct. I smile, knowing not even the eye of God can weep now.

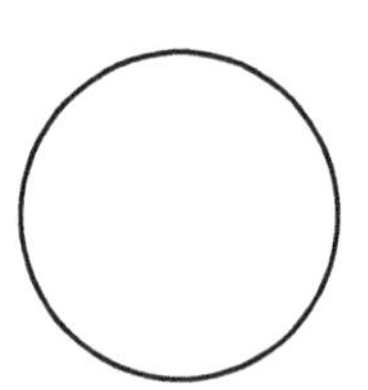

About the Authors

ALLEN ASHLEY

Allen Ashley is a British Fantasy Award winner. His short stories, poems, flash fiction and articles have been widely published in anthologies, magazines and online venues in the UK, USA, Canada and Spain. His books include the novel "The Planet Suite" (TTA Press 1997; reprinted Eibonvale Press 2016) and the anthology "Humanagerie" (Eibonvale Press, 2018, co-edited with Sarah Doyle). He works as a critical reader and creative writing tutor and is the founder of the advanced science fiction and fantasy group Clockhouse London Writers. www.allenashley.com

CHRIS EDWARDS

Chris Edwards is from Glasgow and has several stories about to come out with different publishers. He's co-writer of the audio-drama podcast "Tales from the Aletheian Society", which is now onto its third series. He has also written extensively for Live-Action Roleplay, including being a founding member of Shadow Factories and writing plot for Profound Decisions, as well as many others. He lives with his delightful partner and angelic offspring, who inexplicably love him despite his grumpiness. He enjoys tabletop roleplaying and reading in his spare time.

HANNAH HULBERT

Hannah Hulbert lives in urban Dorset. She is on a permanent sabbatical from reality as she raises two children and devotes her time to visiting imaginary worlds, some of her own creation. You can find her tweeting and doodling when she should be writing as @hhulbert on Twitter.

DAVID TURNBULL

David Turnbull is a member of the Clockhouse London Writers group of genre writers. He writes mainly short fiction and has had numerous short stories published in magazines and anthologies, as well as having stories read at live events such as Liars League London, Solstice Shorts and Virtual Futures. He was born in Scotland, but now lives in the Catford area of London.
He can be found at www.tumsh.co.uk

A.N. MYERS

Andrew Myers was born in London and educated in Reading and Oxford. Since completing a MA in Prose Fiction at Middlesex University, he has won and been shortlisted for several literary prizes, including *Momaya, Dark Tales,* and *Hammond House International Literary Prize*, and his short fiction has been seen in such publications as *101Fiction.com, Speculative66,* the *Alien Days Anthology* from Castrum Press, and the British Fantasy Society bulletin. *The Ides,* his gripping YA science fiction novel, published under the pen name of A.N. Myers, is available from Amazon and his website www.anmyers.com. He is a member of Clockhouse London Writers.

SIMON CLARK

Simon Clark is the author of many novels and short stories, including *Blood Crazy, Vampyrrhic, Darkness Demands, Stranger, The Fall, Bastion* and the award-winning *The Night of the Triffids*: his adaptation of the novel has been broadcast as a five-part drama series on BBC Radio 4 Extra. He has also edited two Sherlock Holmes anthologies for Robinson Books.

ALIYA WHITELEY

Aliya Whiteley writes novels, short stories and non-fiction and has been published in *The Guardian*, *Interzone*, *McSweeney's Internet Tendency*, *Black Static*, *Strange Horizons*, and anthologies such as Unsung Stories' *2084* and *This Dreaming Isle,* and Lonely Planet's *Better than Fiction I* and *II*. She has been shortlisted for the Arthur C Clarke Award, a Shirley Jackson Award, British Fantasy and British Science Fiction awards, the John W Campbell Award, and a James Tiptree Jr award. She also writes a regular non-fiction column for *Interzone* magazine.

TERRY GRIMWOOD

Terry has never been to the moon, but looks at it longingly whenever it's in the sky and finds it a strange and haunting place to contemplate. When not moon-gazing, he teaches at a college, plays harmonica and sings at the Ain't Nothin' But The Blues Bar, and writes. His work has appeared in numerous magazines and anthologies, including *Sensorama*, *Where are We Going* and *Creeping Crawlers*. His short stories have been gathered into two collections: *The Exaggerated Man* and *There is A Way To Live Forever*. His latest novella, *Joe*, is inspired by true events.

STEPHEN PALMER

Stephen Palmer is the author of fifteen genre novels, including his 1996 debut *Memory Seed*, the surreal slipstream steampunk *Hairy London*, and in 2015 his AI book *Beautiful Intelligence*. In 2016 Infinity Plus published his alternate-world steampunk *Factory Girl* trilogy, then a WW1 novel, *Tommy Catkins*. Presently he is working on an AI novel and another steampunk trilogy. His short stories have been published by many and various publishers. Stephen lives and works in Shropshire, UK. He likes Fleet Foxes, tea, The Byrds, and agitating against patriarchal dominion.

PAULINE E. DUNGATE

Pauline E. Dungate is the author of many published short stories and the co-editor of *Something Remains* (Alchemy Press), an anthology produced as a tribute to Joel Lane. Often her stories reflect places she has visited on travels, although she has yet to visit the moon. In the guise of her alter-ego Pauline Morgan, she is a poet and a prolific reviewer. When not writing or reading, she may be found either in the garden or, on sunny days, walking along the River Cole counting butterflies for Butterfly Conservation. Her husband, Chris, puts up with her eccentricities.

DOUGLAS THOMPSON

Douglas Thompson's short stories and poems have appeared in a wide range of magazines and anthologies, including Ambit and New Writing Scotland. Variously classed as a Weird, Horror, Sci Fi, Literary, or Historical novelist, he has produced 12 novels and collections of short stories and poetry since 2009, from various publishers in Britain, Europe and America. His 13th book, 'Barking Circus' is due out this year from Zagava of Dusseldorf, billed as a 'quantum novel' it returns to the fragmented fusion of short stories within a novel story arc, as was pioneered in his debut 'fractal' novel 'Ultrameta'. https://douglasthompson.wordpress.com/

ALEXANDER GREER

Alex has always gravitated toward the strange and the baroque, and has been writing on a small literary blog for years, but only recently ventured into the realm of submitting for publication. Alex lives in the Western United States and you can find some of his odd, unpublished work at raptorpatton.wordpress.com

NIGEL ROBERT WILSON

Nigel Robert Wilson spent most of his life doing international logistics. Now retired and beyond his allotted three score years and ten, he devotes his time to heritage and literary projects. He reviews history books and fantasy fiction. His particular interest is in systems of belief, both religious and political. He has been published before in The Silent Companion, The Rochester Tales, BFS Horizons, Wordland, and The Records of Buckinghamshire.

GARY BUDGEN

Gary Budgen is a London based, and possibly London obsessed, writer whose stories have appeared in many magazines and anthologies including *Interzone, Fur Lined Ghettos* and *Humanagerie* from Eibonvale Press. His collection of short stories, *Chrysalis,* is published by Horrified Press. More information can be found here: https://garybudgen.wordpress.com/

ELANA GOMEL

Elana Gomel is a professor of English literature who has taught and researched in universities around the globe, including Tel-Aviv University, Venice International University, and Stanford. She is the author of six non-fiction books and numerous articles on subjects such as science fiction and narrative theory. As a fiction writer, she has published three novels and more than fifty fantasy and science fiction stories in *Apex*, *Fantasist*, *Zion's Fiction*, *People of the Book*, *Apex Book of World Science Fiction* and many other magazines and anthologies. Her latest novel is *The Cryptids* (2019). She can be found at https://www.citiesoflightanddarkness.com/

ANNA FAGUNDES MARTINO

Anna Fagundes Martino was born in São Paulo (Brazil) in 1981. A graduate from University of East Anglia, she is one of the founders of Editora Dame Blanche, one of the first

Brazilian publishing houses specialised in speculative fiction. She has had works performed on Radio BBC World and in a number of Brazilian venues, such as "Trasgo", "A Taverna" and "Mitografias". She's also published three Fantasy novellas in Brazil. You can find more of her work at annamartino.com

CHARLES WILKINSON

Charles Wilkinson's publications include *The Pain Tree and Other Stories* (London Magazine Editions, 2000) and *Ag & Au*, (Flarestack Poets, 2013). A full-length book of his poems is forthcoming from Eyewear. His collections of strange tales and weird fiction, *A Twist in the Eye* (2016), and *Splendid in Ash* (2018) appeared from Egaeus Press; a chapbook, *The January Estate*, is to be published by Eibonvale Press. He lives in Powys, Wales, where he is heavily outnumbered by members of the ovine community.

THOMAS ALUN BADLAN

Thomas Badlan has been an aspiring writer for as long as he can remember. He studied Creative Writing at the University of Derby. He is a long standing member of Manchester's Monday Night Writers Group and currently works as a literacy teaching assistant. This is his second published story.

ADRIAN CHAMBERLIN

Adrian Chamberlin was born in Wales and lives in south Oxfordshire. He is the author of the critically acclaimed supernatural thriller novel *The Caretakers* as well as numerous short stories in a variety of anthologies, mostly historical or futuristic based supernatural horror. He co-edited *Read the End First*, an apocalyptic anthology with Suzanne Robb (author of the acclaimed thriller *Z-Boat*) and the 2016 supernatural warfare novella collection *Darker Battlefields* for the Exaggerated Press, and his novella *The Silent Towers* was a finalist in Independent Legions Press's 2018 Inferno Award. Further information is on his website www.archivesofpain.com

Lightning Source UK Ltd.
Milton Keynes UK
UKHW040723130121
376857UK00009B/39/J